RIDE A
SHADOWED TRAIL

By

Eunice Boeve

PublishAmerica
Baltimore

First printing

This is a work of fiction. Names, characters, places, and incidents either are the product of the author's imagination or are used fictitiously. Any resemblance to actual persons, living or dead, events, or locales is entirely coincidental.

ISBN: 1-60563-059-4 (softcover)
ISBN: 978-1-4489-1840-9 (hardcover)
PUBLISHED BY PUBLISHAMERICA, LLLP
www.publishamerica.com
Baltimore

Printed in the United States of America

In memory of my brother, Daniel "Danny" Goyen

ACKNOWLEDGMENTS

A special thanks to the following: John Boyington, DVM, our local veterinarian, for his expertise; My children, always my first readers: Katherine Boeve-Pensabene, Kandice Boeve, Kelly Leiker, and Ron Boeve, Jr.; My sister, Mabel Beebe, who, well versed in the ways of livestock, gave me pointers; My husband, Ron, who supports me in all ways; and Margaret Borland (1824-1873), Victoria, Texas, who took a trail herd to Kansas in 1873 and on whom I modeled the Martha Rawlins character in this story.

CHAPTER ONE

The night shadows dimmed Josh's view of the man riding up behind his mama's adobe. Instinctively he ducked behind a small scrub bush. A lot of the men who came to see his mama did not like to see a small boy hanging about. They got funny looks on their faces and some kind of shuffled their feet, looking everywhere but at him. Mama didn't want him around either.

She would tell him to go play, her smile gone, her hand pushing at the air, pushing him away.

Some of the men paid him no mind at all or else they teased him, grins smeared across their faces. They asked him where he got his curly hair, or if he had a horse, or if he'd been roping any longhorns lately. They usually teased him about things like that, but sometimes they teased him about something he didn't understand. He could tell by their grins and their voices they were poking fun at him. Even before Mama could come out and send him away, he'd back up and turn and run toward the bay. At the water's edge, he'd grab up pieces of wood washed up on shore or anything else he could get his hands on, sometimes just fistfuls of sand, and hurl them out into the waves until his arm was tired and his anger gone.

He wondered why the man with the long, pale hair that hung down from beneath a wide-brimmed black hat, had not left his horse out on the street in front of the saloon, instead of tied up behind Mama's adobe. He wondered why the man stayed so close to the walls as he moved around to the door and why he turned to look over his shoulder every few steps. Did he think someone was following him, or did he not want anyone to see him?

When the man was inside with his mama, Josh stood up and turned his attention to the horse the man had left, the bridle reins wrapped around one of the posts that held up the open lean-to where Josh often slept. He walked as close as he dared, talking softly. The horse eyed him, neck arched, ears pricked forward.

Mama had scolded him about getting too near the men's horses. "You maybe scare him and he jerk free and run away, or maybe he kick at you."

Josh stayed back out of reach and watched the horse while the horse watched him. A dark bay with black stockings on all four legs, Josh noticed a white spot on its forehead that looked like a thick letter J, like the first letter of his name, only turned backwards.

He could read and write his own name. Floss had taught him that. She said she didn't know enough to teach him how to read so she'd ask Birdy to give him lessons, but she must have forgotten because Birdy never did. Maybe she forgot, too. He still missed Floss even though he was only six when she died, two whole years ago. She'd lived upstairs over the saloon with Angel and Birdy and had come everyday to see him. She always hugged him against her softness and gave him his "blessing kisses" as she called them, one on each cheek and one on his forehead. She always said he was a good boy and she knew he'd grow up to be a fine, upstanding man.

Mama said his father could write his own name, but she had never learned to write hers. It pleased him to know that his name was the same as his father's. He loved to take a stick and write Joshua Ryder in a patch of soft dirt. Just looking at the name written out made him feel good and somehow closer to his father.

Mama said his father's favorite horse had been a big bay, maybe a lot like this horse with the thick white backward J on his forehead. He smiled to himself as he pretended this horse was his father's and the redheaded man had untied the reins and mounted was leaning down to help him up

8

behind the saddle. Pressed close to his father's back, his arms around his waist, they rode away, his father urging the bay into a lope.

Someday he would get a horse. He wished Mama would get him one now, but she said he was too young. But, shoot, lots of other boys his age and even younger had horses to ride. He liked to go over to the street and stand at the corner of a building or sit back under the steps of the mercantile. He could be there half the day and not be noticed. He liked to listen to folks talk to each other and watch the buggies and wagons and horses and riders going up and down the street. Whenever he saw a boy with his father and near his own age, he'd pretend he was that boy and the man his father.

He wished he could remember how his father had looked. Mama said he was his father's image, except his hair was black and curly instead of straight and red. He would be tall, she assured him, just like his father, for already he was nearly as tall as she was and he was only eight-years-old.

Mama said he was just a year old when his father took sick with yellow fever and died, so it was no wonder he didn't remember him. She told him the sickness came over his father while he was at a ranch near Victoria, looking to get a job working cattle and a cook's job for her.

The ranch people buried his father in the cemetery at Victoria, but Mama didn't know exactly where because she had not had enough money to buy a tombstone.

He missed not knowing his father. He often thought about where they might be now, if his father had lived. He was sure they'd be living on a ranch and he'd have his own horse to ride and he and his father would be working cattle side by side. When the work was done, they'd ride back to the ranch house where Mama would be smiling and happy and they'd sit down and eat together. With his father around there would be no men coming to see Mama and no broom outside the door to keep him from going inside.

He talked to Mama a lot about his father. He wished he could talk to her about horses and ranch work, too, but she didn't know anything about either one. Orphaned as a small child, she had lived with her grandparents and they'd raised sheep. He wasn't interested in sheep.

He was pretty sure that those boys who came to town with their families, and maybe even the boys who lived here in Indianola, knew a lot about horses and about ranch work. He wished one of them could be his friend. He often watched the boys outside the school building, chasing after one another, laughing and shouting.

Mama wouldn't let him go to school, no matter how hard he begged.

"Those boys they will fight you and call you bad names."

"I can fight, Mama," he'd told her. "I'm not a baby."

"You cannot fight five boys or six," she'd said. "They do not care about being fair. They will hate you for being you, and hate, it has no fairness to it."

He asked about the Mexican boys he saw on the streets. He did not see those boys at school. Could he play with them?

"You are white, not Mexican," she'd said. "Still you are not the same as other white boys."

When he asked why he was not the same as other white boys, she told him it was something he would not understand until he was much older.

"Do the Mexican mamas and fathers care if I play with their boys?" he asked.

"I do not know about Mexicans, but you do not speak like them and they not speak like you. You cannot be friends with boys you do not understand."

He had often heard Mexicans talking in their language and wished he could know what they were saying. He had picked up some Mexican words from listening to the men he saw around town.

He knew a *reata*, was the Mexican word for lariat or lasso, a rope used to catch horses and cows, and *caballo* the Mexican word for horse.

He must have been five, or maybe even younger when he told his mama that when he grew to be a man he would need a *caballo* like other men so shouldn't he have one now so he could start learning to ride."

"Horse," she'd said, frowning. "We do not speak Mexican." His mama was never cross with him for long and her face and voice soon softened. "Someday, maybe," she'd said, smiling. "It still be many years 'til you become a man."

He always tried out his new words on Mama and soon learned that hell and damn and son-of-a-bitch were bad words. She did not get angry with him for those words, saying only, "Josh, bad words are not for boys to speak." The word, *whore*, though, was something more than a bad word, for it made Mama's dark eyes turn hard and gave her a voice that matched her eyes. "You do not say that word! You hear me, Josh? Never!"

She would not explain why the word was so bad, but he knew he would not ever say it in front of her, again. But he would like to know what it meant. Maybe when he heard it again, he would also learn its meaning.

Lost in thought, Josh was startled when the man's bay horse tossed his head, rattling the bridle chains. He had better go. The men never stayed long with Mama and he did not want the man to see him looking at the horse.

"I have to go now," he told the horse. He could tell by the way the bay's ears twitched that he was listening to him. "But maybe I will see you again."

He backed away a few steps and was pleased when the horse whinnied a soft low sound. He grinned. *The horse liked him.* With that happy thought, he turned and ran down the narrow, dusty path to the water.

He had fished the bay early this morning and caught two small ones for breakfast. His mama had fried them with hot peppers, picking out the bones before wrapping them in a tortilla. Just the thought of how good they had tasted made his mouth water. He wished he had even a plain tortilla. He wished he could go back and ask his mama for something to eat, but the man might still be there, the broom still outside the door. He'd wait a while to be sure the man was gone.

He sat on the sand and watched the white-topped waves ride the dark waters in to the shore. He liked to watch the waves and feel and smell the clean air blowing in off the sea. He liked the sounds, too, the waves splashing the shore, the ships' horns announcing their arrival into port, and the many bird cries, from the piping call of the sandpiper to the gulls' harsh scream. He felt more at home here on the beach than in his mama's adobe.

He pulled up his legs and rested his chin on his knees. After a while he grew sleepy and he curled up on his side on the soft stretch of sand. The soothing sound of the waves filled his ears and he slept until the moon rose to cast a shimmering glow across the water.

When he got back to the adobe, the horse was gone and there was no broom beside the door. He lifted the latch and pushed the door open. It was dark inside. The usual smell he'd come to think of as man smell, lingered, but there was a new smell, a stronger smell that prickled the hairs on his neck.

He backed out and closed the door behind him. He looked across the alleyway toward the saloon and the outside steps that led to the rooms on the second floor. Mama must have gone up there to see Angel and Birdy. He wondered what their home above the saloon was like. He thought maybe he'd been up there when he was little. He seemed to have some dim memory of it, but he couldn't be sure. Even when Floss was alive, he'd not been allowed to go there, but had to wait for her and Angel and Birdy to come down and see him. When he had asked Mama why, she'd said that some things were not for boys to know.

He decided he might as well go to bed and went around to the lean-to behind the adobe where the man had tied the horse. He rolled up in his blanket, facing out so he could count the stars to make himself sleepy, but tonight hunger gnawed at his belly, and he was awake long into the night, never before so conscious of the moon's slow journey across the sky.

He woke with the sun and scrambled out of his blanket. *He was so hungry.* He hoped Mama had something good cooked for his breakfast. There was still no broom outside the door, so he pushed it open and stopped, puzzled. *Why was Mama on the floor? When had she come home?* "Mama," he called. She did not answer him. She did not get up from the floor. She did not move.

"Mama?"

He forced his suddenly weak legs to take small steps into the room. "Mama?" He squatted down beside her. She lay on her side, her black hair falling over her face. *Was she sick?* He touched her shoulder. It felt stiff. Cold. He pulled back...touched again. "Mama?" he whispered.

"Josh!" Birdy was beside him. Her shaking hands touched Mama's hair. Birdy's hands and head shook all the time, now. They didn't used to. He often wondered what had made them start shaking, but he'd never asked. Birdy stood up and her shaking hands lifted him to his feet, "Come with me," she said.

Outside, he looked up at her. Her head was bobbing and bobbing, her hand holding his was shaking and shaking. He asked why Mama did not get up off the floor, even though he knew the answer. He had seen animals—last week a gray cat... There was blood on Mama, too, wasn't there? His mind shied away from that thought. *No!* He must have imagined it.

If Birdy answered him, he did not hear her. She led him toward those outside stairs leading up to hers and Angel's home above the saloon.

In the room, he saw a man standing at the top of some inside stairs. Birdy let go of his hand and ran at the man, hissing like an angry cat. "Git! Git!" she cried. The man's eyes got big and his mouth dropped open and he almost fell trying to get turned around and back down the stairs. Josh tried to laugh, but a sob came out instead.

Birdy sat down and pulled him onto her lap. She held him against her sharp bones and rocked him like he was just a little baby. He wasn't a baby and he would insist on getting down off her lap, but he was so tired. He shut his eyes, squeezing back tears. When he opened them again Angel was there. Her eyes looked dark, angry, and her lips were set straight and hard. He knew she was mad at whoever had hurt Mama.

"Listen to me, Josh." Birdy pulled him away from her and looked at him, her head shaking and shaking. "Your mama has gone to be with the angels in heaven."

"She died," Angel said. "The Law'll be here soon to talk to you."

The Law! Josh shivered. *What was the Law and why was it coming for him?*

Birdy drew him close again. She looked over his head at Angel and said in a hard voice, "You got no call to worry the boy about that. Not now. Not yet."

"He's got to know," Angel said.

Josh was relieved when *the Law* came to see that it was just the sheriff. He had seen him around town and the man had sometimes spoken to him, quiet like and gentle. Even though he had to stop, sometimes, and take big gulping breaths, Josh told him everything.

The sheriff asked about the man who had tied his horse to the lean-to. "What did he look like, son? Did you see his face?"

"No." Josh tried to make the word sound strong, but in spite of himself, he whimpered and had to bite his lips to keep from crying. Inside his head, the man with the long, pale hair and the wide-brimmed black hat moved around the adobe, turning his head every few steps to look back over his shoulder.

"Do you always sleep under the lean-to, son?" the sheriff asked. So Josh told him about the broom and when the broom wasn't beside the door, he slept inside on his pad on the floor.

"Damn shame," the sheriff said. He turned to Angel and Birdy. "I know a widow with boys, maybe she'll take him 'til we can find him a place. Maybe he can work for his keep, doing small jobs 'til he grows bigger." He paused and added, "I'll pay the woman a little something in the meantime."

Birdy and Angel nodded, and Birdy said, "We'll send you the money for his keep."

Someone brought his blanket and his extra pants and shirt and the sheriff took him to a big house where a woman lived who kind of reminded him of Floss. She was big like Floss, but he soon found out she wasn't anywhere near as nice.

Mrs. Dunkirk's boys, all three bigger than he was, started in right away saying mean things to him. His mother had been right when she said white boys would call him names.

"You're just a dirty snot-nose Mexican," one said.

"Yeah, a stupid snot-nose, dirty Mexican," said his brother.

The tallest boy said he knew what Josh's mama was.

"What?" Josh asked, confused. *What could she be? Wasn't she just his mama?*

"A dirty Mexican whore," the boy said and all three began to chant, "Dirty Mexican whore. Dirty Mexican whore."

Josh bit his lips and stared at the floor, fighting tears. Maybe his mama was a Mexican. She did look a lot like the Mexican women he saw around town, but she was never dirty and she couldn't have been a whore. That word had made her snap at him, so it had to be something really bad. It was the first he'd heard that he was a Mexican, too. But he couldn't be. His Mama always said he was white, just like his father. He couldn't even talk Mexican or understand it either.

At the supper table, the woman slapped a little dab of thick stew on his plate. He noticed she filled her own plate and her boys' plates right up to the edges and laid a big chunk of bread beside their plates, but, somehow, she forgot his. He wanted to remind her, but he was afraid to say anything. Maybe when he cleaned his plate she would give him more stew and maybe she'd remember to give him some bread, too. His mouth watered he was so hungry. He picked up his spoon and took a quick bite.

The woman reached a long arm behind one of her boys and smacked him on the back of the head. "We thanks the good Lord 'fore we go to feedin' our faces," she snarled. She lowered her head and mumbled something under her breath and then crossed herself as he had seen his mama do at times.

That night the woman instructed him to sleep on the floor back under the table "So's I don't falls over you when I gets up to get the fire started for breakfast." He was glad to be alone. All day he had struggled to hold back tears, and now he could let them go, his face burrowed in his blanket to muffle the sound.

He lasted three days and two nights in that house. Mrs. Dunkirk still put just dabs of food on his plate while she filled hers and the boys' full, even allowing them seconds. A leather strap she'd taken to her youngest boy one day, kept Josh from complaining.

The boys continued to call him names and say that bad thing about his mother. They called him a pissant, turd-face, and a shit-head. They shoved and punched him and yanked his curly hair. "He's got curls like a girl," they said to each other with leering grins. "Bet his whorin' ma curled his hair ever' night soon's she got done entertainin' her men."

So they knew that men had come to his mama's house. That puzzled him. How could they know that?

"Hey, little girly-girl." Leon pushed his face so close Josh smelled the raw onions from supper on his breath. "You don't start to be a man and fight, we gonna strip you jaybird naked and put Ma's dress on you."

That was when Josh knew he had to run away. Mrs. Dunkirk would never give him any more to eat and her boys would never stop being mean to him. It terrified him and made his face burn with shame at the thought of being stripped naked and having to wear one of Mrs. Dunkirk's huge dresses. He was sure she'd fly mad and yank her dress off him and take the strap to his naked bottom.

He decided to leave in the night after everyone was asleep. He would lie awake and listen until the house was silent except for the rumble of Mrs. Dunkirk's snores, but try as he might, his eyes closed and he slept.

He dreamed he was rolled up in his blanket under the lean-to behind the adobe and his mama was frantically calling his name, "Josh! Josh!" He scrambled out of his blanket and ran around the adobe. A huge broom stood crosswise blocking the door. As he stared in confusion and fear, a man with long, light-colored hair and a black hat, opened the door and walked through the broom. The shadowy form of a horse stood nearby and as the man mounted the animal, it took a step toward Josh, stretched out its neck and lowered its big head so Josh could see the white spot, like a thick backward J in the middle of its forehead. Josh reached out to touch the spot and horse and rider vanished in a puff of smoke.

He woke from the dream, tears scalding his cheeks. Wiping his runny nose on his shirtsleeve, he rolled his extra pants and shirt up in his blanket and started for the door. Hungry as always, his thoughts turned to the half of a bread loaf he'd seen Mrs. Dunkirk put back in the cupboard after supper. At supper, he'd eyed the bread, his mouth watering, but as usual, she'd just sliced off some for herself and her boys. His hand searched the dark cupboard for the half loaf of bread, touched it, and felt beside it a full loaf. He wanted to take both loaves, but he would take only the half. He was not a thief. He was just awful hungry. Letting himself out of the house, he ran down the silent streets, past dark houses until he reached the bay.

The moon cast a shimmering light across the dark waters and tipped the white crested waves with silver. Afraid of being seen, he climbed the bank and squirmed in under a tamarisk tree where he cried until the sound of the water lapping against the shore and an owl's soft hooting call soothed away his tears and lulled him to sleep.

Chapter Two

When he woke he was hungry again. He had eaten half of the bread last night before he fell asleep. Now he finished it off. Thirsty, he wished he could drink the salty ocean water. He thought of the cistern where Mama got their water, but he didn't want to go anywhere near the adobe and there was no time, anyway. He needed to leave Indianola before Mrs. Dunkirk woke up and found him missing. She was sure to go right to the sheriff.

He decided he'd go to Victoria and maybe find the ranch where his father was when he took sick. There might still be someone there who would remember a redheaded man named Joshua Ryder. Sometimes he imagined his father was still alive, that somehow there had been a mistake. He thought it was possible that some other redheaded man, had died of the fever and not his father at all. He could not think of why his father would have forgotten to come back to them, but there might be a good reason, just one he didn't know about, yet.

A lot of buggies, wagons, and riders traveled the road leading from Indianola to other parts of Texas. The Mexicans came with their huge carts pulled by ox teams. He had heard they brought gold and silver from their mines in Mexico to send out on the ships anchored in the bay. Freight wagons carried supplies from the ships, not only into Mexico, but also to Victoria and other places. Since he didn't know many Mexican words, and he wasn't sure if the Mexicans even took their big carts to Victoria, he would try to get a ride with the freight wagons.

He wished he could see Angel and Birdy before he left, but they would still be sleeping. He knew they would be upset if they knew how mean the Dunkirks had been to him. He wished he could stay with them, but for some reason he couldn't. He knew that. What he didn't know was why.

Birdy said this mama was in heaven. Mama had told him about Heaven and Jesus and God, and angels. He thought that probably after Birdy took him away, his mama had turned into an angel, growing wings so she could fly. Or maybe there were steps hidden somewhere that led to Heaven and it was only when you were dead that you knew where they were.

Mama had told him that everyone was happy in Heaven. He was glad she was happy there, but he missed her so much his heart hurt. If he could find out something about his father, it might make him feel better. It was scary to think of going all that way alone, but going back to the Dunkirk house scared him a whole lot more.

As Josh hurried along the streets to the main road, he saw the dim glow of lamplight in a few houses and he quickened his pace. Dogs barked and one came at him growling. He turned and walked backwards his eyes on the dog. Any minute, he expected a door to open and someone to shout at him to stop. The dog followed him awhile before losing interest. When it stopped to sniff along the edge of a fence, Josh took off running.

He hear the rumble of the freight wagons before he saw them and he took to the weeds at the side of the road. Squatted down out of sight, he watched the wagons roll past, the men calling to their mules, their long, black whips snaking through the air above them.

Each wagon that passed, he told himself he would jump up and call out to the next one, but it wasn't until the last wagon came up beside him, that he scrambled out of the weeds and called to the driver, "Could I ride along with you, Mister?"

The man hauled back on the leather lines and yelled at the mules. They stopped a little ways up the road and Josh ran the short distance. The driver, a big man with a black beard, spit out a dark stream of tobacco juice and extended his hand. "Climb aboard, boy," he called cheerfully. "Where ya'all headin' to?"

"Victoria," Josh said. What he was going to say next, he had to say first in his mind, for he'd only said the word out loud to himself, never to anyone else. He wished his mama had called his father, pa. The boys on the street called their fathers, pa. He'd heard them plenty of times. "Yes, Pa," they'd say, or "Sure thing, Pa." He loved the sound of the word. Taking a deep breath, he looked sideways at the man and said, "I'm going to meet my pa."

"All by your lonesome?"

"Yes, sir. He doesn't know my mama just died, or he'd of come and got me."

The man made a throat clearing sound and said, "Sorry about your mama." He looked over at Josh. "Name's Hudson. Nate Hudson."

Josh told him his name and Nate Hudson sent him a sidelong grin and a howdy do, before turning back to the mules. He yelled and sent a blacksnake curling through the air, the ends of it popping as loud as a gunshot. The mules lurched forward and soon narrowed the distance between them and the next wagon.

At midday, Nate shared cold biscuits and jerky with him. There was plenty and for the first time since he'd eaten the fish at his mother's, his stomach felt comfortably full. The food made him sleepy and he dozed, jerked awake, and dozed again.

He woke from a solid sleep when Nate yelled, "Whoa, mules. Whoa!" He looked up to see that the wagons ahead had come to a stop.

"What's wrong?" Josh asked.

"Not sure." Nate said, hauling back on the long leather lines strung from the mules' harnesses. "A hold up of some kind. Reckon I'll go check." He climbed off the seat and dropping to the ground, walked to the wagon ahead.

As Nate approached the wagon, three horsemen appeared and pulled up to talk to Nate and the other driver. Josh's heart leaped. *That one man was the sheriff! He had seen him ride that same gray horse in Indianola. Was he looking for him? Had he come to take him back to Mrs. Dunkirk's? Would he put him in jail for taking that half loaf of bread?*

His eyes darted to his blanket rolled and tied that he'd set on the floorboards at his feet, and up again at Nate talking to the sheriff and his

19

men. A cold chill passed through him when he saw Nate glance back at his mules and the wagon, and at him.

Certain the sheriff had come for him, he grabbed up his blanket roll and leaped from the wagon. Bent low, he made for the weeds at the side of the road and with one swift glance back, resumed his hunched over run on to a small stand of trees. When he was hidden from sight, he straightened his back and legs and ran on, expecting, at any moment, to hear shouts and the beat of horses' hooves, and a hand grab his hair or the back of his shirt. He walked and ran all that day.

By the time the sun had crossed the sky and was dropping behind the rim of the earth, Josh was stumbling from weariness. He came to a small stream lined with brush and trees and decided to stay the night. Tomorrow, he'd head back toward the road and maybe he could hitch another ride to Victoria.

He slept without dreams, waking to a light rain. He set out in the direction he had come, his stomach growling with hunger. He wished he knew if he was going the right way. When he'd run from the sheriff, he'd just run, without thinking about how he'd get back to the road. He looked for his tracks, but any sign his bare feet might have left had dissolved in the rain. He was lost and probably he'd never find his way to Victoria and never find anyone who knew his father.

When the rain stopped the clouds cleared to show the sun high overhead. Josh pulled his extra pants and shirt from his bedroll and dressed in dry clothes and carrying his wet ones, he set out again to find the road.

Some hours later, his eyes now blurred with tears he could no longer hold back, he would have walked right out in plain sight of a small weathered wood house, a corral, and some outbuildings, if he hadn't heard the horse whinny.

He jerked back and dropped to the ground. On hands and knees he crawled to the protective cover of some brush and rocks and peering over the rocks, saw a white horse standing inside a corral.

Josh turned his eyes from the horse to look over the rest of the place. Besides the corral and the house, there was a long shed with a slanted roof attached to the corral and beyond the corral two other small buildings.

He wondered if it would be safe to go down and ask whoever lived in the house if he could have something to eat. His stomach growled constantly and sometimes, if he moved too fast, he got dizzy. Undecided, he blinked back tears and waited. The white horse waited, too.

Josh dozed, jerking awake when the white horse whinnied again. He blinked the grogginess from his eyes and peered over the rock. A man with a jumpy kind of walk had come out of the house and was headed towards the corral. He watched as the man went to the horse and mounted its bare back by climbing part way up the side of the corral and swinging a leg over. The horse carried the man away. When they were out of sight, Josh looked back at the house.

The man would have food in the house, but he might have a wife in there, too. Josh kept his eyes on the house for a while longer and when no one else came out, he ran down to the corral.

He waited there a few minutes, vaguely aware of the odor of horse manure. A redbird called, startling him, and a little wind teased the dirt into a dust devil at his feet. Finally, not hearing or seeing any signs of life, he darted over to the side of the house. The window was too high for him to look inside, so he pressed his ear against the wood and listened. Hearing no sound, he went to the door and knocked lightly. When no one came to the door, he lifted the latch and went inside.

A pan half full of cornbread cut in pieces sat on a cold stove. Josh stuffed a piece in his mouth. The bread, dry and crumbly, nearly choked him and he grabbed up a dipper full of water from the bucket set on a stand in the corner. He gulped the water, in his haste, slobbering out bits of cornbread. As he started to hang the dipper back he thought of his mother and what she would say. "Josh! You not leave that dirty!" The ache of his longing for her brought stinging tears and a small whimpering sound from his lips. He swallowed, knuckled away the tears, and looked for a towel. Seeing none, he took the tail of his shirt and wiped out the bits of soggy crumbs his mouth had spit back into the dipper. Afraid if he stayed any longer the man would return and catch him, he stuffed his pockets with the rest of the cornbread and stepped to the door.

He eyed the narrow path the man and horse had followed, aware of the now total silence. The wind that had danced the little dust devil at his feet had died away, leaving the leaves in the tree beside the house to hang motionless. Even the redbird was silent.

Josh closed the door and hurried past the corral, up into the brush and rocks, and on to the trees beside the small stream. He dug the crumbs of corn bread from his pockets and ate until there was none left. His stomach satisfied, he rolled up in his blanket and slept through the rest of the afternoon and all through the night.

A shaft of morning sunlight piercing the branches and leaves overhead brought him awake. He sat up conscious of the now familiar hunger gnawing at his belly. He would have to wait until later in the day, if the man took the horse for a ride at the same time every day. But maybe he didn't. Maybe today, he was already gone. He hurried over to the rocks and heaved a sigh of relief when he saw that the man was already mounted. As soon as they were out of sight, he ran down to the house.

His heart leaped at the sight of a plate on the table filled with meat and beans and on the side, two big biscuits. Within minutes, he had cleaned the plate, eaten one biscuit, stuffed the other in his pants pocket for later, gulped down a dipper full of water, and was out the door.

Back in the shelter of the trees, his stomach pleasantly full, Josh dozed in the warmth of the sun filtering through the leaves overhead.

When he woke, the sun was low in the sky and he knew it was too late to start out to look for the road to Victoria. He would have to stay this one more night. He wondered if he dared go to the man's house again. The man must be wondering who was eating his food and he might try to sneak back and catch him. Maybe this time—this last time—he had better grab up what he could carry and bring it back here to eat. He ate the biscuit he'd saved, rolled up again in his blanket, and slept. In his dreams the man with the jumpy walk stood over him.

CHAPTER THREE

Pete Waters decided he'd best bring the boy in this morning and find out why he was sleeping nights in the trees and raiding his house while he had Snow out for her exercise.

Snow was too old to be carrying a foal and he cursed himself a dozen times a day for putting her to stud. She and the other mares had thrown some good, clean-limbed offspring, which he'd sold after breaking them to ride. The colts and fillies had given him enough to live on. It didn't take much and he had some salted away for his and Snow's old age, which, for both of them, was coming up mighty fast. He'd sold off the last mare two years ago, but he'd kept the stud, a big buckskin, until he could put him in with Snow one last time. He hadn't minded selling the other horses, but he'd had Snow seventeen years—since she was a three-year-old. He could no more have sold Snow than he could have sold his own flesh and blood. He'd kept Spook, too, not that he was so attached to the gelding, but he was a good riding horse and several years younger than the mare. This would be Snow's last foal, but he wished he'd heeded his better judgment and had let the gray filly she'd dropped three years ago be her last.

He'd been graining the mare for months and lately had taken to keeping her in the corral for fear she'd drop the foal when he wasn't around and maybe need his help. He took her out twice a day to stretch her legs and eat some grass. Sometimes he wondered if he should be riding her, although he didn't think it hurt her any and maybe even kept her stronger. 'Course she wasn't carrying much weight with no saddle and skinny as he'd come to be in his later years—not that he'd been a big man to start with—but age had sure whittled him down to pint size. He hoped when the time came, which would be only a matter of days, now, that she would breeze through the ordeal like a young mare.

He needed to get this business with the boy settled soon, for when Snow birthed she and the foal would have to be confined to the corral for a while and the boy couldn't wait that long for his grub. He wasn't likely to show with him and Snow around all the time and he might head out for other parts. The neighbors, except for the Pinõs family, were few and far between. If he'd happen to stumble on to Miguel and Rosita's, they would take him in, but he might go right past their place and wander around until he starved to death.

He hated having to scare the boy by sneaking up behind him and holding his gun on him and, of course, the gun wasn't loaded, but the boy wouldn't know that. He knew with his gimpy leg and sixty-five years, he was no match for the little rascal if he took off scrambling through the brush. In the dim moonlight he'd studied the boy fast asleep tucked back in under a tree and judged his age to be eight or ten, too damn young to be wandering around alone, stealing food from folks and sleeping outside nights.

He'd studied on it most of the night and couldn't figure out another way, short of roping and hogtying the boy. Once he'd been good with a rope, but rheumatism had stiffened up his hands some, and he was sure out of practice. It had been a heck of a long spell since he'd done any real roping. He might yet be good enough to rope a small boy, especially if he caught him unawares, but there was the possibility of the loop going wide and missing him. Even if he carried another rope, it took time to shake out the loop and by then the boy'd be gone. It wasn't like riding after a steer, your horse carrying you along, keeping you in range, while you shook out another loop.

Checking his pistol again to be certain it was empty, Pete stepped out on to the porch and sidled up against the wall until he could step off the far side of the porch and slip around the house. He'd make a wide swing up into the rocks and brush and come down behind the boy.

* * *

Josh watched the door of the house. The man was still inside and the sun was climbing higher and higher in the sky. It worried him that the man hadn't gone for a ride yet. Maybe the man wouldn't be riding the horse at all today. That thought brought the sudden sting of tears. He was already so hungry his stomach hurt. He ran a sleeve across his eyes and squinted hard. He wouldn't cry about it, anyway. He had already cried way too much. He was done crying like a baby.

"Hold it, boy." The man's voice came from behind him. He swung around and stared up at the man, his heart banging against his chest. *The man from the house below! The man with the white horse!* He jumped to his feet, ready to run.

"Don't move," the man said. "I've got you covered."

Josh's eyes leaped from the man's face to the barrel end of a pistol aimed straight at his chest. Fear made his legs tremble.

The man stuck the pistol in the waistband of his gray pants, and with a jerk of his chin, said, "Come on down to the house. I've got some grub waiting. We'll talk then." He motioned Josh ahead of him, "Reckon you know the way."

Josh nodded.

The white horse whinnied at them as they walked past the corral.

"It's all right, Snow," the man said. "We'd stop to chew the fat but we've got a hungry boy here."

The man's cheerful words eased Josh's fear and put some strength back in his legs. The gun had scared him, but the man's eyes, blue, he remembered, hadn't looked mean at all. *Had the sheriff been here looking for him? Had he asked the man to catch him, so he could take him back to Mrs. Dunkirk?* Anger tightened his stomach. If he had to go back, he'd just run away again, but this time he'd take more food and he'd run farther and faster.

At the door, the man reached around Josh, lifted the latch and pushed. Josh's eyes fell on the now familiar room, the table and cook stove, a couple of chairs, and a door that opened into another room.

"Sit," the man said, motioning toward the table, "and I'll rustle you up some grub."

The man took the gun he'd stuck in the waistband of his pants and laid it up on a shelf. "Reckon I won't be needin' this no more. " He grinned at Josh. "It' ain't loaded anyhow." His grin faded and he added, "Hated like the very devil to have to use it, but figured you'd take off into the brush like some wild critter 'fore I could explain things. Stoved up as I'm gettin' to be, you'd of left me eating your dust."

Josh took the chair the man indicated. His eyes followed the man as he shoved a chunk of wood in the stove, set a heavy skillet on top, and began slicing bacon. His mouth watered at the aroma rising up from the pan. When the bacon was done, the man put it on a blue tin plate, added eggs to the grease and in a few minutes scooped them up and put them on the plate along with a slab of bread. "Eat," he commanded.

As Josh bent over his plate, the man took two cups from the cupboard and filled them with coffee from a battered looking, black pot on the stove. "You like coffee?" he asked.

"I don't know," Josh said. "I've never had any."

A smile spread across the man's face and twinkled in his blue eyes nested in a web of wrinkles. "You'll like this. I put in a good sized dip of lick."

"What?"

The man chuckled and the last of Josh's fear slipped away. "Guess most folks call it molasses. On roundup some years back, we had a fella called it lick and I just sort of kept it up."

Josh took a cautious sip of the coffee and smiled up at the man. "I like it," he said. "It smells good, too."

When he had mopped the plate clean with a piece of bread crust, chewed and swallowed it, and drained the last sweet drop of coffee from his cup, the man had a bunch of questions for him. First he wanted to know his name.

Afraid the sheriff was still looking for him, he decided he'd better not use his own name. Angel always talked about a brother named Billy Clyde. He'd use that name if this man knew the sheriff.

"Just in passing," The man said when he asked and then added with a grin, "You ain't a wanted man, are you? You ain't gone and held up no bank or stage, have you?"

"No sir." *A wanted man? Shoot, he wasn't even a man yet. But he was a thief.* He shivered and taking a deep breath, confessed to the half loaf of bread he'd taken from the Dunkirks. He felt shame heat his face. "I came in when you were gone and took your food, too."

"You was doggone hungry, I reckon," the man said.

Josh nodded, ducking his head to hide the sudden welling of tears.

"So it's all right. You was just trying to survive. Many's the man who's come upon an empty cabin and helped himself to the fixin's there, mindful that he don't take too much and that he returns the hospitality should the opportunity come to him."

Josh blinked back his tears and looking back up at the man's open face and friendly blue eyes, the words poured out of him in rushes of sound, like tidal waves splashing again and again against the shore.

He began with his name, his real name, forgetting he had even considered another. He told about the man with the long, light-colored hair that hung down from under his black hat and about the bay horse with the white backward J on his forehead. He tried to tell about his mama, but he couldn't get more than a stuttering of words past the choking feeling in his throat.

The man helped him. "You found your mama dead and you think that man killed her?"

He nodded, although he hadn't until then thought that the man might have been the one. *Had he? Or had someone come later, after the man with the pale hair was gone?*

"And then what?" the man said.

So Josh told him about Birdy taking him up the back stairs of the saloon, to the rooms where she and Angel lived, but he didn't tell about her holding and rocking him like a baby. He told about the sheriff coming and asking questions and taking him to Mrs. Dunkirk. He did not tell the man what the Dunkirk boys said about his mama, or that they threatened to takes his clothes and put their mama's big dress on him, but he did tell him that the boys called him names and that he never got enough to eat. He ended his story with the sheriff and his men riding up to the freighters that morning and his fear that they had come to take him back to Mrs. Dunkirk.

The man listened, once in a while nodding, but not speaking. Josh held his jaws so stiff against the threat of tears that they hurt when he finally stopped talking.

The man chewed awhile on his lower lip and then said, "I guess I forgot to tell you my name. It's Pete Waters. I live here by myself. The white horse in the corral is a mare I call Snow. I have a bay gelding, name of Spook, staked out on some good grass. Named him Spook 'cause he's got a real nervous side to him. Used to be skittish as all get out, especially when he was a youngster."

"Did you name your horse Snow because she's white?"

"Never really gave it much thought, but, yes, I reckon so. Where I growed up, up north in a place called Michigan, it snowed all winter long. Deep snows, too. Deep enough to bury this little o' house clean up to its rooftop. I've got some real fond memories of playing in the snow with my brothers and afterwards thawing out in front of Ma's cook stove, putting away her warm, sweetened milk and buttered light bread biscuits."

Josh thought he'd sure like to see that snow Pete Waters talked about.

Pete Waters went on to tell Josh he had come to Texas when he was a young man and right away got work on a ranch.

"My pa used to do that," Josh said, surprised that he had said pa so easily.

"Worked cattle? Where?"

"I don't know. Mama said when I was about a year old, he heard of a place up near Victoria needing a man to do ranch work and someone to cook. So he went to ask about the jobs."

"He was going to hire on as a hand and see if your mama could be the cook."

Josh nodded. "Except he took sick and died. Mama said it was yellow fever. The ranch people buried him in the cemetery in Victoria. Mama wanted to buy him a tombstone, but she didn't have the money."

As he spoke of her, he could see his mama's dark eyes looking soft on him, her lips curving into a warm smile. Almost, he could hear her say of his pa, *"His heart it was good, Josh. Time it go by and you grow up, you not forget."*

Pete Waters jarred Josh back from those warm thoughts by saying as he stood up and reached for Josh's empty plate. "I reckon now you'd like to make Snow's acquaintance."

Josh jumped up. "I sure would, Mr. Waters," he said.

"Pete," the man said, turning back from dropping the plate into a blue enamel wash pan. "Call me Pete."

"Yes, sir, Mr. Pete," Josh said.

Pete laughed. "Just Pete. No mister, no *Senõr*, just Pete."

"Pete," Josh said, a warmth filling him. He sure liked this man named Pete.

Josh could hardly believe he was at last getting to touch a horse. It surprised him that the mare's mane felt coarse under his fingers, not soft, like hair, like he thought it would feel. It pleased him that the mare liked him, or at least that was what Pete said, grinning like it sure pleased him a lot, too.

He laughed when he held out his hand and the mare touched it with her soft, mouse-colored muzzle, snuffing a little and breathing warm puffs of air on it. He stepped closer and ran his hand along her shoulders and sides shooing off a couple of flies. Except for the swish of her tail and occasional stamp of a hoof, Snow stood still. Josh breathed in the smell of her and again felt her warm breath when she swung her head around to nuzzle him on the shoulder, like she was smelling of him, too.

For the first time since his mama's death, Josh felt content. He hoped he could stay awhile, a day or two anyway.

"She likes you boy," Pete said. "Want to go with me to take her for a walk? I like to give her a little workout a couple of times a day to keep her in shape. She's a little old to be having a foal."

Josh felt his heart give a little skip. "A foal? That's a baby, isn't it?"

"Sure is," Pete said. "She'll be dropping it any day now." He grinned at Josh. "Do you want to ride her?"

Pete's words made his heart leap. *Did he want to ride the horse? Oh, yes. He'd been waiting all his life to ride a horse.*

"If you'll give me your foot, I'll boost you up," Pete said.

It felt strange being up on the mare's back. He sat so high he could look down on the top of the gray hat covering Pete's bald head.

Pete tied a short rope to the horse's halter and showed him how to neck rein her, but he never had to use it for she followed Pete like a pet dog. He noticed that Pete had changed from his old scarred boots to a pair of moccasins. Probably so he could walk better. His jumpy walk made his head bob up and down almost as much as Birdy's shook.

At first Snow's back felt as slippery as though she'd been greased with tallow and he kept a tight grip on a handful of her white mane, but, he soon got used to her movements and he began to relax and enjoy himself.

When they left the narrow road and headed off toward a stand of trees, Pete said. "Garcitas crick is just ahead. We're only a few miles from Port Lavaca. Maybe about where the town of Linville used to be. The Commaches looted and burned the place back in the '40s and those who survived moved a ways south and started Port Lavaca. That's where I go to do my trading."

Now high up on Snow's back, Josh looked down on the crown of Pete's hat. "Are we going to Port Lavaca today?"

"Not today. We'll wait until after Snow has her foal."

When they came to the creek, Pete said, "Slide off and let Snow get herself a drink and graze a spell. You and me can take our ease over there in the shade. Should of brought us 'long a fishing pole." He squinted at Josh. "You ever go fishing?"

Josh nodded. "I had a pole, but I didn't bring it."

"Never did much fishing myself," Pete said.

* * *

That evening Pete took him to where he'd staked out the bay gelding he'd spoken of earlier. Pete boosted Josh up on the horse's back and he rode him to the corral. "Guess I told you I named him Spook 'cause he'd spook at anything, even his own shadow," Pete said as he walked his jumpy walk along beside the horse. "He's pretty calm now, but you ought to have seen him when he was a youngster, shying and snorting at ever'thing. Any excuse, a fence post he'd forgotten about, or a bird flying up, would set him into pitching like a wild bronc." He grinned up at Josh. "I'm shamed to say it, but I've had to pull leather a time or to, riding him in his young days."

"Pull leather?" Josh asked, puzzled.

"Grabbed the saddle horn. Now if I'd of been in the company of some other fellas, I'd of gotten bucked off and got a snoot full of dirt 'fore I'd have shamed myself that a-way."

A warm feeling filled Josh. Pete's "snoot full of dirt" brought a laugh bubbling up out of him and made Pete grin. He'd remember that about not grabbing the saddle horn.

They had fried potatoes, beans, and biscuits for supper. Afterwards, they cut wood for the wood box. Pete gave him a hatchet to cut up kindling while he took an ax and split up some large chunks of firewood. That done, they sat outside on the porch. A big live oak tree shaded the porch from the western sun, now past the horizon, leaving a faint flush of red in the sky. A slight breeze cooled the air. They'd carried their chairs from the table to the porch. Pete tipped his back against the wall, but Josh kept his flat, afraid he couldn't balance it right and it would fall over and make him look the fool. If he was going to stay, and he sure hoped he was, for a while anyway—at least until he was ready to look for someone who could tell him about his pa—he'd practice tipping his chair back when Pete was gone off to town or someplace.

Pete talked some about the foal Snow was to have any day now, but mostly they sat in silence as they watched the nighthawks and bats glide through the evening air.

Josh fell asleep almost as soon as he tumbled on to the small rawhide sling cot across the small room from Pete's tarp covered bed. He pulled his blanket up close to his face and the next thing he knew, sunlight was streaming through the small window and Pete's bed was empty, the tarp smoothly in place.

He had been with Pete a few days when one morning at breakfast, Pete, handed him a plate of fried mush soaked in molasses, or lick as he, too, had begun to call it, and said,

"Well, you've had a chance to look over this two-horse outfit, reckon you want to sign on and ride with us?"

"You mean stay?" Quick tears threatened making his words sound funny and he knew he was going to start bawling, but the fork he'd picked up in anticipation of tasting the sweet-flavored mush saved him by slipping from his hand. It clattered against the table and dropped to the floor. By the time he'd picked it up, he was all right again. "I'd sure like that," he said and forked up a mouthful of the fried mush.

Pete grinned. "Well, I reckon you and me's got what it takes to get along and Snow and Spook seem to like your brand."

31

A rush of happiness fluttered up in Josh's chest. If he couldn't be with his mama, then he'd like to be here. Someday, but not now, he'd leave here and go looking for his pa again. But for a while, at least until Pete tired of him, he had a place to stay and plenty to eat.

"Guess it's a done deal then," Pete said. "Slick up that breakfast and we'll get started on our work. I've been thinking you're gonna need some roping lessons. That is if you're aiming to work cattle someday, like me'n your daddy did."

"Really?" Josh could hardly believe his ears. "What am I gonna rope?"

Pete grinned. "First, the snubbing post in the corral, " he said.

Picturing himself roping the post, Josh laughed, and nearly choked on a mouthful of mush.

Chapter Four

Pete watched the boy eat, so filled with emotion, that if not for the coffee to wash down the lump that kept rising in his throat, he wouldn't have been able to swallow his breakfast. Etta Jane would have been so damned proud of this boy. He'd give most anything to have her here to mother the little fella.

Over the years, Etta Jane had sort of faded out of his dreams, but she slipped back in the night the boy came as if she'd never been gone. She sure did want him to have the boy. Coming awake in the dark from one of his dreams, he'd held silent arguments with her and with himself. *He's awful small. It's a big responsibility, taking on a boy. What if I can't raise him up right and he turns out bad?*

He remembered how she used to look when she disagreed with him, one eyebrow cocked a little higher than the other and he almost thought he heard her say, "Nonsense, Pete. You're just scared."

That was true. 'Course he knew he was just foolin' himself. The boy had his heart roped and hogtied already. So why was he arguing with himself, and with her? Sure seemed to please the little fella, too, that he wanted him to stay. 'Course, he didn't have much choice, either him or those Dunkirks, or the road again. He might not care so much for his benefactor, but it sure did beat the alternative.

For months after Etta Jane died, Pete's dreams had been filled with her, and even now, twenty years later, he still dreamed of her on occasion.

Now, since the boy had come, she was back in his dreams as real as she had been those first long, lonely months after her death and he could swear she was talking to him about the boy. Each time he woke from one of his wife's night time visits, he'd listen to the boy's soft even breathing from across the room and he'd let his tears go, tears he'd held back too many years. Tears for the children they never had, tears that in his younger years he'd been afraid would make him less of a man, tears that flowed like rivers down the crevices of his old, weather-beaten face and soaked into his pillow, tears that released him to sleep again, untroubled by dreams.

He'd sure enjoyed this past week having the boy around. Some old regrets, long buried, had surfaced, but that was natural, giving as how he and Etta Jane had wanted a child.

The boy didn't talk none about his mama. Not since that first day, and Pete had sure been curious to know what had happened to get her killed. He would like to go into Indianola and ask around, but he couldn't take the boy along and where could he leave him while he was doing the asking? Besides he didn't want to leave Snow that long. She might drop her foal before they got back. He'd just wait. Whatever the news was, it wouldn't be going away. Someday he'd find out what had happened to the boy's mama.

As it turned out, he didn't have long to wait. Josh was starting out of the house one afternoon when two men came riding up, one on a stocky, barrel-chested gray, the other on a long-legged sorrel. The boy recognized the sheriff and ducked back inside, his face blanched out as white as Etta Jane's "going to town" shirtwaist.

"It's the sheriff," he whispered, fear filling his big, dark brown eyes. "You won't let him take me back, will you?"

"I sure won't," Pete assured him. "Leastways," he added, with a small grin, "not without a fight."

The boy was too nervous to see any humor in Pete's words and with one anxious glance in the direction of the approaching riders, he disappeared around back of the house and didn't return until the men had ridden away.

When Pete told him about the boy, the sheriff said he's sure been wondering. "One of the freighters, a feller named Hudson, said he figured the boy was just hiding, although he couldn't figure out why 'til I told him. He figured the boy'd come out of his hiding place, soon's me and my men left. But he must'a just kept on running 'til he run on to your place."

"You weren't after the boy?" Pete said. He couldn't believe the law would take time for a small boy, but thinking about it, he thought they probably should. Small boys should be as important as outlaws.

The sheriff laughed. "No, we wasn't wantin' him, we was after some crazy galoot who shot up a saloon and killed the bartender in the process. We got him, too," he added, with a touch of pride.

Pete stirred up some biscuits and reheated some beans for the two men and while they ate, the sheriff told him about Josh's mama, how she'd worked out of that little adobe after the boy got too old to stay upstairs above the saloon.

Pete knew the saloon right away. He had visited one of those rooms on the second floor a few times after Etta Jane died. Sick with grief and loneliness, he had needed someone to hold him, he realized, later, as much, or maybe even more than the coupling, which was fast and unsatisfying. He'd had the woman called Floss that first time and so the few times he returned, he'd asked for her again. He did not remember seeing a Mexican woman, but that was twenty years ago. Likely she'd still been a child then.

The sheriff took a swallow of coffee and said, "The boy told us about the fella with the light-colored hair and the black hat. He might be the killer, but whoever it was must have been nursing a grudge, 'cause he sure beat the hell out of her." He paused and reached for his tobacco sack and papers. "Damn near broke every bone in her body and beat her face to a pulp. Strangest thing. He left a big o' skinning knife in her belly."

As he was leaving the sheriff said, "Those two upstairs above the saloon were sure worried about the boy. They'll be right glad to hear, he's got himself a place."

Pete mulled over the sheriff's words as he watched the two men ride away. So the boy had been born in a sportin' house. And the two whores there cared enough to worry about him. Funny, they hadn't taken him in. The boy was used to the trade, living as he was in his mama's home. Probably she sent him out when she got a customer, and couldn't they do the same? But the boy'd be harder to keep corralled upstairs in their rooms and he was getting a mite too old not to know what was going on. Hard to tell what would have happened if his mama'd lived. He wondered who'd killed her, probably some lickered up fool with a short fuse. Odd that he'd left a skinning knife in her. A fella skinning out hides for his living wasn't likely to leave the tools of his trade behind.

The sheriff thought it was a grudge killing. That the way he'd beat her up had sure made it seem personal. Said he hoped it wasn't the boy's old man. The boy said his pa was dead, but his mama may have just told him that, not knowing, most likely, who'd planted that particular seed.

Pete wondered if the boy knew yet what his mama had been. If not, maybe he'd never have to know. He was only eight years old, but, he might, as he grew older, begin putting it all together and, if he asked him, he'd have to tell him the truth. It didn't never do no good to lie. That was one thing he'd learned in his advanced years. Once you lied you had to keep on lying and that got to be a hard trail to follow. If and when the boy did get to figuring it out, he hoped the anger and shame wouldn't go to eatin' on him. Anger and shame could turn a good boy bad. He'd have to watch for that and turn it aside if he saw it coming.

Ordinarily, Pete Waters didn't hold with sportin' women, even though he'd used that one in Indianola. But he figured for some it was mostly a matter of survival. And they sure could ease a fella's natural urges. His natural urges had been fed quite well those eight years he'd been married to Etta Jane. He sure had enjoyed having her in his house when he came home and, Lord, the pleasure he'd taken in their bed, all but lost in the softness of her body. Now he was too old for the blood to go racing too hot through his veins and the pleasures of the flesh had faded, but the memory still remained.

When the need had come upon him, after Etta Jane's death, he had bypassed Port Lavaca, where he was liable to run into someone he knew and had gone on to Indianola. A couple of drinks for courage and to dim the memory of his wife, he'd turned to the big one called Floss and tried to lose himself in her. Not that it ever worked. If she would have allowed kissing, maybe, for he had always enjoyed kissing, craved it even, but Floss would jerk her head aside, so his kissed always landed in her yella hair.

Etta Jane told him when she lay dying, that he ought to marry again. "Forty five ain't all that old for a man," she'd said. "Find yourself a young wife that can get you a son."

He'd hushed her. Kissing her forehead and smoothing back her brown hair, he'd assured her he had no wish to marry again. Sometimes he made light of it, saying no sane woman was gonna look at a sawed-off, bowlegged, bald-headed, banty rooster of a man with a gimpy leg. Other times he assured her that she was his sweetheart and always would be, whether here in this world or on the other side of the divide. He would never hurt Etta Jane by confessing to wanting that nameless, faceless woman who could bear him a son. Yet, when Etta Jane was gone and he was free, he never looked for that nameless, faceless woman. Sometimes he thought it was the fear that she, too, would lose their babies and he'd have to live through that slice of constant misery all over again. Sometimes he thought it was guilt for having lied to Etta Jane, not only on her deathbed, but through half of their marriage. Each time a baby died in her womb and when the last one, the fifth, a little boy who lived a few hours giving them hope in spite of the evidence to the contrary, he assured her, as always, that he did not need a child, a son. He hoped he had convinced her of his lie, but he was never sure.

The others had died unseen, sloughed off in blood, a small handful of matter, not yet a child, and carried away by the old Mexican woman who attended Etta Jane. Only the last one, that tiny, perfectly formed boy, too weak to grasp the nipple Etta Jane offered with tears flowing down her cheeks, had he seen and held in his arms. That one had ripped a hole in the already thinning fabric of their marriage.

"Let me let you go," Etta Jane said, several weeks after they put that little boy in the cemetery at Port Lavaca. "I will sign whatever papers they've got that says we're no longer married. Then if you'd drive me to Fort Worth… My oldest sister, Anna Mae, is widowed. She writes how awful lonely her days have come to be. I know she'd be real glad if I was to come live with her."

Although he'd wanted to, he could not let her go to marry another, but if she died, he would be free. May he burn in hell for those thoughts for the gods of evil must have read his mind, for shortly afterwards she began to fail.

At first she thought it was another baby on the way, but something else grew inside her, something that soon took her life and set him free, but it was a freedom he couldn't take and he had put aside his dreams of a son.

Now, at this age, maybe even past his ability to sire a son, one had come to him. A son, given to him by the gods and a Mexican whore, or, maybe, Etta Jane. Some folks believed that those who have gone on, to wherever folks go after death, have an influence on the living. If they did, then Etta Jane would have worked her heavenly fingers to the bone to get him a boy. So maybe it had all been her doing. Who was he to say?

After he talked to the boy about staying on, the vivid dreams of Etta Jane ceased. That night he woke, not remembering the words she had spoken, but with the feeling that she had just told him goodbye. His throat thick with tears, he left his bed, careful not to wake the boy, and stepped outside. As he looked up into the night sky, a star shot across the heavens. Tears stinging his eyes, he whispered, "Thank you for the boy, Etta Jane."

Chapter Five

Pete woke with a full bladder and a dream of Snow and rose up on an elbow to see that the mare was down on the floor of the shed, stretched out on her side. Light from the full moon and Snow's own white hide made it easy to see. Slipping into his moccasins, he left the boy asleep on the blankets they'd brought from the house last night and stepped out of the shed. The moon was high overhead, the stars bright gems in the night sky. Buttoning his pants, he went back in to the mare and squatted beside her.

"You doing all right, girl?" he asked stroking her neck. "You gonna get us a baby here a'fore long?"

Snow raised her head and rolled her eyes back at him. He eased away from her a few feet and sat down to wait. He'd decided not to wake the boy until the birth was a little closer to being a done deal.

Two days ago Snow had begun to come into her milk and all day she had been restless. By dark, tonight, she was constantly switching her tail and a light sweat bathed her flanks.

He grinned to himself, remembering how the boy's dark eyes grew wide when he told him Snow was about to foal. Excited, he'd rattled off questions faster'n a prairie fire in a high wind, and had to be reassured a dozen times that, yes, Pete was certain the foal would be here by morning. He'd also wanted Pete's opinion, just about as many times, as to whether the foal would be a colt or a filly? Also what color did he think the baby would be and was he going to start raising horses again? He'd tried to stay awake to answer the boy's questions, but he'd kept nodding off.

He wondered how long it had taken the boy to settle down enough to sleep. He was sure dead asleep now, his head rolled off the pillow of hay and hanging down in a way that would guarantee a stiff neck in an old man.

Sitting there watching the mare, Pete dozed off, jerking awake when Snow got up on her feet and walked out into the corral. He stood up and followed her. She paced the corral several times around, before coming back in to lower herself down again on the hay covered dirt floor and stretch out on her side. In a few minutes she began to strain.

Intent on the mare, he jumped when Josh, hovering at his elbow, his hair tousled, his brown eyes wide, spoke. "Is she having her foal, Pete?"

"She sure is, son. Reckon we'll be getting us a new baby, right soon."

The boy settled down beside him and they watched together, waiting. He was glad Josh was out of questions. He was too worried to have the patience for questions now. Snow had rolled over on her back a few times and that wasn't a good sign. Time wise, too, it wasn't good, either. Her offspring should have come by now.

Gut sick with worry, Pete silently cursed himself. What was it about him that wanted babies, whether human or horse? He should have left Etta Jane alone and spared her the pain of losing another child. He should have gone to Indianola to satisfy his needs. She might still be alive, if she'd not had those babies to drain away her strength, her happiness in living. Sometimes he wondered if wanting a baby so bad had caused the tumor. The doctor said it wasn't his fault, or hers, that those things just happened. If there was any blame, it should go to the tumor growing in her belly. Still, he could never shake the idea that his wish for a child, especially a son, had created the growth that, for a time, had mimicked a baby and then grew to kill her.

Forcing his mind away from thoughts of Etta Jane, he turned his full attention to the mare. There should have been some progress by now. He'd best give her some help. Telling Josh to stay put, he went over and squatted behind Snow. She raised her head and looked back at him. He shed his shirt and reached for the can of tallow he'd brought out, in case it was needed. Greasing his right hand and arm, he felt inside the mare. Through the birth sac he could feel a head and one tiny hoof. Where was the other one?

He called on Etta Jane for help, whispered pleas inside his head, as his fingers felt along the shoulder of the foal searching for the other leg, the mare's contractions bearing down hard on his arm. When he found the leg, turned back along the body, he knew he'd have to tear the birth sac and pull it back around. He grasped the slippery little leg just above the hoof and pushing back on the body of the foal, he carefully maneuvered the leg around until it was next to the other forward limb. He pulled his arm out and waited. Soon the foal's long legs emerged, then the head, nose first. "It's coming, Snow," he said. To his ears, his voice sounded high-pitched and overloud. "Push it out girl. Push it out."

"Look, Pete! Look!" Josh cried in a shouted whisper, as the foal, dark and wet, slipped out of Snow.

Pete touched the colt and a shiver ran through the little horse, followed by a deep shuddering breath. "He's breathing, Josh," Pete said. "Get that feed sack over there and dry him off."

The awe and amazement shining in Josh's dark eyes and glowing face, as the boy rubbed the little horse's wet coat, tickled Pete. "A perfect little fella, ain't he?" Pete said.

"He sure is," Josh whispered, his eyes never leaving the colt.

The colt raised his head and Josh drew back, feed sack in hand. He grinned up at Pete when the little horse shook his head a couple of times, wiggled his ears back and forth and snorted air through his small nostrils.

"He's trying to figure out if everything on him's working," Pete said, feeling his own grin crease his face.

Snow raised her head and nickered to her offspring.

"Your little fella's doing okay, Mama," Pete said, patting the mare as he got to his feet. "You rest a spell. The boy and I'll scoot back and give you some breathing room."

Outside the shed, he sluiced water from the tank over his arm, wiped off with a gunny sack, and donned his shirt. The boy had followed him, watching, solemn-eyed and silent. His face broke into a grin when Pete winked at him.

They sat back on their blankets, backs against the wall, eyes on the mare and colt. Snow was on her feet now, licking her baby. Josh laughed when the colt tried to stand up on his little hooves. Every time he moved his forelegs out in front of him and tried to stand, they would quiver and give way, and he'd fall back again. Seconds later, a shake of his little head and he was trying it again. With each new try the colt grew stronger and finally, he was up, standing on his long, wobbly legs.

As the little horse took his first staggering steps, Snow stayed beside him. The colt ran his nose over her, starting at her tail and moving along her side. She turned her head to watch him and the two touched noses. Snow nickered softly. From his mother, the colt moved to the side of the shed to investigate a coil of rope hanging on the wall.

"Let's go to the house and get some breakfast," Pete said. "If I don't get some grub in me soon, my belly's gonna rub sores on my backbone,"

"Is that the same as my belly thinks my throat's been cut?" Josh said, his grin shining in his dark eyes.

"Same as," Pete said. It pleased him that the boy was teasing him about his old sayings. He must be feeling to home here.

Although the boy hadn't thought he was too hungry, he sure put away the batter cakes and bacon. When he got his belly full, his long, dark lashes went to blinking and he was looking dangerously close to unhinging his jaw with his yawning, but it wasn't a-tall likely he'd chose sleep over that brand new colt and when Pete said, "Reckon we'd best check on 'em," the boy hopped off his chair spry as a grasshopper.

They walked back to the corral, the sun just breaking over the rim of the earth and spreading a pink flush across the eastern sky. Snow and her offspring were still under the shed.

"You sure got us one fine baby," Pete said, talking softly to Snow as he looked her over carefully. He didn't realize Josh was watching intently, until he turned from the mare and said, "She looks fine to me." Josh let out a whoosh of the breath he must have been holding. Maybe it had occurred to him that death could claim the colt's mama, too. In sympathy, Pete touched the boy's shoulder. "Reckon we can take our bedrolls in. I could sure use some more shut-eye."

"Can I stay here?" Josh asked, his eyes following the colt as the little horse nosed Snow's flank and finding a teat began to suck, his stub of a tail swinging back and forth.

Pete grinned. "Suits me," he said. "I guess I'll stay, too, if you don't mind an old man snoring in your ear."

Josh flashed a quick grin. "You don't snore, Pete. Leastways, not much."

When Pete woke, Josh, Snow, and the colt were out in the corral, the colt feeding again and Josh perched on a top rail watching. Pete yawned and stretched. He was surprised to see that the sun stood midway in the sky. He hadn't slept that good for a long time. Clapping his hat on his head, he stepped out of the shadows of the shed into the bright sunlight and walked over to Josh.

"Would you like to pet him when he's done feeding?" he asked, smiling up at the boy.

"I sure would," Josh said, swinging off the top rail and jumping backwards to the ground.

"It's okay, little fella," Pete said, as they approached Snow and her colt. "We ain't aiming to hurt you. We just want to get acquainted that's all." Snow swung her head back to keep an eye on the colt crowded up against her.

"The instincts of motherhood will make her wary for a few days," Pete said. "Just take it slow."

When he was a couple of arm's length from the colt, Josh stopped and held out his hand. The colt took a step toward him and stretched his neck until his nose touched the boy's hand. Then he shook his head and backed up, nearly falling over his long legs. Laughter bubbled up in Josh, erupting in a snort that gave him the hiccups and startled the colt into crowding even closer to Snow.

"I 'spect Peanut here'll shed off that muddy brown color," Pete said. "Could be white like his mama, but I doubt it."

"Don't white horses get born white?" Josh asked around two more hiccups.

"Never knowed of one that was. They're generally a dark color and shed off to white. Knowed a fella once named his colt Cloud. Thought he'd be light gray like his mama, but he turned out to be a bay."

"Did he call him Cloud, anyway?" Josh asked, around another hiccup.

"Yep. Hard to change a name once you get used to it."

"Are you naming him Peanut?" Josh hiccupped again, his eyes on the little horse.

Pete saw right away that the name didn't set too well with the boy. Course he hadn't planned on naming him anyway.

"How about if you name him?"

"Me?" Josh jerked his eyes away from the colt to stare up at him.

Pete felt a little catch in his heart as he looked down into the boy's small, earnest face. "It'd be right for you to name him, since he's gonna be yours."

"He...He...He's gonna be m...mine?" the boy stammered.

Pete grinned. "When that little fella gets growed big enough to ride, I 'spect all I'll be ridin' is a rocking chair."

"Gosh, Pete. Thanks!" Josh swung around to look again at the colt, his hiccups vanishing in this moment of joy.

"Looks like your hiccups been cured," Pete said.

Josh laughed, his face a mirror of his happiness. Then he sobered. "What color do you think he'll be? Do you think I should know that before I name him?"

"Don't know as it matters. Just give him a name you like. Far as his color goes, I'd put my money on buckskin, like his sire." Pete put a hand on the boy's shoulder. "He's a mighty good-looking colt, whatever color he turns off to be. I reckon he'll be as fine a ridin' horse as his mama."

"I know he will," Josh said, his words all wrapped up in joy and a bit of pride.

* * *

Pete thought he saw a change in Snow toward evening of the next day. Slightly off her feed, she appeared listless. The colt was prancing around pert as you please, so there was nothing wrong with him. Maybe he was just imagining things. He sure hoped so. He didn't say anything to Josh, but the boy was quick to pick up on anything out of the ordinary and that night lying in their beds in the dark, Pete, sure the boy was asleep, was surprised when he said, "You think Snow's all right, Pete? She don't act quite the same. Like she don't feel too good."

"I don't know, son," Pete told him. "I've noticed a change in her, too. Maybe we'll know more tomorrow."

Snow was no better by morning and as the day progressed, she grew increasingly listless. Standing with her head hanging, she was pretty much ignoring her colt. She hadn't eaten or taken any water to speak of since morning and Pete knew he was loosing her. Of all the horses he'd owned, she had always been his favorite. It made him sick to his stomach to think of what he'd soon have to do. The best he could do for her was to make it quick, one bullet in the middle of her head, just above the eyes a little, so it'd hit her brain.

He was pretty sure the birth had done some kind of slow damage to her insides. Maybe that little leg turned backwards had poked a hole in something while he was pulling it around. Several times she'd kicked up her hind leg, striking her belly, like a horse does sometimes when it's hurting. She looked bloated and her sides felt tight as a drum. Every time he ran his hand along her stomach, she jerked her head to look back at him, so he was pretty sure she was in pain. The hell of it was, there wasn't anything he could do for her.

"Is she going to be all right, Pete?" Worry showed in the boy's brown eyes. Although he hated like the devil to tell Josh his colt was about to be an orphan, Pete knew he had to give an honest answer.

"No, she ain't, son. I'm going to have to put her out of her misery. She's hurting and she's not eating or drinking. She won't have milk for the youngster much longer. I want you to go over to the Pinõs' and bring Miguel. Ask him if he can part with a fresh nanny for a few weeks and a lamb's bottle, too, if he's got one to spare."

* * *

Pete gave him directions to the couples' home, a small adobe house with goats and sheep everywhere, some in the yard, the rest scattered out over the land. It was nearly five miles to the Pinõs' home from Pete's, and Josh ran most of the way. Pete had considered sending him on Spook, but the gelding was too unpredictable and Josh too green of a rider.

Miguel Pinõs, a young, thin-faced Mexican man, saw him and came out of the house to meet him. The man greeted him in Spanish, but switched when Josh answered him in Anglo, explaining that he'd come from Pete's.

"You live with Pete?" the Mexican man asked, his eyebrows lifting in surprise.

Josh nodded. "Snow's sick. She had a colt and now she's sick. Pete'll have to shoot her." He blinked back a sudden gathering of tears and swallowed hard before he could find his voice again. "Pete wants you to come and bring a nanny goat if you got one fresh and a lamb's bottle if you got one to spare."

"*Si.* I do," Miguel said. "Both goat and bottle." He jerked his chin in the direction of the adobe. "Come. Meet my Rosita. You are hungry, no? You eat. I get the goat."

Rosita Pinõs, small and thin with dark eyes and long shiny, black hair, reminded him of his mama and the ache he carried in his heart, rose up with a rush of tears he barely managed to keep from spilling over.

A solemn-faced baby, resting on his mama's hip, fixed his black eyes on Josh and followed his every move even as Rosita sat the baby down on a mat and turned away to fix Josh a tortilla filled with scrambled eggs, onions, and peppers.

Even Rosita's food tasted like his mother's and he swallowed tears with the first couple of bites. When he could manage the words, Josh told Rosita about the colt. "Pete says I can name him, but I haven't thought of one yet."

Rosita smiled. "No worry. The name it will come."

Josh hoped she was right. Already he had thought of lots of names, but none that had come to mind seemed to suit the little horse. He wished he'd asked his mother the name of his father's horse.

Miguel called from outside and Josh, thanking Rosita, went out to where the man sat astride a donkey, a bottle with a black rubber nipple sticking out of his pocket and a nanny goat stubbornly pulling back on the rope in his hand. "My foot, it make a stirrup for you," Miguel said. Josh put his bare foot on the man's sandaled one and grasping his arm, swung up behind him.

They found Pete down over a small rise of ground back of the shed digging Snow's grave. As they approached, Pete saw them and tossing out another shovel full of dirt, stopped and wiped a sleeve across his sweaty face. "I ain't leaving her for the damned wolves and buzzards," he said.

Miguel jumped down into the hole and reached for Pete's shovel. "You go rest," he said.

It was approaching dusk when they finished the grave and Pete went to the house and brought back the long-barreled, single-action Colt he'd held on Josh that first morning.

"Keep the colt back 'til I get her out," Pete told Josh, as he led Snow out of the corral. The rough sound of his voice, made Josh give him a quick glance. What he saw in Pete's face brought a welling of tears and he squeezed his eyes tight and bit down on his lip to hold them at bay.

The colt whinnied and tried to follow his mother, but Josh waved his arms and talked to him until he had the corral poles back in place. As Pete led the mare away, the colt ran up to the bars and called, his whinnying shrill with confusion and fear. The mare did not answer. When she was out of sight, the colt whirled and raced along the sides of the corral, calling to her over and over, his small hooves beating against the hard packed dirt of the corral.

Chapter Six

The colt gained on the goat's milk. They made a team, the two of them, Pete milking the goat, Josh holding the bottle while Pete filled and capped it with the black, rubber nipple, and Josh feeding the colt. One night when the boy was about to fall asleep on his feet, Pete offered to take over the feeding and let him go back to bed, but Josh insisted on doing it himself.

"He's mine," the boy said. "So I should be the one to feed him. Besides," he added, looking up at Pete, "you're tired, too."

The colt needed to be fed every two hours for the first week, then the time between feeding could be gradually lengthened until he was old enough to wean. The boy never complained about the feedings whether it was night or day, but by the end of the first week, he was looking hollow eyed and often fell asleep over supper.

It wasn't long before the colt saw the boy as source of that good, warm milk and he followed Josh around like a pet dog. The colt liked the goat, too, but she seemed wary of him. Josh wondered aloud if the goat realized her milk went to feed the little pest who bucked and jumped around her, as he did around him, trying to get her to play.

Pete enjoyed the heck out of watching boy and the colt run around the corral, dodging in and out of the shed, chasing and being chased, until Pete wondered if the colt would soon get to thinking he was half boy with a little goat thrown in. They'd tried putting Spook in the corral with him for a few hours a day, but that didn't work for the gelding had a tendency to get irritated at the little fella and usually tried to nip or kick him.

Josh couldn't even step out of the house, now, without the colt racing to the corral gate and nickering for him. If they didn't keep him confined to the corral, he'd be poking his nose in at the front door, looking for Josh. In fact that was how he finally got his name. "He follows you around like he's your shadow," Pete said to Josh one day.

"Shadow!" Josh exclaimed, his face glowing. "That's his name! Shadow!"

"Well, I'm sure glad you finally picked a name for him," Pete said. "I was beginning to think you was gonna be riding him after longhorns a'fore he got his true name."

"I was worried, too," Josh admitted.

Pete had been thinking for some time about getting a gentle old mare for the colt to have for horse company and for Josh to ride until Shadow grew old enough. When he asked the boy about going with him to Port Lavaca, the boy's eyes grew as big and round as a full moon. "For me? A horse! A saddle! A bridle! For me? Gosh, Pete. For me?"

"Sure thing. How else are you gonna become a rip-snorting *vaquero*?"

* * *

At Will Shippley's livery stable, Pete bought Josh a small dapple-gray mare and a saddle and bridle.

"She's a bit smooth mouthed, but gentle and fair riding. Name's Molly," Shippley told them.

The mare was good about taking the bridle bit and keeping her head down so Josh could slip the headstall over her ears. Pete helped him throw the saddle up over the mare's back and checked to be sure he'd drawn the cinch up snug so the saddle wouldn't slip.

Josh had to stand on tiptoe to get his foot in the stirrup and slipped a hand in under the saddle below the pommel to pull himself up and get his leg on over.

Grinning at the boy sitting on the mare, pleased as a hound dog with a new bone, Pete reined Spook over and leaning over patted the boy's leg. "Ready to ride?" he asked.

"You bet," the boy answered and lifting the bridle reins, touched his heels to the mare's side. The colt trotted along at her side.

* * *

Shadow took an instant liking to the mare, but he still preferred Josh, which still worried Pete. "I believe I'd best take over your feeding chores and send you over to live with Rosita and Miguel for a week or ten days," he said. "Give these two a chance to get acquainted without some two-legged boy confusing the issue."

Although Josh missed the colt and Pete, too, and thought often of the mare and the saddle and bridle he'd barely used, the time he spent with Rosita and Miguel and their baby boy, Ramon, were pleasant days and he began to grow accustomed to their language and was soon speaking a few words of it, himself. He felt guilty, sometimes, knowing his mama had wanted him to speak only Anglo, but he did not say anything to the Pinòs. He did not want them to think his mama had been ashamed of being a Mexican. He still wondered why the Dunkirk boys had called her a dirty Mexican whore. She had not been dirty, but she had been Mexican, for she had looked like Rosita and the other Mexican women he'd seen, but as to being a whore he still did not know what that word meant. Several times he tried to get up enough nerve to ask Rosita, but he was afraid that it was such a bad word that she would fly mad at him like his mama had. He hoped it wasn't any worse than being a Mexican and as far as he could tell there was nothing wrong with that.

Maybe his mama just wanted him to be Anglo because she wanted him to be just like his father. She always said he looked just like him.

One sunny morning he told Rosita what his mother had told him, about looking like his father...his pa.

"Ahh," she said, a smile warming her eyes. "your *padre* must be good man. Handsome, too, I think."

At her words, a warm feeling rushed over him and he ducked his head to hide his tears.

* * *

From the day Josh left, Pete missed the boy more than he could ever have imagined. Every waking moment seemed filled with the boy. Each morning the boy sat at the table with him, and in his mind's eye, poured lick on his battercakes or fried cornmeal mush, and drank his coffee rich with the sweetener. All through the rest of the day, the boy dogged his footsteps, and at night seemed to breath his deep night sleep into the room.

To Pete it seemed nothing short of a miracle that the boy had stumbled upon this place. He could've cut through the brush a half a mile to one side or the other and not even seen the place. It was darn near a miracle all right.

He remembered some of the Bible preaching he'd gotten as a boy, sitting on a hard pew between his brothers. His ma had sure been a stickler about attending church. He always thought Pap had gone along more to please Ma than God. Pap always grinned at his boys when they went to belly aching about being cooped up inside a stuffy old church and said it was God's plan to make 'em appreciate the good old outdoors more. Pap always let them have Sunday afternoons off except at haying or calving time. Those Sundays, they didn't even go to church. That sure worried Ma. She was sure church going was the prime leverage a person had with God. Pap always said that God favored being decent to other folks and good as Ma was to everybody, he reckoned she'd have no problem getting past those pearly gates, even if she did miss church a few times.

After Ma died and Pap married the Weber witch, they still went to church, but there wasn't no talk of him and his brothers having Sunday afternoons off, no sir. She had more'n enough chores to keep them and Pap busy. *God, but he'd hated that woman.* She was all saintly and pious sitting in church on Sundays, but the minute her butt got sat down on the buggy seat to go home, she shed her sainthood like a snake does his skin and went to raking Pap and them over the coals about whatever she could think up that they might of done wrong.

Eva Weber was the reason he went to Texas. It hadn't been more'n two months after Ma's passing that the witch got Pap to marry her. She'd cast a quick loop and pulled him in, acting sweeter'n clover honey. He doubted that the marriage bed was hardly cooled off before Pap realized he'd made a pact with the devil's mistress and was caught tighter'n a bronc up against a snubbing post.

In those months Eva Weber shared his bed and bossed his household, Pap grew old and stooped with hardly a word to say to anyone. He just shriveled up inside and a few months shy of two years after Ma's passing, he up and keeled over dead while he was slopping the hogs. Those damned hogs was a-chewing on him a'fore he and Ralph went out to see why he hadn't come in to supper.

Alvin and Ralph was wanting the place bad enough to stay on and live with the witch, though he bet they were damned thankful when she finally kicked off. His brothers wrote about her passing. In that same letter they asked him to come back and they'd share the farm with him, but, by then, he was happy doing what he was doing, riding for the Bar Two outfit and courting Etta Jane.

Probably because of his own good mother and his witch of a stepmother, he thought a lot about Josh's mother. She must have been a good woman, despite her line of work, to have brought such a fine boy along this far. Whenever Josh said something about his mama he talked like she'd been awful good to him. He missed her, too, wasn't no doubt about that, even though, the little fella didn't ever say so, but he'd seen the boy look off into the distance, and a couple of times had seen a tear leak out a'fore he could brush it away.

Odd, her being a good mother and a whore at the same time. He'd sure like to know more about her. He told himself he ought to know, on account of he was raising her boy.

One day, when Josh was still at the Pinõs' and Miguel had come by with a sweet cake Rosita had baked for him, he persuaded Miguel to see to the colt while he went to Indianola.

"It not change the boy," Miguel said when he explained why he wanted to go. "He be who he is, no matter what you find about him."

"I know you're right, but I've got to do it." Pete, himself, could not really explain his need to know. He only knew it tugged at him like a pup worryin' a bone.

Pete had to admit that he was glad those two women at the saloon in Indianola had not been there when he visited Floss those many years ago. It wasn't anything he was real proud of even these women knowing. Josh had called them, Angel and Birdy, odd names that somehow fit them. Right away they offered to help with the boy's keep, Angel jumping up to get some cash money from a small bag tucked away in a drawer. Although he declined their help, Pete thought their offer spoke highly of them.

They told him what Josh's mother had told them, when she first came, maybe carrying the child, but not telling them until she began to show and then never saying who the daddy was. When the boy got old enough to know, she made one up for him. A good, decent daddy she had die off with yellow fever so she wouldn't have to produce him.

"We knew the fella who dropped her off on our doorstep," Angel said. "Told us he found her wandering along this side of the Rio Grande near dead from exhaustion and starvation. Guess she told him it was lucky the river was low that time of year for she'd had to swim some to get away from three men who had killed her grandparents and were looking to kill her."

"I think she told Floss more than she told us," Birdy spoke up in her thin, reedy voice.

Angel added, "Said her name was Maria, but it took her awhile to answer to it natural like."

"She went to work within a month of coming here," Birdy said. "The father could be one of her first customers, but Josh was a good sized baby, so it wasn't very likely that he wasn't full term. I've often wondered if the father wasn't the man who brought her to us. He was a tall fellow with red hair just as she later described Josh's father to him."

Angel added that she knew for a fact that Floss has asked her if she'd ever been with a man not wanting to throw her into the job if she hadn't. "She said yes, but she didn't give us no details. She didn't have to work after she got to showing too much."

"You took care of her," Pete said.

"Yes," Birdy said. "We were a family of sorts. Of course, we took care of her."

Pete liked the way these two women talked to him, straight forward and honest, not working their sex on him like he thought some whores probably did. He wondered what was wrong with Birdy to make her head and hands shake all the time. He wondered if the Angel woman helped her eat. He bet she couldn't pick up a fork and keep it still long enough to get any food on it, let alone get it up to her mouth. No wonder she was all bones. It sure must cut into her trade. Some men wasn't gonna be paying out hard cash to lay with a woman shaking like a leaf in a wind storm and a bony one at that. She sure sounded educated though. Made him wonder how come she ended up in a sportin' house. The other woman, Angel, which was some odd name for a whore, was on the skinny side, too, but hard eyed and brittle as poorly tanned hide. He bet when she got riled she was a regular wildcat. She'd probably cut your throat cool as you please, but the hell of it was, he liked her.

"Lookin' at him, we could see he wasn't all Mexican," Angel said. "So his daddy's got to have been white." She paused, narrowing her eyes. "She was a good girl and we all liked her. We thought a whole lot of her boy, too. She did have some real funny ways about her, though. She was Mex plain as daylight, but learned Anglo quick as she could. Never let the boy speak Mex."

"Floss influenced her there," Birdy said. "She thought the boy would get along better if she raised him as a white boy. Floss asked me to teach Maria, so Josh would learn proper English from her." She laughed. "Maria's first language would often over-ride her English, so I tried to model the language for him."

"My ear tells me you've had schoolin'," Pete said.

Birdy smiled and regarded him a moment before saying, "I have. I regret I didn't try to teach the boy some reading and writing. I could have done so." She lowered her eyes and added in a quiet voice. "For a few years I did not suffer this affliction well, and I had no time for anything, but my own selfish thoughts."

"Maria was just fourteen when she came to us." Angel jumped in with her words like she was being quick to take his attention away from Birdy. "She was a sweet girl. Never did get that tough look about her. Guess it's 'cause she learned to escape. Said she went away in her mind to her grandparents' sheep farm and watched the lambs play."

On his way out, they followed him and stood on the small landing outside the door.

"We certainly appreciate you coming by to tell us about Josh," Birdy said. "The sheriff told us you'd taken him in. We do thank you for your kindness."

"It's been my pleasure," Pete said. "He's one fine boy."

As he stepped off the bottom step, Angel called down to him. "See that adobe hut? That's where they lived. Maria sent him outside when she had work to do."

When he turned back to acknowledge Angel's words, she added, "You take good care of our boy, you hear, or we'll come and beat hell out of you."

Startled he gave her a quick look. Both women were smiling.

Pete touched the brim of his hat. "I will," he said.

Angel and Birdy's story sure helped to ease his mind about the boy's mother. They had liked her, and given the circumstances, it was likely she'd had no other way to make a living. Being Mexican and growing a belly to boot, and so young. He'd bet any amount of money anyone would put up that she'd been a good mother, the way the boy mourned her.

* * *

The day Josh was to come home, Pete was up before dawn. He figured Rosita would insist on giving the boy breakfast before letting him go. He hoped Josh would want to come home. Miguel and Rosita were sure nice people and it wouldn't surprise him none if the boy would want to stay with them. It'd be a whole lot nicer to live with a young family instead of an old codger like himself. But even if he didn't want to come back to him, Pete thought, Shadow would draw him. He wasn't going to stay away from that colt any longer than he had to.

The sun was just above the horizon, when he heard Josh coming, running and calling his name. "Pete! Pete! I'm back, Pete!" Bursting inside, he danced around like he had hot coals in his britches and then he was out the door calling, " Shadow! Shadow!"

His heart light with the knowledge that the boy had come to him first, Pete stepped outside to watch the reunion. The boy's arms flew about the colt's neck and hugged tight, then the two burst apart and went running around the corral, one leaping, jumping, arms flung wide, the other kicking and bucking. Molly watched awhile before nickering softly to the colt. Shadow stopped, turned, and trotted back to her. The boy stood still, watching. Molly stretched out her head and the two touched noses briefly before the colt turned again to the boy.

Chapter Seven

Shadow had turned out to be a buckskin with black mane and tail as Pete had predicted. When the colt was old enough to be ridden, Josh, under Pete's guidance, had taught him to accept the saddle and bridle. Now Shadow and Josh moved as though horse and rider were one. Watching them, Pete thought sure his old heart would swell up with love and pride 'til it busted. Which it might be planning on doing, pretty damn soon.

He was sure draggy and tired these days and his wind capacity was plumb pitiful anymore. Hell, just chopping an armload of firewood left him weak and breathing like a wind-broke horse. 'Course he was closing in on seventy-five years. A man couldn't plan on living forever.

* * *

Josh turned Shadow toward home putting the buckskin into an easy lope. It worried him to leave Pete now that he was so sick, but Pete insisted on it. So twice a week, since he'd turned fifteen, two and a half years ago, he'd worked for Will Shippley at his livery stables in Port Lavaca. Shippley, crowding ninety, was no longer able to do the heavy work, but he would not give up.

"The day I leave my horses, you can plant me out yonder in the graveyard," he muttered to Josh one day after his daughter, now gray-headed herself, pleaded with him to give up his stable and come live with her and her husband.

Josh liked working at the livery stable and Shadow enjoyed the company of the other horses, so he had no worries about work, but Pete had had some bad sick spells lately and it seemed to Josh as if each day he moved slower and spent more time in bed.

Miguel and Rosita often came over with their boys. Ramon was ten years old, now, and had three younger brothers, the latest one was just crawling, a big-eyed boy they'd named Pete. Rosita often brought their supper and helped Josh clean the house.

One day, busy shoveling manure, Josh overheard some men talking about a doctor in Victoria they thought was extra good at curing folks. The next day, he asked Will Shippley for the time to take Pete to the doctor and the Pinòs for the use of their donkey cart. Rosita made a bed in the cart soft with blankets and patted Pete's arm in a gesture of goodbye, her dark eyes filled with tenderness. Miguel had insisted on going along and driving the donkey, so Josh had ridden beside them on Shadow.

The doctor, a small, slender man, his brow wrinkled in a perpetual frown, didn't mince words. "Your old heart's failing you, Mr. Waters. I can't do a thing for you. Just rest all you can and make amends if you've got any to make."

Josh tried not to let Pete see how the doctor's words had slammed into his gut.

The doctor put Pete in a room off from his office for the night and Josh and Miguel took the donkey cart and Shadow to the edge of town and made camp.

Just before turning in for the night, they reheated the coffee over a bed of glowing coals. Neither had said much the whole evening, but now Miguel, his eyes on the fire, said, "*Senòr* Pete he is a good man. My wish be that my sons grow up to know him. He see not Mexican or Anglo. He see people who earn what they come to be."

"My mother was Mexican, my father, Anglo," Josh said, turning to look at Miguel.

Miguel smiled. "A good mix you are, too. You do both proud."

Josh turned back to stare at the dying embers. He wondered if Miguel knew *all* of his story. Knew what his mother had been. He knew now what a whore was. He'd learned that when, at thirteen, he had gone to Indianola to see Angel and Birdy, but had found them gone and two others in their place.

"Reckon they're dead," the big blonde named Myra said. "Had a bitch name of Jewel when we come, but she took the fever and didn't last long."

Those two in Angel and Birdy's rooms above the saloon had both scared the hell out of him, especially the one named Myra. He knew now that if he'd asked, Pete would have gone with him, even if he disapproved, and Myra wouldn't have grabbed him through his pants. He had to grin about that now, but it sure as the devil hadn't been funny then.

Finishing their coffee they rolled up in their blankets and Miguel was soon snoring. Josh stayed awake far into the night his thoughts on Pete. He remembered the doctor's words about Pete making amends, if he'd any to make. It was hard to imagine that Pete had ever done anything to get folks riled up. Yet, he had once told him that most folks by the time they were grown, usually have something back along their trail that they weren't too proud of. Josh bet that if there was anything like that back along Pete's trail, it cast a mighty small shadow.

He and Pete had talked about those shadows the year Josh had ridden alone into Indianola and found out about his mother. But it was the year before that he first got to really thinking about the man with the light hair and the black hat and wondering if he had been his mother's killer. He'd worried it over in his mind awhile and then had asked Pete if there was any way of knowing if the man who had killed her had ever been caught. Pete must have seen how much it was bothering him for he took him into Indianola to see the sheriff.

The sheriff still remembered him. "Sure was sorry about your mama," he said when Pete introduced Josh and told his story. "Sure glad you found you a home, though." He smoothed his black mustache. "Sorry I didn't know how ornery that Mrs. Dunkirk and her brood were when I put you there. Had the oldest one in my jail not too long ago. Doubt I've seen the last of him and won't be surprised if I see one or both of his brothers."

"You never found the person who killed this boy's mother?" Pete asked.

"No, but evidence points to a real bad one name of Cole Slade. He's been terrorizing border towns from El Paso to Brownsville and up along the coast all the way to Louisiana. He'll rob anything, a stage, a bank, a store, a hotel. He plays no favorites that way. And he ain't shy about killing neither. Men, women, makes no difference to him. He strikes a place and then disappears. Sometimes it's two, maybe three years before I hear of him again and I get to hoping he's cashed in his chips. Then I get word that he's robbing and killing somewheres else."

"What evidence do you have that this Cole Slade might have killed this boy's mother?" Pete asked.

"Nothing real solid. Just a minute." The sheriff turned away and took a handful of papers bound with a heavy string from his desk drawer. He'd licked his thumb and flipped through the papers, until he'd found the one he wanted.

"This is my report from a stage holdup some years back. A man name of Sam Hughes was on that stage and got robbed of his watch and all the money that was on him, which, he said, was considerable. He said the feller that did it had a bandana pulled up over his nose, but what little skin Sam saw between the man's bandana and the black sombrero was real pitted, like he'd survived a good case of small pox." The sheriff paused in the making of a cigarette and said, "Hughes came to me some six months later and said he saw the fella again out back of that adobe the night this boy's ma was killed."

Again the image that was burned forever in his memory flooded Josh's senses and again the man with the long, light-colored hair moved close to the walls of his mother's adobe, every few steps casting a quick glance over his shoulder, and the sheriff's next words, sent a sharp chill through him.

"Sam said he was a tall man. Had long, curly yeller hair sticking out from under his black sombrero and that does sure fit Cole Slade's description. Said he saw the horse he rode, too, and it had the same markings as the one the outlaw rode when he held up the stage. But he did admit that it was pretty dark out, so he couldn't be dead sure."

"Where does Hughes live now?" Pete had pulled off his hat when he entered the sheriff's office and was slapping it lightly against his leg.

"Maybe someone should talk to him again."

"'Fraid he's been dead a couple of years."

"Damn," Pete said.

Josh remembered the heat of the sun that day as he walked out of the sheriff's office with Pete. He'd looked up at the clear blue sky dotted with a flock of screaming gulls wheeling in from the bay, and promised his mother that when he got big enough, he would learn to handle a gun and go after Cole Slade. When he found him, he would make him tell why he had killed her. Then he would shoot him dead.

Pete bought their noon meal in one of the eating houses that day and all the while Josh wanted to ask Pete if they could walk over and see the adobe behind the saloon and climb those outside stairs and see Angel and Birdy, too. Although the memory of his mother lying on the floor so cold and still had faded some along with his grief, the fear that it might start up all over again stayed his tongue and they had ridden home, the secrets of the adobe hut and the upstairs rooms above the saloon, kept from him for another year.

In his thirteenth year he'd had several vivid dreams. Usually they were about his mother, but often the man with the light hair and the black hat, the man certain to be Cole Slade, and the horse with the thick, white backward J on his forehead, also appeared.

His dreams spilled over into his daytime thoughts, taking him back to the night his mother was killed. Some days, he could hardly think of anything else and Pete would have to ask him twice to do some chore, like fill the wood box or go to the spring for water.

In one dream, a long line of men stood outside his mother's adobe and just before the one closest to the door walked in to see his mama, he would turn, look Josh in the eye and smile. In another dream, he was down by the bay when he heard screams and knowing it was his mother, he'd run up the path to the adobe, determined to save her, but just as he'd reached the door, he'd looked up into the blue sky and saw a gull flying overhead and knew the screams had only been the gull's cry.

With his dreams came memories—memories of how the men had come to see his mother, always men, never a woman, unless it was Birdy, or Angel, or Floss, before she died. He could stay inside the adobe with

Mama when they came, but never when the men were there. Once, he had refused to go, but she'd pushed him out, her face and voice harsh with anger.

He remembered the Dunkirk boys' taunts of "Dirty Mexican whore." He still hated those boys for their cruel tongues, but his hate for them paled along side the hate that was growing inside him for the man who had killed his mother...a tall, blond, pockmarked man named Cole Slade. At first just the thought of the name burned inside him until sometimes he thought he could stand it no longer. Now, he still hated the man, but the seething anger had been walled off into a cold place in his heart.

The sheriff said he hoped the man was dead and, in a way, he hoped so, too, but he would also like to face him when he was grown up enough to carry a gun and had practiced enough to be good at shooting it. If Slade was still alive then, he'd hunt him down and, if he had to, he'd shoot him, but he'd rather bring him in to whatever town was the closest to be hanged.

Those dreams and his thoughts grew a hollow, lonesome feeling inside him and kept him angry all the time. Pete didn't have to more than open his mouth to make him mad, and although he was ashamed, afterwards, of lashing out at Pete, he couldn't seem to stop. He started spending his days on Shadow, aimlessly riding through scrub oak, laurel, prickly pear, and mesquite, his mind on his mother and the man who had killed her. At night he returned knowing Pete would come looking for him, if he wasn't home by dark.

He asked Pete, shortly after their visit to Indianola to see the sheriff, if they could go back again and see Birdy and Angel. He thought they might have remembered something they hadn't told the sheriff. Angry over Pete's answer, he began the wall he eventually built between them.

"It's not likely they'll know any more than they did the day he questioned them," Pete told him, adding that it would be nothing more than a wild goose chase and that he'd be better off, hard as it was, just to let it go.

It was on one of his solitary rides, that he decided to go alone to Indianola and see Birdy and Angel and maybe the sheriff, too. He might have some fresh news of Slade. *Pete didn't know everything.* So he told Pete he wanted to stay out overnight, sleep under the stars and fry his breakfast over a campfire. Pete seemed to study him for a moment and then said he guessed he was old enough to stay out by himself. He surprised Josh by bringing out the long-barreled Colt he had held on him that first day and had used to put Snow out of her misery.

"I'd sure feel a whole lot better if you'd carry this," Pete told him. "It ain't likely you're gonna need it, but you might run onto a hydrophoby coyote, a mean tempered javelina, a sidewinder or a cottonmouth, or, though it ain't likely, some thieving two-legged critter."

Pete gave him lessons, having him shoot at empty tomato cans, wood targets, and finally rabbits, grouse, and quail. Pete floured and fried his kill in hot bacon grease for their supper. Pete praised him, calling him a natural-born shot.

Pete had helped him tie his bedroll on behind the cantle along with a sack of cold biscuits, bacon, coffee, and a frying pan and coffee pot. Guilt over lying to Pete had nearly waylaid him that morning when swinging up on Shadow, he'd looked down and saw suspicion in Pete's face. Pete somehow knew he was lying, but wasn't calling him on it. He'd almost confessed, right then, but something kept him from it and reining Shadow around, he'd ridden away.

Just before the ranch would disappear from his sight, he'd turned in the saddle to look back. Pete was still standing by the corral. He'd almost turned around then and several more times before he reached Indianola, he had almost given up and turned Shadow back toward home.

He'd known Pete's leg was acting up again and that had bothered him. Pete had taken a musket ball in his right leg in the last battle of the Texas and Mexican war and it had caused him to limp ever since. Now, rheumatism was giving him a lot of pain and although he never complained, Josh could tell by the set of his jaw when his leg was hurting him. And it had been hurting him that day.

Pete had fought in that war back in '36 and had barely escaped with his life. He had been with Colonel Fannins' Texas troops when they were captured and imprisoned at Goliad. Told they were going home, once outside the prison their captors had opened fire. "They shot us down like rats in a barrel," Pete told him. Only a handful had escaped. Pete had been one of them. A bullet had grazed his arm, but otherwise he was unhurt.

"I wasn't hurt," Pete told him. "But I was boiling mad! I couldn't wait to get back into the fracas and kill ever last one of them Mexicans." Stealing a horse the next day he had joined Sam Houston's army in time for the final battle at San Jacinto. That battle had brought defeat to Santa Ana and his Mexican forces and left Pete with a game leg.

He had often wondered how a man could kill and almost be killed by Mexicans and then have friends like Miguel and Rosita. He wished Pete could have known his mother. He knew Pete would have liked her, too.

He'd made camp just out of Indianola and rode in the next day. Leaving Shadow at the hitching rail in front of the dry goods store and steeling himself against a flood of memories, he'd walked around behind the building and down a back street to the small adobe hut. The door hung open, sagging on its leather hinges. It was empty except for a litter of dried twigs and rodent droppings. A ragged scrap of curtain drooped from the tiny window. His eyes swept the floor, stopping on the spot where he had last seen his mother lying cold and still.

Blinking back tears, he'd jerked his head out of the doorway and looked up at the stairway leading to the second floor of the saloon, suddenly anxious to see Angel and Birdy.

On the narrow landing at the top of the stairs, he removed his hat as Pete had taught him to do in the presence of women, and rapped on the door, weathered with age and the elements. He'd smiled anticipating the sight of Birdy's thin frame and smile of welcome, and Angel's big eyes framed by her dark hair, peering over Birdy's shoulder. He could almost hear their voices. *"Oh, Josh! Oh, my, how we missed you. Come in Josh tell us all about yourself and your new life."*

"Yes?" The woman who'd opened the door was not Birdy, nor Angel either. She'd worn a dress pulled tight at the waist, but loose at the top— so loose he could see her flesh down to the tops of the rounded mounds of her breasts. His face flushed hot and his tongue got tangled up, so he stammered when he asked for Angel or Birdy.

The woman had laughed, a cold, bitter laugh. "Why ya little pecker. Ya been here before. My gawd! Ya'll was a baby, wasn't ya? Hell, ya'll still a baby!"

Josh had stood in silent confusion. *What was she talking about, calling him a baby?*

The woman laughed again and wrapping a long-fingered hand around his arm had pulled him inside. "Nell," she called back over her shoulder. "Come see what I found."

Nell, short with narrowed eyes and pinched lips, stepped out of another room and regarded him with a scowl.

The woman with the tops of her breasts showing, sat down on a bed, letting the front of her dress fall open so he could see every bit of her legs, and said gleefully, "This little runt's been up here with those two old bitches that used to be here. Lord, Nell, what ya think, them two's been gone near on to three years, ain't they?" Not waiting for Nell's answer, she went on, "Them two was awful long in the tooth for this here little runt, wouldn't ya say?" She grinned again, showing remarkably white teeth. "So Nell, ya'll want to take him? I figure ya being a mite younger, ya'll might be more suitable." She leaned toward him and the top of her dress inched open a little more. "Ya'll got any money on ya."

Josh, totally bewildered, had shaken his head. "No."

Anger sparked in the woman's eyes. "Those old hens wasn't taking ya'll for free, was they?"

Again Josh shook his head, as confused as ever.

"Tell ya what," the woman said, suddenly good natured again. "Let me feel of that little o' thing."

He'd just about died of shock when the woman's hand snaked out and cupped his manhood through his pants. Fear raced through him and instinctively he'd reached down to protect himself, touched her hand, and jerked his own back as quickly as if he'd touched hot coals. The woman released him then and turned to her companion. "Ya'll ought to come take a feel of this little o'thing. Why it hain't no bigger'n a baby's." Her head snapped back to stare at him, her eyes darkened and her face puckered into a mean frown. "Ya'll ain't Mexican is ya? Got no use for greasers."

"S-sort of," he'd stammered.

"Well, " The woman chuckled. "Sorta's okay. 'pect ya'll's white blood thinned out the greaser shit." She winked at him. "Come here, baby. Let o' Myra take ya for a tumble."

Josh stepped back, stumbled over a footstool, righted himself and stood staring, his heart beating like a tom-tom, his mouth dry as dust.

"Oh, so now ya'll's turned scaredycat." Myra taunted him. "Spect ya'll lyin' about laying with them two old whores. Bet ya'll ain't never been with no woman."

The one named Nell grew impatient. "Quit foolin' with him, Myra," she'd said. "We don't need no snot-nosed brat up here. 'Pecially one with no money."

"Say!" A spark of interest showed on Myra's face. "Ya'll ain't the brat, of that greaser gal, got herself killed, some years back, is ya?"

Josh nodded, hope rising in his heart. *Maybe this woman did know something. Maybe she had even known his mother.* But when he asked, she snorted. "That was before my time, honey. 'Sides, Nell and me don't work with no greaser whore."

Bracing himself for Myra's loud scornful laugh, and stammering so he could hardly get his words out, he'd asked what a whore was.

It was the one called Nell who'd laughed that time. Myra, the big woman just raised her eyebrows and stared at him, until Nell said, "Tell him and kick him to hell out of here, 'for gawd sakes. He's innocent as a new born lamb."

"Okay, boy." Myra heaved herself up off the bed. "I'll tell ya and then ya'll get your sad, little ass out of here, pronto. Ya hear?"

"Yes'm." He'd had to fight the urge to bolt for the door and freedom. He'd felt as if he'd landed in a nest of snakes, their venom already coursing through his body.

"A whore lays her body down for men to use and they pays her money. That's what a whore is. She lets him use her body—ya know, like a male animal does a female animal to get offspring. Except there ain't usually no offspring with whores." She paused and canted her head to one side. "Ya ma must have slipped up to get ya'll. Either she was too stupid or too soft in the head to get rid of ya while she still had time."

"You don't know!" Josh had shouted in defense of his mother, anger overriding his fear as he spilled out the story of his father going to Victoria and dying of yellow fever.

Nell made a sound of exasperation and then let him have it. Cold and grim, she let him know that it was more than likely that he had no father, leastways none his mama could have put a name to. She told him his mama had lied to him and that it was time he grew up and learned how life was. She left him with nothing as he fumbled his way to the door and stumbled down the stairs, dry-eyed, but as blind as if awash in tears.

This time, he did not look toward his mother's adobe where the men had come and paid money to lie down on top of her, but he could not have been more conscious of it.

Shadow nickered softly when he saw him coming. Quickly, he untied the reins from the hitching post and throwing the off rein around the buckskin's neck, swung up in the saddle. He reined the horse around and urged him into a dead run, desperate to put distance between himself and the women upstairs.

He was out of sight of the town before he remembered the sheriff. More than ever he wanted to hunt down the man who had killed his mother. If he had only let her live, Josh imagined that he would have taken her away, just as soon as he'd grown old enough. He thought they might even have gone to Victoria to that ranch that had needed a hand to work the cattle and a cook to feed the men. Maybe he'd have done what his father couldn't. Now, there was nothing left to do, but find that mean, murdering Slade.

Fighting tears and hoping those two above the saloon would not come down to the street and see him, he swung Shadow around and rode back into town.

He had arrived at the man's office just as he was coming out the door. Facing the sun, the sheriff pulled his hat lower over his eyes as he looked up at Josh, still seated on Shadow. It had taken him a moment to recognize Josh from a year ago.

"No, son, I ain't heard a word of him," the sheriff said. "Don't reckon he's in these parts no more. But if he's alive, he's raisin' hell somewheres." For the space of several heartbeats, he'd paused and then added, "Sure sorry about your ma, though."

Josh nodded. He wondered if the sheriff was really sorry, or just thought of it as one less whore in the world.

On the way home, the two women, upstairs above the cantina, rode with him. He tried to shake them off, but they stuck closer than a burr to a saddle blanket, as Pete would say. The big one's words echoed over and over inside his head. *"Ya ain't the brat of that greaser gal, got herself killed is ya?"*

Pete was down at the corral, sitting in under the shed out of the sun, oiling the leather on a bridle when Josh arrived home. "You have a good ride?" he asked as he stepped out into the sunlight and squinted up at him.

"It was all right." Josh swung down from Shadow and throwing a stirrup up over the saddle horn, busied himself with unsaddling the buckskin.

"Well," Pete said, turning away, "I'd better get on up to the house and throw some grub on the table. I expect you're getting on to half starved."

CHAPTER EIGHT

Lying in the donkey cart, going home to die, Pete Waters thought about the time Josh was thirteen and had come home from his overnight trip, saying he'd been up on the Guadalupe, but had really been to see those sporting women at Indianola. Pete had hoped the boy would have let that part of his past die, but he'd been bound to know. Still the truth, even a hard truth, can settle a notion once and for all, and clear the way for getting on with living, if one's a mind too, though some folks get to liking bitterness and hate too much to let go.

Ever since the boy had learned the truth about his mother's work and that the renegade outlaw, Cole Slade, had probably been her killer, he had rarely mentioned his mother, but he often mentioned Slade and the hope that the sheriff would catch him.

He'd added his hope to the boy's, for if they ever caught him, a swift hanging would follow. It worried him some that after Saint Peter passed him through those pearly gates, or sent him the other way, whichever he had a mind to do, that the boy would hear that Slade still lived and would head out looking for him. If he found him, the boy wouldn't stand a chance.

He'd seen right away, when Josh got back from that overnight trip, that something had saddled him and was ridin' him hard. Moody and cantankerous before he left, the boy now carried a hard anger that followed him from daylight to dark. Something had happened he knew, and the only reasonable explanation was that he had been to Indianola and had learned about his mother's occupation. He'd had a time getting the boy to talk, in fact it had taken several days and he'd finally had to get tough to get it done.

He'd waited until night when they were sitting out on the porch, chairs tipped back against the wall, watching the night cast its shadow across the land. The nightly ritual, over the years, had given them a time to speak of anything that might be on their minds. He smiled to himself remembering how the first few days Josh had sat his chair straight-backed and then one evening, had tipped it back his bare feet perched on the bottom rung as casually as if he'd been doing it every evening. It had sure tickled him and he wondered if the boy had been practicing or if he'd just gotten the courage to give it a try.

They sat awhile, not talking at all and he saw they weren't ever gonna make any headway that-a-way, so he started talking about a couple of calves their range cattle had dropped that day. He'd been buying cows until they now had a fair sized herd, big enough to give the boy and his horse some experience.

The boy had answered just what needed answering and no more, so he'd said, "What's the problem, son? You got something setting heavy on your chest?"

His, "*It's nothing.*" had sounded to Pete's ears like a big something, so he tried another tack. "You ain't told me any particulars about the ride you took or exactly where you set up camp."

"I went up towards Victoria on the Guadalupe."

"Did you lay your soogans over a prickly pear while you was there?"

The boy had thrown him a quick, startled glance, dropping his chair forward, his boots hitting the porch floorboards with a thud. Pete had bought the boy his first pair of boots in Jay Close's mercantile that first Christmas. The boy's eyes got as big as the rowels on a pair of Mexican spurs when he first laid eyes on the shiny black footwear, and he near broke his face grinning as he clomped out of the store in them. On the way home, Josh riding Molly with a leggy Shadow tagging along behind, and himself on Spook, Josh'd kept stiffening his boots in the stirrups and holding them out a little, so he could admire them. He half expected the boy to wear them to bed. He didn't, but he did line them up so perfectly beside his bed, that if lines had been drawn on the floor in front of the toes and behind the heels, they'd have both been straight as arrows. He'd given the boy spurs the next Christmas and a new pair of boots, too, for he had outgrown the other pair by then.

Ordinarily, Josh would have grinned at the image of his soogans laid over a prickly pear, but that night, he'd turned his face once again out toward the dark and muttered a quiet, "No."

He'd pushed the boy a little more. "The way you're acting," he said, " makes me think you've got a burr of some kind stuck under your saddle. I 'pect any minute to see you duck your head and go to buckin'."

"I'm all right," Josh had answered, but he'd sounded far from all right. He had thought about touching spurs to the boy, like you did a horse that wasn't wantin' to go where you was aiming for him to, but he'd been afraid to push too hard. So he'd let it go, hoping the boy would open up to him in a few days.

He'd waited a week and Josh was still giving no indication that he was ever going to talk, if he didn't force the issue. The boy was still as prickly as a dog that had nosed a porcupine and it sure was getting on his nerves. It shamed him to remember how he'd lost his temper with the boy. Still, it might have been the only way he'd ever have jarred his tongue loose and got him to talking and letting the poison out of his system.

It had been hard for the boy to tell him, but the more they'd talked about it over the course of some days, the more Josh had worked out the kinks. Today, at going on to eighteen, he seemed to have come to accept what his mama had been, knowing she had been a good mother and that he had no right to pass judgment on her without knowing what circumstances, or shadows lay back along her trail leading her to the life she'd lived.

He opened his eyes and looked up at Josh riding Shadow beside the donkey cart. He sure was proud of him. He reckoned even a true son of his own blood could not have pleased him more. Etta Jane would have been proud of him, too. Hell, she'd of come near to busting her buttons over the boy.

* * *

Josh saw Pete open his eyes and look up at him. He forced out a weak grin, tears dangerously close to the rim of his eyes, and was rewarded with the touch of a smile on Pete's lips and in his blue eyes before they closed again.

Josh blinked hard and looked up into the sky, swept with wispy clouds, and rode for a time watching a hawk circle in a slow, gliding, searching sweep of the sky. When he looked down again at Pete, lying flat on his back in the donkey cart, his thin, old body barely raising the colorful blanket Rosita had knitted for him from carded sheep's wool, his thoughts ranged forward to the day when Pete would leave him. The thought made his stomach go hollow and fill his chest with an aching sadness. Although he was a good head and shoulders taller and many pounds heavier than Pete, he felt like he still wasn't grown up enough to live without him.

Pete had been his anchor ever since he'd taken him into his home. Pete had accepted him as he might a son and had taught him the things he would have taught a son. Not just to ride and rope and work cattle, but to look at a situation and the people involved with an open mind. It was Pete who had helped him come to accept his mother's trade as probably all she could have done at the time.

When he'd come home from seeing those two women who had taken Angel and Birdy's places above the saloon in Indianola, he had been embarrassed and angry and darned hard to live with. Pete had let him get by with it for a few days before he had demanded to know what was eating him. That first night he'd have bawled his head off if he'd tried to tell Pete about seeing those two old whores. As they did every night, he and Pete had sat out on the porch, looking out toward the dark. When Pete questioned him and he couldn't answer, Pete got to his feet and went inside to bed.

The next few days, Pete hadn't asked him any more questions or seemed to notice his bad attitude. He'd been half grateful to Pete for not getting after him, but, at the same time, he wished Pete would force him to tell. Finally, he got his wish.

They were in the shed where Shadow had been born, sitting on an old bench Pete had made years ago. Pete was teaching him how to braid his own *reata.* "You're getting mighty handy with a rope," he'd told him, "and I reckon it's time you got one of your own. Could get you a store bought one, but seems to me every *vaquero* ought to have one he's braided with his own hands."

Josh tried to concentrate on pulling the rawhide strips taunt with each interweaving motion, but he couldn't seem to focus and Pete had to correct his work several times. *What good would it do any way. He wasn't ever going to amount to anything. He was the son of a whore, the worthless son of a whore and he had no real father, just some man who'd paid her money to lay on top of her. Like Myra said, his mother had probably lied and there had never been a redheaded man named Joshua Ryder.*

Pete had started questioning him again and when all he'd give back were sullen mutterings, Pete had jumped to his feet and slapping a strip of leather against the bench had yelled, "Okay. Let's get it out! Something's got you on the prod and I ain't putting up with it no more."

He had known then he was trapped and the story spilled out of him. He didn't remember everything Pete said that day, but he remembered clearly what he'd said about his mother. And how Pete had cautioned him against keeping poisonous thoughts inside.

Anger raging through him he'd spit out, " My mother was a whore, just like those Dunkirk boys said. A dirty, Mexican whore."

"That's damned harsh talk," Pete said. "Too harsh to use about her, I'm thinking. She loved you and tried to raise you right. If circumstances would have been different."

"If I'd of had a pa," he'd ground out through gritted teeth.

He'd nearly cried then and Pete had given him a minute or two before saying, "Sometimes, we catch a raw deal. Could be of our own making, could be not, but I reckon your mama was a pretty fine woman who got a raw deal."

Pete had confessed then to going to see Angel and Birdy back when Shadow was a colt and Josh had been staying with the Pinõs.

What he saw as Pete's betrayal had angered him even more and he'd had to swallow a throat full of tears before lashing out at Pete. "You sneaked off! Went behind my back!"

Pete hadn't defended himself at all, he'd merely said, "Yes, son, I did.

And I can tell you those two women were good people, just like your mama, I imagine."

Josh started to ask why Pete had kept that from him, and then he knew and the anger drained out of him. He'd been eight years old. You didn't tell a boy his mama was a whore when he was only eight years old.

He'd almost lost his grip on his tears then, feeling some sorry for himself, and a little scared of what Pete might really think of him.

As if he could read his mind, Pete had said, "Do you think I thought any less of you because of what your mama did for a living? Do you think I thought any less of her?"

"Did you?" Josh had asked choking back tears.

"No," Pete said. " You're a good boy, one I'm proud to call my son. The way I see it, someone in your bloodline had to have been a thoroughbred. A scrub horse mated to another scrub horse, most often throws a scrub foal instead of a prize winning filly or colt. I'd say your pa and your mama, or at least one of 'em, had good bloodlines 'cause your mama sure threw a prize-winning boy."

His eyes swimming, he'd ducked his head. He'd had no words to express how Pete had lifted his burden of shame.

Pete let him have some time before asking him again about those two women who lived and worked above the saloon. He called them sportin' women and told him that most folks marry, but some don't and nature gives a man a real strong urge to be with a woman and those who aren't married sometimes visit those women who make their livin' that-a-way.

"Were you ever married?" Josh asked. An unwanted image of Pete lying down with a woman, a woman who looked like Myra, made him duck his head embarrassed.

"Yes," Pete said. "She was a good woman. Etta Jane was her name."

Josh picked up the long strips of rawhide and began again to work at braiding his reata. They had sat in silence a while, then Pete said something that Josh figured would stick in his mind the rest of his life.

"You know, son," he'd said, "most all of us at one time or another rides a shadowed trail. Ain't no one's got a clear, unblemished past or family ties they're always proud of. So your mother worked at a job most of us look down on, but do you know why? Did you know her life? Do you know what shadows lurked back along the trail she'd come up to get to where she was?"

Josh had had to admit he didn't, but he wasn't quite ready to forgive her and with a new rush of shame and anger intertwined, he'd muttered, "I bet she could of done something else."

Pete had laid a hand on his knee. "I'd slack up some on that rope you've got on your mama and dallied around your saddle horn, leastways 'til you know the shadows in her life. When you know them shadows, then I reckon you can judge."

"Why didn't she take in washing or something."

"According to Angel and Birdy, she was awful young. Just a little older than you are now and it must have been damned confusing knowing what to do." Pete shrugged. "She told them she'd come from Mexico, that some men had killed her grandparents and were fixing to kill her and she had to swim the Bravo to get away from them. She was half dead when a tall redheaded fella found her on this side of the river. He's the one took her to those women over the saloon."

That bit of news had shocked him. *Had that man been his father? Had he made her grow a baby inside and because she was Mexican didn't want to marry her, so he had just dropped her off with Floss and Angel and Birdy?*

"Maybe he was my father and he didn't want me," Josh said, biting his bottom lip to hold back tears.

"Now whoa, son," Pete said. "Don't no one know, now that your mama's gone."

In confusion and anger, he had lashed out at Pete. "Mama said he was a good man. One to be proud of. I bet she lied to me, like those sonsabitchin' old whores said."

"Son, I wouldn't go to dwelling on them kind of thoughts or using them kind of words," Pete said, his blue eyes narrowing under the frown creasing his brow. "Don't go imagining what you've got no right to imagine, not knowing the facts. Falling into that bottomless hole makes for a sorry life."

Slowly, over time, Josh began to forgive his mother for how she had made her living and for her lies about his father, if they had been lies. Later he had come up with the idea that maybe the redheaded man had been his father and had left Mama with Floss and Angel and Birdy, but just to go see about a ranch job and something had happened, like maybe he did get the fever and die. Mama not knowing why he never came back to her, could have changed the story just a little bit for him, so he'd feel like he'd had a real father, if only for a year. Or maybe his mama's story was true. He decided then that one day when he was older he'd try to find that ranch where his mama said his pa had gone to look for work. Maybe someone there would remember him. Those two above the saloon said his mother mostly likely didn't know who'd sired him. But how could they know when they weren't even there? Besides he doubted if they could be counted on when it came to telling the truth.

While they were in Victoria in the doctor's office, Josh wondered where the cemetery might be. If Mama had told him the truth, his pa's grave would be close by. It would probably be a wild goose chase, but someday, he'd come back and ask around. See if anyone remembered a Joshua Ryder. But for now, Pete needed him and he needed to be with Pete for whatever time he had left. Even if they didn't share the same blood, Pete was his real pa and always would be.

CHAPTER NINE

When the doctor sent him home to die, Pete Waters worried more for the future needs of the boy he loved as dearly as he would a son of his own flesh and blood, than he did of his own impending death. He had lived a good long life and it didn't seem right to ask for more time. The boy was grown. He could get along without him now. He and Josh were not bound by blood or legal document, but he considered him his son and as his son, should have what little Pete would leave behind. Chances were after he died, the boy could just stay on here and nothing would ever be said. He'd feel a whole lot better, though, if the place belonged to Josh legally. He tried writing out a will, but his fingers were too clumsy to hold the pencil and he couldn't figure how to spell most of the words he wanted to use. He seemed to have forgotten most of the four years of schooling he'd had back in Michigan. Finally, he sent Miguel into Port Lavaca to ask around for a man who knew how to write. Miguel had brought out a woman instead.

"I have a legible hand," she said, "and my spelling is as good as anyone's and better than most." She was a young woman, the wife of a traveling preacher. Her clothes were threadbare, but her dignity was certainly intact. Pete half fell in love with her the hour she was there to take down his last wishes.

He wished he had a big ranch to leave Josh with a thousand or so head of fat beeves and some blooded horses, but all he had was this small spread and the twenty head of range cattle he'd bought for Josh to learn the cow business on, and, all the horseflesh he was leaving the boy, except for Shadow, was old Spook, now that Molly, the mare, had died. Danged if he could remember now if Molly had died this past fall, or the one before.

"You feeling like supper?" Josh stood at his bedside. Nearly eighteen, he'd grown tall, six feet anyhow. He was a good-looking boy with his dark brown eyes, thick, black curly hair, and that deep cleft in his chin. He wondered if Josh's mother or the man who sired him had had that same distinctive chin, or if it went back a ways to another generation.

He watched Josh pull up a chair and take up a bowl and spoon to feed him. He sure hated that he couldn't feed himself no more. Hell, he was as weak as a newly dropped calf. In the past month or two, Rosita had taught Josh to cook. One day, she'd brought over an old hen and showed him how to cut off its head, clean, and cook it. He'd listened to her give the boy advice.

"It make good broth for *Señor* Pete. He need soft foods. Eggs be good. I bring you some *mañana.*"

The broth tasted good to him and was about all he cared to eat, so Josh brought home some hens to stock Etta Jane's old chicken house. Josh had entertained him that night with the story of Shadow's reluctance to tote the sacks of chickens home.

"I wish you could have seen him, Pete. He eyed those sacks like he thought they were stuffed full of rattlesnakes and it took all he had in him to stand still while I tied them on behind the cantle. On the way home every time one of those hens gave a flop, he'd go to trotting sideways trying to keep his eye on the sacks and still get us home."

Those chickens were what got him to thinking about the boy's future. What was the boy going to do? Sit here on this place and raise chickens? Lord, he hoped not. A youngster had no business settling for that. Besides, how long was he gonna be content, living here with only Rosita and Miguel and their youngsters for company, raising a few cows and a bunch of chickens. And even if he was some content for a while, he'd bet a gold piece to a horse turd, he wouldn't be for long. He sure hoped not anyway, 'cause it sure as the devil wouldn't be good for him. He needed to get out and learn about the world. Get acquainted with some of life's lessons and rub elbows with a whole bunch of folks, maybe even someday meet a girl who'd make him a good wife and raise him some fine youngsters. The boy needed some excitement, some adventure under his hide. He needed to be in the company of other young men. If he stayed here, his world would grow way too narrow. It helped some that he worked for old Will Shippley, but Will did the talking to the customers and Josh mostly got acquainted with horse manure and hay stacks. The boy worked for one old man and played nursemaid to another. It was time he got out with other young folks and got some seasoning under his belt and a cow outfit would sure do that. Miguel would keep an eye on the place for him, keep out any would be squatters.

He hoped the boy would find a good outfit to ride for. He sure had some good memories of a couple of spreads he'd worked for. The last one when he married Etta Jane. He'd hoped she'd be content with him working the ranch, but she pretty well had her heart set on them getting a place of their own. For a couple of years they'd been real happy, him raising horses and her with her milk cow, some chickens, and a garden. Then she started in losing those babies.

He shook off those old memories and turned his thoughts back to Josh's future. Folks were saying there was a big market for cattle in the east, now, and the railroads had come west as far as Kansas, and a lot of the ranches were driving their cattle to markets there. Maybe the boy could hire on with an outfit going to Kansas. That would season the boy all right.

He knew his own time was running out and he'd soon be waking up in that sweet by and by, his mother used to sing about. He didn't mind going. He was too damned tired to stay on this old earth, anyway, but he sure hated to leave the boy. He hoped if there was a hereafter, like his mother had believed, he could poke a hole in the sky and see the boy now and then. Maybe he could catch the flash of his grin, the shine in his brown eyes, or see him on Shadow, the buckskin loping along in that easy gait he had. It pleased his eye to see Josh and Shadow together. That boy rode like he was part of the horse and he was handy as hell with a rope. Yes, a cow outfit was the place for the boy now.

He slept and woke at dawn. He turned on his side and saw that the boy was gone from his bed, slipped out in his stocking feet, so he wouldn't wake him. His boots were lined up as neatly as he had lined up that first pair. His boots held spurs now, and the boy slid his feet in and out of them without removing his spurs. The clomp, clomp of those boots and the jingle of those spurs had got to be pure music to his ears. "Ain't no way you gonna be sneaking up on me, son," he'd said one day when Josh had come in from outside.

"Don't reckon I got a reason to sneak up on you, Pete," Josh had answered with a grin. "But if I do, I'll sure remember to tiptoe up behind you in my stocking feet."

When he bought the spurs and explained to the boy that he needed to get a file and work off the points until they were blunt and dull, the boy hadn't said a word but there had been a question in his brown eyes. "Never could understand why spur makers don't just make them thataway," Pete told him. "A good *vaquero* don't ever abuse his horse, but uses his spurs when his bronc needs a gentle nudge. Sometimes a horse has got different ideas than the fella sitting on his back and he don't want to go where plainly they're headed, 'specially if the horse is plumb worn to the nubbin and wants to call it quits, or he gets it into his head that the ground's too steep or rocky, or brushy, or there might be a spook hiding in it somewhere."

"Shadow always goes where I want him to," Josh had answered.

"Could be you'd find yourself on a different bronc, sometime. All horses ain't as accommodating as Shadow. Some's stubborn, mule-headed critters, just as knotheaded as they come. But even then you don't need no sharp spurs. They get the message with dull ones. Fellas who cut their horses with spurs sure didn't last long around a cow camp."

"Do they get let go?" Josh asked.

"Sometimes. But if they don't, they get such a cold shoulder turned to 'em and the air gets so chilly around them that they get scared of freezing to death, so they pack up, draw their wages, and leave."

"Anybody hurt Shadow and I'd shoot 'em," Josh said, his face expressing the horror of that unthinkable deed.

Around a chuckle, Pete'd said, "I might just go along with you and put my own slug in him, myself, 'cept we only got the one gun between us."

Josh had returned his grin. "Well, I'll tell you what. You get to shoot if the fella's abusing your horse and I get to him shoot if he's hurting mine."

"Sounds like a deal to me," Pete had said.

Now as the pale light of early morning crept into the room, he heard Josh rattle the stove grate to shake down the ashes, before laying down kindling to start the morning's fire.

When he figured Josh had the fire started and the coffee on, he called, "Josh, come here a minute."

"You all right, Pete?" Josh was through the door in an instant, his face plainly showing his fear.

"Yeah."

The boy thought he was breathing his last. Well, it wouldn't be long now until he would be. Each morning it seemed to Pete that he was weaker. He thought this might be the day. Maybe he ought to have Josh shave him, just in case. 'Course they could do it afterwards, but he'd like to die clean-shaven.

Josh had been shaving himself now for practically a year and had lately grown a mustache. The black mustache took some of the boyish look from his face so he looked his eighteen years. He was sure a good-looking young man. Ought to drive the women crazy. He grinned to himself and ran a hand over the stubble on his cheeks and chin. Maybe after Josh got him shaved, he'd have him wash his face and bring him a little of that thin gruel Rosita had taught him to make for his breakfast. It had little taste to it, but it went down easy and made Josh and Rosita both happy.

Rosita would be over a little later this morning to wash whatever she thought needed washing and to give him a sponge bath and straighten up his bed. She always smiled and kissed the top of his bald head when she asked if he'd eaten anything and he could tell her that, yes, he had.

He brought his attention back to Josh standing beside the bed, waiting. "I've been thinking that when I'm gone, you ought to head out for Victoria or somewheres and join up with one of them cow-outfits there. It'll give you good experience and teach you more'n you can learn on your own."

"What about this place?" Josh said, his brow furrowing in a frown.

"Miguel will look after the place. Give him Spook and sell the cows. Use some for spending money and sock the rest away 'til you need it. Give Rosita the chickens. Someday, if you ever want to come back, you can. If you don't, you can sign the place over to Miguel and Rosita, or maybe by then, to Ramon."

"I'd like to stay on here," Josh said.

It pleased him that the boy wanted to stay on here, but he was too young to settle for few head of cows on a ranch no bigger'n a man's shirt tail. "You need to see how other folks do things, Josh. Get a little experience under your belt."

"I thought if I stayed here I could run a few more head and make some improvements over time. But if you'd rather, I'll go find some ranch work."

"That would please me a whole lot. I ain't meaning you can't come back some day, but I want you to look around first, see what there is to see. You're young. You've got years to settle down. Take your time. Could be you won't want to come back and if you don't, just sign the place over to Miguel and go on about your living. But if you're still hankering to settle down here, well, the place will be waiting for you."

"If that's what you want, Pete," Josh said, shrugging, a slight frown creasing his brow. Plainly uneasy, he changed the subject. "I've got the coffee on. Could you drink some this morning?"

CHAPTER TEN

Josh closed Pete's eyes, unseeing now and straightened the blanket, although barely rumpled, over the gaunt body almost as small now, as Gordo's, the Pinõs seven-year-old. Tears filled his eyes, blurring his vision. He had sat beside Pete's bed all night, listening to his shallow breathing, certain each breath would be his last. Towards morning Pete woke, looked at him as if checking to see that he was still there, sighed, and took his last breath.

Miguel came out of the goat shed to meet him as Josh pulled Shadow up into the shade of the Pinõs' adobe and dismounted.

"*Senõr* Pete he is gone?" Miguel dark eyes looked questioning up into his.

Josh nodded.

"Come," Miguel gestured toward the doorway, "Rosita, she make you breakfast."

As Josh ate, Miguel and Rosita probed him with gentle questions about his last night with Pete and where he thought Pete would want to be buried.

Josh knew that Pete's wife and infant son were buried in the cemetery at Port Lavaca and he was sure Pete would want to be buried there beside them.

"We help you with Pete," Rosita told Josh as he finished eating and pushed back from the table. She turned toward ten-year-old, Ramon and spoke to him, Josh catching enough of the words to figure out that she was leaving him in charge of the other boys while she and Miguel were gone. All were solemn faced, even little Pete who, although too young to know that the man whose name he carried was gone from their lives forever, had matched his mood to his family's.

Josh carried in water and set it on the stove to warm for Pete's final bath. "He not care if the water cold," Rosita said with a soft little smile, "but Miguel and me, we do."

Miguel and Rosita washed and dressed Pete, insisting Josh find something else to do, so he went to find Shadow. He had turned him and old Spook out to graze and the two had not strayed far. As he approached, Shadow looked up, nickered, and came to meet him. Facing him, Josh put his hands on each side of the horse's jawbones and leaned his head in to touch his forehead against Shadow's and, as they breathed in some of each others air, he let the tears fall.

Two weeks later, Josh had quit his job, sold his cattle, buried most of the money under a corner of the house, told the Pinõs goodbye, and on Shadow was headed for Victoria.

Although a part of him wanted to stay at Pete's place, he could not help but be excited about hiring on with a cow outfit and maybe finding something out about the red-headed man, who might or might not have fathered him.

In Victoria, he rented a room in one of the boarding houses and kept Shadow at the livery stable while he wandered the streets, asking at each place of business if anyone remembered a tall redheaded man of some seventeen years ago. When he had inquired at every place of business, including the doctor's office and the undertaker's, he decided to see if he could learn anything from the sheriff. If the sheriff could not give him any information, he'd start riding from ranch to ranch.

Josh found the sheriff late one afternoon, returning to his office after having been out two days investigating the killing of a man who got caught changing brands.

He shook his head and sank down wearily in his office chair when Josh asked about the redheaded man.

"Can't say as I've ever heard of a Joshua Ryder. Too bad he wasn't wanted by the law. I've got a handful of bills on those fellas. I save 'em all, even if the the fella in question has been apprehended or isn't alive anymore."

A sudden thought brought a quickening to Josh's chest. "You don't have a poster on a Cole Slade, do you?" he asked.

The sheriff looked startled. "You know Slade?"

"No. But I think he killed my mother when I was just a boy."

"I'm sure sorry, son. He's a mean son of a bitch. Most of these fellas outside the law, don't hold with killing women folk, but that bastard don't care. Uses little girls, too. Especially little Mexican girls."

Josh's heart lurched. "Mexican girls?"

"Yeah. Picks 'em up and carries 'em away."

"Why Mexican girls?"

The sheriff shrugged. "Quien Sabe? Heard he picked up another one last month. They say his gang knocked off a bank in Brownsville some weeks ago and was high-tailing it out of town, when Slade spurred his horse around behind a building and grabbed her up. She wasn't more'n twelve years old according to the report I got." He shook his head.

"Later, I heard her body was found with a bullet through the head."

All the way back to his room at the boarding house, Josh rolled the sheriff's words over in his mind. *So Slade was still alive.* He thought of abandoning his search for the redheaded man and going after Slade, but he'd need to practice his shooting first. It would do no good to go after Slade and be such a poor shot that he'd get himself killed and Slade could just go on raising hell and spreading misery. No, he'd best stick to his original plan and if Slade was still alive then, he'd find him and shoot him, if he had to, or bring him in to the sheriff to be hanged.

He wondered about Slade taking young Mexican girls. *Was that why he had come to his mother? Had he meant to kidnap her and she'd fought him? She hadn't been a young girl though. The sheriff said Slade favored young girls.*

* * *

On a bright sunny day in early February, Josh bought a canteen and more ammunition for Pete's old gun and started his search ranch by ranch from a list the sheriff had given him. A few weeks later, not sure how long, himself, as the days had slipped by without much notice on his part, he had been to all but one ranch. He had made a wide loop as far north as the Colorado River and as far south as the Nueces. Every evening while it was still light, he made camp and practiced drawing his gun and clicking on an empty chamber. Shooting, he figured would attract attention and maybe bring someone in to snoop around at night and make off with the small sack of coins he had stuffed in with his change of clothes. As soon as he finished practicing, he reloaded in case he'd need to protect himself, but the only thing he'd ever had to shoot at was a coyote sneaking off with his grub sack.

He had bypassed the Lazy R, a ranch near Victoria, when he heard it was run by a woman, but it was the only ranch left so he'd have to ask there as well. In general women made him nervous. If they were all like Rosita he would not be so tongue-tied when he had to talk to them, but he was always afraid of running into a woman like the two who lived and worked on the second floor of the saloon in Indianola.

No one, so far, had been able to recall the tall, redheaded man of seventeen years ago, nor had anyone recalled needing a ranch hand and a cook at the same time. One ranch owner said he might have needed a hand about that time, especially for their cow hunts, but his cook was a second generation one. Another ranch owner told him he had needed a cook about that time, but ended up getting married and he'd added with a grin, "So I got me a cook in the bargain."

At first Josh was surprised to be invited in to eat, if he arrived at mealtime. A later arrival and he was given coffee and biscuits or a slab of buttered bread or whatever else the cook or lady of the house could rustle up in a hurry. Once he accepted an invitation to stay for the night and had slept in the bunkhouse. Used to hearing only Shadow move about in the dark, the snores, rustlings, and deep breathing sounds of a half dozen men, kept him awake most of the night. The next morning, at breakfast, one of the men remembered working with a redheaded man called Rusty down near Brownsville.

"I 'membered him when I woke up this morning," the man said. "His last name was Richman. That was some years ago, though...maybe ten, twelve years or there 'bouts. Ain't seen nor heard about him since."

Discouragement sat heavy on Josh as he turned Shadow toward the Lazy R. "If no one at the Lazy R knows anything," he said to Shadow, "I guess I'll have to give it up."

Shadow flicked his ears as if acknowledging his words and Josh leaned forward to pat the buckskin's neck.

CHAPTER ELEVEN

As he reined Shadow up by the front porch of the ranch house, a dark-haired woman stepped out of the doorway to greet him. "Tie your horse and come on in. Have you had your supper yet?"

"No, ma'am," Josh said, "But I'd like to water my horse first, if I could."

"By all means. There's a barrel by the corral. Pull off his saddle and put him in the corral, if you'd like and come on up. We've just sat down to eat."

When Josh got back to the ranch house, a young girl with long, dark brown braids was waiting for him. With a shy smile, she said, "Mother sent me to wait for you." Josh followed her inside to a room where the Rawlins family and their ranch hands were eating at a long table filled with bowls and platters of food. The woman who had greeted him earlier sat at the head of the table. She looked up with a smile and motioned him to an empty chair beside a boy near his own age who sat next to the little girl with the braided hair.

Like those at the other ranches he visited, no one asked him his name, nor offered theirs. They just nodded a hello to him and turned their attention to the plates in front of them. Josh was passed a platter of beefsteak, biscuits, bowls of mashed potatoes and gravy, and some kind of tangy green stuff that tasted surprisingly good.

The men ate in silence except for an occasional comment among themselves or in answer to Mrs. Rawlins when she asked them a question about the ranch.

Josh noticed another girl who resembled the girl who had met him at the door. Like the boy, she looked to be near his age or a little younger. Long, dark hair framed a very pretty face, but it was her eyes that caught his attention. He thought they had to be the biggest and bluest he'd ever seen. The girl caught him looking at her and smiled. He ducked his head, and felt heat creep up his neck and bathe his face. A little later in the meal he heard Mrs. Rawlins call the girl Belle.

One of the men at the table, and older fellow with a thick drooping mustache the color of dry sand, called the boy sitting next to Josh, Lee, and asked him if he thought the roan gelding was broken to saddle well enough to take on the drive.

Lee said he thought so.

Mrs. Rawlins smiled at Lee before turning her clear blue eyes to Josh. "We're about set to take a herd up the trail to Wichita, Kansas. There I hope to sell them to buyers for the eastern market who will ship them out on railroad cars." She paused, a small frown knitting her brow. "Have you worked cattle before?"

"A few head. My…" he stopped, he couldn't call Pete his pa, and he was more than his friend. He cleared his throat and said, "The man who raised me ran a few head."

"I see." Mrs. Rawlins turned her head and spoke to the man who had asked Lee about the horse. "Could we use another hand to ride drag, since Shorty's broken his arm?"

The man nodded. "We could," he said.

Josh had noticed a man across the table, a bandaged right arm looped through a sling to hold it. Evidently it was the one he used most of the time, for he ate awkwardly and slower than the rest.

"I'm plumb sorry about this," Shorty said, holding up the arm as though he wanted to be clear what he was sorry about. "Sure didn't reckon on no rattlesnake jumping up under O' Speck's hooves. Should have been on my toes."

One of the men laughed. "Sure was a sight, seeing old Speck going one way and Shorty here another. Confused the rattler so, not knowing who to bite, he just pulled in his fangs and slithered away."

Everyone laughed, even Shorty although his face flushed red.

As the laughter died away, Mrs. Rawlins turned toward Josh. "Would you want to throw in with us? The trail drive will take about three months and then you'll be free to come back. I pay a dollar a day, payable when the herd is sold and loaded into the railroad cars. You will ride drag, which is at the very end of the herd. I'm told the rider breathes in a lot of dust, so if you've ever had lung problems."

"No ma'am. I never have," Josh said.

"You ain't worked more'n a few head," one of the men spoke up.

"No. We had a real small spread."

"Well," Mrs. Rawlins said, addressing the men. "He sits his horse well and took care of him before coming in to eat. That says a lot about a man." With a flash of a grin at Josh, she added, "I bet you were getting pretty lank, too."

Josh returned her grin. "I sure was, ma'am. Pete, the fella who raised me, used to say when he was real hungry, 'My stomach must think my throat's been cut.'"

Mrs. Rawlins waited for the chuckles to die down before saying, "So what is your answer?"

"Well, well..." he stuttered, "I sure do appreciate the offer, but I'm trying to find someone who knew my pa. His name was Joshua Ryder, the same as mine, only folks call me Josh."

"Well hello, Josh," Mrs. Rawlins said. "I'm Martha Rawlins and these are my children. Lee, and Kit next to you, and this, she gestured toward the blue-eyed girl, is Belle."

From Lee and Kit, the young girl who'd met him on the porch and brought him into supper, Josh turned to the big-eyed girl and felt the world fall away. Her blue-eyed steady gaze and beautiful full red lips parted in a soft smile, wrapped him up in a spell so deep it seemed minutes before he could tear his eyes from her and listen to her mother, who was introducing the men at the table. Rattled by the girl's presence, he ended up getting only a few of the names.

Shorty's last name, he learned, was Ellis and the man with the drooping, sand-colored mustache, who had asked Lee Rawlins about the horse, was Charley Whitcomb. The only others he could put a face to their names, were Slim Rafters, a thin man with a large nose, Joe Saunders, a man with twinkling blue eyes behind a pair of spectacles, and a Mexican man Mrs. Rawlins introduced as Ruberto Gomez. She smiled, "But we call him Sugar."

Mrs. Rawlins turned her attention to a large colored woman who had entered the room with a big platter filled with cuts of pie. The woman paused beside Mrs. Rawlins who took the first piece and moved on around the table.

"Thank you, Lucy," Mrs. Rawlins said, when everyone had their pie and the colored woman was heading back to the kitchen.

"You is shore welcome Miz Rawlins." The colored woman smiled back at her, a fondness showing in her dark face. "I's be back with more coffee."

Picking up her fork, Mrs. Rawlins paused and turned to Josh. "You say your father lived around here?"

"Yes, ma'am, he came up this way looking for work," Josh said and told her the story his mother had told him.

When he finished, Mrs. Rawlins shook her head. "I don't recall ever meeting a man by that name. You say it was seventeen years ago?"

"Yes, ma'am. About that. I just turned eighteen and my mother said I was just starting to walk."

A thoughtful look crossed Mrs. Rawlins' face, followed by a small frown. "We've hired a number of cow hands over the years, but Lucy has been our head cook for more than twenty years. I don't recall ever hearing that name." She smiled and added, "That is until today. "Seventeen years is a long time, Joshua."

Josh felt the color rise up in his face. She was telling him it was a foolish mission. That he should take her up on her offer and forget about his search, at least for a while. Maybe she was right. Maybe he should go on this cattle drive. It was what Pete had wanted him to do. When he got back he could take up the search, again. But he had already asked everywhere he could think of to ask. There really wasn't any place else to go looking. A wave of despair swept over him. He had carried the idea of finding some trace of his pa so long that it was hard to think of letting go, but he really had no choice. He had to consider, too, that the redheaded Joshua Ryder had never even existed.

He thought of Cole Slade. He wasn't ready yet to hunt him down. There was no sense in giving that dirty sidewinder any more of an edge than he already had. On this drive, he could continue to practice drawing his gun, although he wouldn't be able to shoot it, not with a herd nearby. After he got back from this drive, he'd stay on at Pete's place and practice his shooting until he could hit a target square every time. Then he would see what the sheriffs at Victoria and Indianola had to say. See if they had even a scrap of information. Anything at all to give him the start of a trail to follow.

He looked at Mrs. Rawlins, conscious of her daughter's blue eyes fixed steadily on him, and said, "I accept your offer. Thank you, ma'am."

She smiled. "Good. Lee can show you the bunkhouse and where we pasture the horses. We're holding the herd out on the range. The men have spent a couple of months rounding up all the cattle they could drag out of the brush, branding the mavericks and what we missed on round up last fall. They're beginning to settle down now, but some are still pretty wild."

"Begging your pardon, ma'am," a man with black hair and dark eyes sitting at the end of the table said, "but you're making this trip sound like a picnic to the boy. Those old mossy horns ain't just wild, they's mean as snakes and quick as wild hogs and, if they're a mind to, they'll gore you or your horse in the blink of an eye if you ain't watching."

"You are so right, Jake." Sober-faced, Mrs. Rawlins turned back to Josh. "You'll do well to respect the fact that these longhorns are truly wild animals that as Jake says will turn on you and your horse and, I'm told, will stampede at the drop of a hat, trampling anything that gets in their way."

"I'll remember, ma'am," Josh assured her.

She smiled. "We expect to pull out at sunrise the day after tomorrow, so tomorrow you can ride out with these men." She nodded at the men around the table who were finishing up their pie and coffee. "They pulled the day watch. We have the night crew out there now."

Josh nodded. "Yes, ma'am," he said. From the corner of his eye he could see Belle eating her pie, but looking at him every now and then with her measuring gaze. Feeling the flush of red again creep from his collar to his face, he ducked his head and forked up a piece of his pie.

A small, lean black man brought out another pot of coffee from the kitchen. Mrs. Rawlins introduced him to Josh as Hector Thomas, Lucy's son. "Hector is going to be our cook on the trail drive."

Mrs. Rawlin's words gave Josh a small start. *She didn't actually mean she was going along, did she?*

The one called Jake grinned at Josh. "Hector's already warned us about complaining about his cooking while we're on the drive. Says he has a stew he makes out of coyote for any of us he hears complaining, so take heed if you're fixing to ride with us."

"That be right," Hector said, smiling at Josh, "And if it gets real bad, I adds the hide, too."

Everyone laughed and Hector with a wide grin went back to the kitchen.

The men, except for Shorty, seemed to finish their coffee in one simultaneous gulp and as one, pushed back from the table. Shorty who had struggled to eat with his fork in his left hand, gave them a quick, anxious look and bending low over his pie, began shoveling it in as fast as he could.

The men trailed out to the porch. Some paused to roll cigarettes before following their companions down the steps. They scattered in several directions. Some headed toward a long, low building that Josh surmised was the bunkhouse, a few walked on down to the corral, maybe, he thought, to check out Shadow. A touch of pride straightened his back and put a small smile on his face. As Pete said, the buckskin was a horse to take pride in; deep chested with a well-shaped head that matched the size of his body, his dark eyes in a wide face were alert and intelligent looking. With his buckskin color, four black stockings and a thick black mane and tail, Shadow was "easy on the eye", as Pete said. He was easy riding, too, his gait smooth, even in a fast trot, and he was quick on his feet, a necessity for a good cow horse.

He would have preferred going to the corral first to hear what the men might say about Shadow, but Lee said, "I'll show you the bunkhouse."

Beds lined the walls of the bunkhouse and a small table and a stove occupied the center. "This bunk's empty," Lee said, indicating a bunk where the thin mattress had been rolled up and tied with twine. "Mother will see to it that you get a blanket and a pillow."

"Thanks," Josh said. "Now if you don't mind showing me where to put my horse."

Shadow raised his head and whinnied when he saw them coming. "Is he a pet or a horse?" one of the men, lounging around the corral, said.

"Both," Josh said. I raised him from a colt when his mama died."

"It's a wonder he ain't a knot-head." Shorty, who had finished his supper and had just joined them, said. "I raised a colt oncet. Had to get him to sucking milk-soaked rags and the darned little rascal was always hungry. Got so I'd do most anything a-tall to get out of feeding the little runt, so my sister took over. He grew up kind of spindly legged and pot-bellied. Regular nuisance, but sis sure liked him. Followed her around like a puppy dog."

"We raised him on goat's milk," Josh said. "Used a lamb's bottle."

"An old Mexican woman told me once that goat's milk would make a fella live to be near a hundred," Slim Rafters spoke up. "Me, I figure if I gotta drink the stuff, I'd as soon kick off a wee bit early."

Joe Saunders laughed. "You should of done it, Slim. It might have fattened you up some and you wouldn't have to stand twice to make a shadow."

"You're just jealous, 'cause the girl's ain't a-swooning over you," Slim said good naturedly.

"I don't know about you fellas," Joe said. "But if I can wade through this stuff piling up around here, I'm going on over to the bunkhouse."

"They always tease each other like that?" Josh asked as he and Lee took Shadow over to the pasture where several head of horses grazed, lifting their heads to eye the newcomer, one giving a welcoming whinny.

Lee grinned. "That's mild compared to how they usually jaw at each other." His face sobering he added, "We've got a good outfit. We like to think of our men as family. If we get one that doesn't fit in, especially a thin skinned one who gets peeved easily, or one too big for his britches, the boys rag on him until they've got him more to their liking, or else he's asking for his pay and moving on."

As they walked back, Lee asked him about his father and Josh repeated what he'd told them at the supper table. "My father's dead, too." Lee said when Josh had finished. "He kept having pains in his chest. Mother wanted to take him to a doctor, but he fought her on it, and one night he just died in his sleep."

"Sorry," Josh said.

"I know why you want to hear about your father, I like to hear about mine, too. Makes it seem like he's not so far away."

"You have memories of him?"

"Yeah. I was eleven when he died. I'm eighteen now."

"I wished I'd have been older," Josh said.

"Yeah. I have a lot of memories."

They lapsed into silence until Lee said, turning his head to look at him, "I just remembered. Come on up to the house. Mother will be wanting to get your name on the payroll."

Josh's heart jumped in his chest. *Would the big-eyed girl be there?* Ever since he had left the Rawlins' house after supper, she had stayed foremost in his mind. Several times he'd said her name inside his head. He thought Belle was the prettiest name he'd ever heard.

He watched for a glimpse of the girl as he followed Lee through the house to a small room where Mrs. Rawlins sat at a desk, going over some papers. Looking up, she smiled and said, "Well, Josh are you and your horse getting settled?"

"Yes. ma'am." It was odd how comfortable he felt with both Lee and Mrs. Rawlins. Almost as though he had always known them. He wished his pa could have gone to work here and his mama, too. He would have grown up with Lee and Belle and their little sister. But he wouldn't have met Pete or the Pinõs, or have Shadow.

He thought of the morning they'd laid Pete to rest in the little cemetery in Port Lavaca. They'd stood awhile, the Pinõs and himself, looking down at Pete's grave mounded with bare dirt next to his wife and infant son's level grassy ones. A breeze blowing in from the bay scattered strands of Rosita dark hair. She wiped at the hairs blowing across her face and said, *"Life, she gives and life she takes away and in both ways she changes our journey."*

He thought, now, of Pete saying we all had shadows back along the trails we ride, and he wondered, as he had since learning of Cole Slade's kidnapping of Mexican girls, if somewhere Slade and his mother had crossed trails before that final time?

"Mother," a soft, feminine voice said behind them. "I can't find that dark brown coat of mine. Have you seen it?"

Josh turned with Lee to look at the girl, his heart hammering in his chest. Belle gave them all the flash of a smile, then her blue eyes locked on his and time stood still.

Mrs. Rawlins broke the spell her daughter had woven around him by telling her to ask Lucy about the coat.

Again a flash of a smile and she was gone.

Feeling almost dazed, it took Josh a second to understand what Mrs. Rawlins was saying.

"I put your name down on the payroll list. I spelled your last name with a y. Is that right? Or is it an i?"

Her words startled and embarrassed him. Under ordinary circumstances, he was able to spell his name, not that he ever had much call to do so, but now, he couldn't remember for sure. Belle's sudden appearance and blue eyes had muddled any knowledge he possessed. Was it a y or an i? Feeling the heat rise up in his face, he ducked his head and mumbled, "You have it right, ma'am." Seconds later, his senses returned and he realized that she'd had it right. If she hadn't, though, he'd have left it at that, rather than appear the fool.

He knew some words. He could pick out stable, cafe, saloon, and knew the long word, mercantile, and what those words meant, but he couldn't spell any word but his name.

Mrs. Rawlins looked at him for a long moment and finally said, "I don't expect you had access to many schools. A lot of children don't. I loved teaching. I should have been a teacher, I guess. If you're interested, while we're on the trail, I could teach you to read and write."

"You're going on the drive?" *So it was true!*

She smiled. "Yes, and so are the girls. You don't think we're leaving this big adventure to you men-folks to enjoy alone, do you?"

Again the heat rushed to Josh's face. "No. No, ma'am," he stammered, his heart was jumping around like a frog at fandango as Pete used to say. *Belle would be going, too!*

Mrs. Rawlins smile was swallowed up in a laugh and with blue eyes twinkling, she turned to Lee. "Have Lucy get you some bedding for this boy and let me get back to my work."

"Lucy and Hector have been with our family for years," Lee told him as they went toward the kitchen in search of the colored woman. "After the coloreds were emancipated, Lucy and Hector stayed on. We've always considered them a part of our family and they feel the same."

"So you gots youself a new cowhand," Lucy said, her dark eyes on Lee as she handed over the blanket roll to Josh. The smile she gave Lee disappeared from her wide mouth as she turned to Josh. "You be working for a good outfit. It's the best they is. And you'd best be 'preciatin' it. You ain't family now, but you work for Mis Rawlins long and you is gonna be family, just like the rest of us."

Josh searched for words to answer the colored woman, but none came to mind, so he just nodded and gave her a small smile, which she answered with a soft chuckle.

As they stepped out on the porch, Lee fished his cigarette makings from his shirt pocket, and said, "Lucy was right about you becoming family if you work for my mother. Just like her offering to teach you to read and write. She draws everyone that comes here to her, like her children aren't enough."

Josh wondered at the lack of hostility in Lee's voice. "Your mother is an awful nice woman," he said.

Lee nodded. "She is at that." He was silent a few moments and then said, "Mother lost her first husband and their two children when the children were just young and then my father, too. I think she's afraid she'll lose more of us and so she draws others to her as a sort of insurance that she won't be left alone." He paused to light the cigarette he'd rolled and blowing out smoke said, "Whether or not you accept her teaching, before this drive is over, unless you've got a bad streak that hasn't shown up yet, she'll tuck you under her wing same as the rest of us."

Josh grinned. "I think I'd like that," he said.

CHAPTER TWELVE

Josh lay on his bunk, his arms behind his head, and watched the men. He listened for a spoken name and tried to place the name with the face of the ones he'd missed while the big-eyed girl was looking at him. The Mexican was already in his bunk and sound asleep, giving off a rumble of soft snores. "Sugar's sure out of it," one of the men had commented as they came inside the bunkhouse.

"We call him Sugar," Charley Whitcomb told Josh, "because he's got a whale of a sweet tooth. The rest of us go to town, we head for the saloon for a cool drink, he goes to the mercantile and buys himself a sack full of candy."

Jake, the tall, thin, dark haired man who had spoken up at supper about the herd being wild, said, "Some folks don't cotton to Mexicans in the saloon, and give 'em trouble. We 'spect Sugar'd be okay 'cause he's with us, but he don't ask to stir up no trouble"

Josh felt his face flush. *Did this man know he was half Mexican? Did it matter to him?*

"Come on, Jake," Charley said, "Let's have a go round of poker 'fore sack time."

Jake sat down at the small table that held a kerosene lamp and began to shuffle a deck of cards. "We playing for matchsticks or money?"

Charley laughed. "Matchsticks, I reckon. You'd take all my money. What little I've got."

Jake grinned. "I've been thinking about getting out of this cow chasing job and getting me a gambling suit, grease back my hair real slick and start using my real talent."

"'Cepting you get downright nasty if you're cooped up in a building too long," Shorty Ellis said, holding his broken arm with his good one as he sat down on his bunk.

"Ain't it the truth," Jake said, a mock frown on his face. "So I'll just stay being a poor o' cowhand."

They bantered back and forth a few minutes more before they settled down to play cards. Two men came in who had sat outside smoking, their chairs tipped back against the bunkhouse wall, like he and Pete used to do in the evenings. Both tall men, they had to duck their heads to keep from scrapping their hats as they entered. Josh noticed they all kept their hats on, even inside, except, of course, inside Mrs. Rawlins' house. That was one thing Pete had sure drummed into his head. "You go into a house where there's ladies, you be sure to take off your hat. Ain't nothing more impolite than keeping your hat on in the house with a woman present."

Despite his certainty that he wouldn't sleep a wink, Josh wasn't even aware when the last man to crawl into bed blew out the lamp.

* * *

It was still dark when Charley's "up and at 'em boys," brought Josh and the others tumbling out of their bunks. Charley relit the kerosene lamp and Slim started a fire in the stove and set a bucket of water on to heat. They took turns slopping water on their faces, tossing out the scant amount they'd used and handing the basin to the next man. Some of the men shaved, peering into a cracked mirror above the small washstand. Watching them, Shorty fingered his growing beard. "Sure wish I could get rid of this itchy brush," he moaned, "But I'm scared I'll cut my throat, using my left hand and I sure ain't gonna trust one of you fellas to do it for me."

"I used to shave the man who raised me when he was sick," Josh said. "You want me to do it?"

"Naw," Shorty said. "Be different if you wasn't going on the drive and could do the job real regular. I reckon 'til this arm gets mended, I'll have to grow me a bush."

"Gives him something to gripe about," Jake said, with a grin at Josh.

Josh had started growing a mustache shortly before Pete got sick, but he used the basin and his razor to scrape the light growth of whiskers from his cheeks and chin.

They all walked together up to the main house for a breakfast of stewed prunes, biscuits covered with gravy, and fried beefsteak. This time Mrs. Rawlins and the girls did not make an appearance, although Lee was there. They ate quickly, silently. Leaving their plates slicked clean, they pushed back their chairs, grabbed up their hats, and went back outside. The horses, including Shadow, were in the corral.

"Our horse wrangler brought them in," Lee explained seeing Josh's look of surprise. The horse wrangler, Josh saw was Sugar the Mexican, who had been asleep by the time he got to the bunkhouse, but he realized now, had not been there this morning when he woke. He was small and thin, his legs bowed as if he'd spent his lifetime on a horse. His black eyes, beneath a wide, high-topped sombero, gray and sweat stained, took note of Josh again, as they had at the supper table last night, and Josh wondered if he recognized the Mexican blood in him.

The men were picking their mounts, Sugar roping the ones they chose with a swift, deft sail of the rope that passed over the horses' heads and settled around their necks. When he looked at him, Josh said, "The buckskin's mine. He'll come to me."

As they swung up on their horses, Jake's, a blaze-faced black, suddenly ducked his head and humped his back. They reined out of the way to give Jake and his horse room as the black gelding leaped in the air and came down stiff-legged, his hooves raising a small dust cloud. With every jump, Jake slapped his gray hat from the horse's rump to his neck. Josh marveled at how easy the man sat his pitching horse, gloved hands tight on the reins. Josh remembered Pete's words from that day long ago about grabbing the saddle horn. *"I'd of got me a snoot full of dirt, for I'd have shamed myself that-a-way."*

In a few minutes the horse had settled down and Jake spurred him into a lope out away from the corral and back again, pulling him up so tight he sat back a little on his haunches.

"'Bout like ridin' a rockin' chair, ain't he?" Slim Rafters said, grinning at Jake from on top of the sorrel gelding he was riding.

"Sure is," Jake answered flashing a grin at Slim. "Makes me homesick for my mama."

Their faces creased with smiles, the men touched their heels to their horses and headed out to take their turn at watching the herd.

They heard the bawling of the cattle before they saw them. Josh was amazed at the size of the herd. Up off their bed ground, the long-horned cattle had spread out across the rangeland to graze, the night crew riding around them to herd back the strays.

"You go with Lee and take the first man's place and Lee'll take the other's," Charley said and turning his bay gelding around, headed towards the west end of the herd.

"You sure have a lot of cows," Josh said, reining Shadow over to ride along side Lee on the black and white piebald he called Ace. "We only ran an average of twenty head."

"We've been collecting for a year now for this drive. Some we already had, but we kept adding to them, popping them out of the brush and taming them down some. But like Jake said, last night at supper, they're still wild as deer and can run like one, too. And mean. If you get one on the prod, why it'd be safer to be tossed into a sack full of wild cats. And branding them? O' boy, you turn one loose and you'd better scoot up on your horse right quick."

Josh grinned. "I'll remember," he said.

"Jake's the only one of us ever been on a trail drive," Lee said. "He says we'll have to watch to be sure they don't get riled up or spooked. Says they'll run in the blink of an eye and before you know it the whole herd will be scattered to the four winds. He says, they tell him a herd can get spoiled that way and want to run all the time." He grinned. "Jake could be stretching the truth some. Listening to him, you'd think we're going to be riding in the most hellish rain and lightning storms old Ma Nature ever produced and we'll be swimming rivers running bank full, the bottoms filled with quicksand that'll grab our cows and suck them down faster than we can get a rope on them and drag them out."

His face sobered. "Jake doesn't think Mother and the girls ought to be going along, but Mother's made up her mind and I think she and the girls will be safe enough in their wagon. "Of course," he flashed a grin at Josh,

"Belle's not the type to stay wagon bound, but neither Charley nor Mother will let her anywhere close to the herd, much as she'd like to."

"She rides?" Josh said.

"Like she's trying to outrun the wind."

Josh smiled and enjoyed the mental picture of the blue-eyed girl racing a horse, bent low in the saddle, her dark hair streaming behind her, as he rode over to relieve a dark-haired, dark-eyed man with the look of an Indian about him.

"Name's Josh Ryder," he said as he rode up to the man who sat a tall, leggy dark bay with black mane and tail. "I'm to take your place for today."

The solemn faced man acknowledged him with a small jerk of his chin. "Billy Redfeather," he said and lifting the reins, clucked to his horse. "Let's get us some grub and a bit of shut-eye, Kola."

The herd moved as they grazed, so by evening they were several miles to the southwest. They would bed down as darkness fell, Josh had been told, a few rising at intervals to move around and graze some more before lying down again.

It proved to be a long day and Josh welcomed the few head who strayed from the herd, for it helped break the monotony. When he turned Shadow after the stray, he imagined Belle Rawlins watching, not only him, but also his horse, quick and graceful on his feet, and in his imagination he'd carry out a larger sight for her to admire; the longhorn running flat out and he and Shadow after it, using all their skill to return it to the herd. His daydreams also found him atop a bucking bronc, sitting easy in the saddle, his body swaying with the horse's movements, his hat in his free hand fanning the horse from shoulder to haunches. He'd never ridden a bucking horse, but he hoped to get a chance one day soon.

He grinned to himself remembering Pete's words about grabbing on to the saddle horn, and knew he'd go flying off before he'd do that. He pictured himself landing on the ground and getting up causal-like, locating his hat and dusting off his britches with it, before clapping it back on his head. He'd look over at her and those big, blue eyes would be wide with admiration. He'd flash her a grin before he climbed back on again.

When the sun was straight up overhead, he untied the flour sack from the back of his saddle and ate the cold biscuits and beef jerky each had been given as they filed out of the house after breakfast. The food filled his stomach, but by the time evening came and Billy Redfeather rode out to relieve him, he was anticipating the platters of food that would soon be on the Rawlins table and the blue-eyed girl who would be sitting across from him.

They talked of little else but the drive at supper that night. Again Mrs. Rawlins and her children ate with them. Josh tried to keep his eyes off Belle, but it wasn't easy. He was careful not to let her catch him looking and sometimes had to jerk his eyes away so fast he felt like he'd jarred them out of their sockets. It excited him to think about her going with them and that excitement kept his heart jumping like a scared jackrabbit. He wondered if he hadn't been wearing a loose shirt, if it could be seen thumping under his skin. He wondered how old she was. Maybe sixteen or seventeen, a year or two behind him. Lee had told him he was the oldest at eighteen, but he hadn't mentioned his sisters' ages and Josh would sure like to know, but he wasn't going to ask and let Lee know he was already about half gone on the girl. Gosh, but she was beautiful. He sure liked watching her. Her beautiful face had so many changes of expression and although it embarrassed him to think about her body, he sure liked how it looked, from the slender, graceful neck to the soft mound of breast that dipped down to a small waist. Her dresses could give him no hint of the hips and legs down to the small feet, or at least he assumed they were small, he had seen nothing of them but a pointed toe encased in black leather.

Aware of his thoughts making his face flush with color, his palms sweat, and the pleasant tingle spread through his lower body, he pulled his thoughts away from the girl. He shifted in his chair and made himself listen to Charley Whitcomb who was talking about the trail drive. Something he should be paying attention to instead of getting all calf-eyed over a blue-eyed, dark-haired girl.

They would be up before dawn, so that all hands would be in place by five o'clock to turn the herd north toward Kansas, Charley informed them. Each rider would have four extra horses in the remuda. Sugar would take care of the horses and Swede Davidson an older, gray-haired man, would drive the wagon carrying Mrs. Rawlins and the two girls, their bed rolls and other necessities.

Charley Whitcomb had assigned the men their places to ride along side the herd. Josh would be riding drag along with Jimmy Letts and Jed Motts. Joe Saunders and Jake Howell were the point men. They'd ride out after Charley, who as the trail boss would take the lead. The swingmen, Charley called them, would be Slim Rafters and Snort Beers, a red-headed man with a ready grin. Charley had assigned Billy Redfeather and Lee Rawlins at flank.

Hector came in from the kitchen with a fresh pot of coffee and as he set the pot down at the end of the table, Charley said, "Well, Hector, you reckon you can keep this bunch of yahoos from straving to death before we get to Kansas?"

"Reckon I aim to try," Hector said, a grin lighting his face. "Yes, sir, I sure do aim to try."

After supper, Josh on Shadow and Lee riding Ace, his favorite, the spotted black and white piebald gelding with blue eyes, they rode out to see the horses that would make up the remuda on the trail drive. As they sat in the saddle, watching the animals graze, Lee cocked his right leg over the saddle horn and rolled a smoke. He offered papers and tobacco to Josh who shook his head and said, "Never took it up."

He knew it was probably because Pete didn't smoke that he didn't either. "To me it was too much trouble keeping track of the makings," Pete said one day when he asked. "I've seen men cuss a blue streak when they got their papers or tobacco wet and be grumpy as hell before they got 'em dried out enough for a smoke. Figured then, I'd save myself the aggravation."

Lee pointed out each horse assigned to Josh. "The two sorrels there, one with the four white stockings and the other with the blaze face, the dark bay and that red roan. Their names are Son of a Gun, shortened to Son, Socks, Topper, shortened to Top, and Rip. They're good horses," he added.

"Son, Socks, Top, and Rip." Josh repeated the names. "They ought to be easy to remember." Thinking as always of the blue-eyed Belle, whose presence had shadowed him ever since he'd met her, Josh said in what he hoped was a matter of fact voice. "Will your mother and sisters be taking along saddle horses?"

"Mother and Kit won't," Lee answered. "Mother rides quite well and so does Kit, but they're leaving their horses at home. Belle, now, that's a horse of different color as they say. She would no more leave her horse behind than she would think of trying to lasso the moon." He grinned. Josh had noticed that Lee had a lopsided grin, the right side of his mouth lifting a little more then the rest.

"Swede will probably have Mother and Kit for company most of the time, but Belle would just as soon be a horseback."

Josh grinned at him. "I'm guessing your sister has an independent streak."

"About a mile wide," Lee answered.

CHAPTER THIRTEEN

Dreaming a wonderful, exciting dream about kissing Belle, when Charley called out for them to be "up and at 'em," at first Josh had no idea where he was or whose voice had prodded him out of his dream. He reached for his gray hat as he sat up on his bunk. Giving his hair a run through with his fingers, he clapped the hat on, shrugged into his shirt and pulled on his brown twill pants, standing to button the fly. All around him, the men were grumbling and needling each other good-naturedly as they dressed.

Slim Rafters blew a kiss toward his bunk, stripped of all but the mattress, the blankets now rolled up into a bedroll under his arm, "My poor o' backsides gonna miss you when I'm out there somewhere laying on the hard, cold ground, tarantulas and rattlesnakes nosing around for a place to get in next to my hide."

Jake Howell, the poker playing man who, yesterday, had ridden his crow-hopping horse with such ease, looked up from stuffing his feet into a pair of high-topped, well-worn, scuffed black boots and said, "Hell, man, ain't no snake or tarantula, lessen they're deaf, gonna be able to stand your snoring. I was damn tempted, last night, to get up and stuff my sock in your mouth."

"Hey Shorty," the redheaded Snort Beers said, turning to the man still lying in his bunk, eyes open staring up at the ceiling. "You'd best be a lightin' on your feet here in a bit, pardner, even if you ain't going with us. I don't mind leaving my ladies in bed, but I shore as thunder ain't gonna let no no-account cowhand lay abed whiles I'm out a-tearing things up."

"I wish you all'd pipe down," Shorty answered just as good naturedly, "so's I could get me some beauty sleep." He pretended to snore a little and then swung his feet out on to the floor. "Sure wish I was a going with you fellas," he said, suddenly sober. "This old bunkhouse's going to get mighty lonesome with just me and Tucker here staying to home."

The man he called Tucker, a black-haired man with gray eyes fringed in long black lashes, had already quit his bunk and was reaching over to turn down the wick on the lamp that had flared up and was sending up smoke to blacken the chimney. Josh noticed he favored his right leg as he walked toward the door. "Gotta get some air," he said, "Getting close in here with all you knot-heads running off at the mouth."

As soon as the door closed behind Tucker, Shorty said to Josh, "A horse fell on him, crushed his leg so it gets to hurting bad when he has to do a lot of riding."

Josh nodded and began rolling up his bedroll.

The bunk beside his was already empty, the bedroll gone. He had not heard the Mexican leave to bring up the horses. He thought of Shadow, probably in the corral now, waiting for him.

Josh was disappointed when he walked into the large dining room with the other men to find that Mrs. Rawlins and her daughters had already eaten and were just leaving. The girls following their mother paused as Mrs. Rawlins turned to speak to Charley. Josh's stomach gave a little lurch when Belle looked straight at him, her blue eyes warming above the quick, little smile on her full red lips.

His dream of kissing Belle still fresh in his mind, Josh felt his face redden and heard only the end of what Mrs. Rawlins said to Charley Whitcomb, "Looks like we're going to have fine, sunny weather to start our drive."

"Looks that way, ma'am," Charley said, "Hope it holds all the way to Kansas."

With Mrs. Rawlins and the girls gone from the room, the men sat down and went to work on their breakfast of beefsteak, fried potatoes, and cornbread.

Around his chewing and swallows of hot coffee, Charley Whitcomb reminded them that the cattle they were about to herd north still had some wild in them. "Remember, it ain't been a great long time since we popped 'em out of the brush, but in a few days they ought to settle down. By then, so Jake tells me, the natural leaders will have taken over and the rest will fill in where they fit in the order of things."

Jake Howell looked up from his plate and said around a bite of cornbread, "A couple of them are bound to be real renegades and they sure can cause a pile of trouble. We had a big red steer on that drive I was on in '73 that kept a-getting the notion to quit our outfit and head for parts unknown. That got the rest of them to thinking likewise and we finally had to cut him out of the herd. We drove him down over into a draw far enough away so's not to excite the herd and shot him." He grinned and took a swallow of coffee. "He'd of made good eatin' if he hadn't been so danged tough."

"If we have one of those, we'll probably cull it out that way, too," Charley said. He stirred sugar into his coffee and turned to Josh. "You and Jimmy and Jed'll be riding drag. The dust is gonna half blind you most of the time and a few head could slip past and we'd go off and leave 'em. You've got to watch for that. We don't aim to lose more'n we have to."

Josh nodded along with Jed and Jimmy and then added, "Yes, sir."

Charley squinted at him over his coffee cup, "Don't need the sir," he said. "Just Charley'll do fine."

Josh nodded and Charley shifted his gaze to take in the other two who would be riding drag.

"Sometimes," he said, "we'll get a stray from some other trail herd. We'll go ahead and take it in and unless they come calling for it, we'll take it on through with ours. Some of ours is bound to get lost and get off into some other herd the same's the strays we pick up. We can't go a riding back and forth exchanging beeves."

As they stepped out of the house and into the clear, fresh morning air, Josh saw that Hector had a pair of brown mules hitched to the cook's wagon. A light-skinned man with a tight mass of curly black hair and a pleasant-looking face, he looked as eager as Josh felt about getting the drive under way.

Swede Davidson was hitching four mules, two grays, a black and a brown to the wagon Mrs. Rawlins and the girls' would use and was now helping load the wagon.

Josh grinned as Kit, pigtails swinging, climbed up onto the wagon seat and sat there looking around, a pleased smile on her small face. His heart did a little tumble and his jaw felt like it'd dropped a foot, when Belle came around from the other side of the wagon and mounted a light gray gelding, swinging a leg up over the saddle and sitting astride.

Jake, seeing his look of surprise laughed. "Ain't those britches something'? " He chuckled. "I guess they ain't real britches, but something Belle came up with when her mama wouldn't let her wear her brother's. Got Lucy to sew 'em for her. Belle likes to ride hard and fast and I expect those long dresses women wear could be a real nuisance."

"I reckon they would," Josh said.

"Lee told us Belle begged her mama to let her help with the herd," Jake continued. "Said she'd ride point, or swing, or flank, or even drag that she wasn't at all choosy, but she didn't get the job done. Her mama put her foot down about that." Jake took a last drag of his cigarette and dropped it to the ground, grinding it under his boot heel. "Sure glad Missus Rawlins got her persuaded. Much as I admire the girl's grit, we don't need no female person lending us a hand. Probably scare hell out of the cattle." He laughed a short snort of admiration. "Belle's a bit head strong, but if push comes to shove, Missus Rawlins just as strong-willed and hard-headed as the girl. You won't find neither one of those two having the vapors."

Josh scrubbed a hand over the lower half of his face, trying to rub off the grin that kept wanting to spread from ear to ear. *He bet Jake was right about Belle being headstrong. He'd bet money she wasn't shy, either, the way she poured those blue eyes all over him and smiled like she was thinking up little devilish thoughts. 'Course he wasn't going to be complaining none. No sir. She could look at him and smile at him all day long, if she wanted to, and he sure hoped she would.*

As he saddled Shadow and swung up on the buckskin, he was still thinking about Belle and trying to rein in the silly grin that kept wanting to pop out and spread all over his face

Sugar had left ahead of the herd with the remuda. He would range the extra horses out some distance from the herd and have them ready in a rope corral by noon and supper time so they could change mounts. Each morning he'd head out before day break to find where they'd wandered in the night as they grazed, and bring them back so each man had a fresh horse to start the day. Talking about it earlier, Josh had wondered how Sugar could keep all of the horses in a rope corral and Jake had explained.

"'Spose if one was to throw a live rattlesnake in amongst 'em, they'd get to snorting and backing into that rope 'til it plum give away. But most times, that rope fence'll hold 'em tight as a corral."

As they neared the cattle, just getting up from their bed ground and starting to graze, Charley made a wide swing around the herd. As trail boss, he would take the lead. When he was some distance away, Jake, the right point man touched the sides of his big, black gelding and rode slowly out toward the herd singing, soft and low, *"Come along you o'cow critters, come along. We're gonna be walking some long, long miles this day. We gonna be foot sore and saddle weary for it ends, but we gonna do it anyway."*

The longhorns, eyed him warily, some turning away, their bodies following the swing of their heads. Others backed up, heads lowered, their eyes on the horse and rider. A few skittish ones bellered and bawled and swung away, wall-eyed, as Jake hazed a black and white spotted steer they called "Old Crook, because of his crooked right horn, along in front of his horse. When Jake reined his horse away to the side, the steer kept moving and several others began to follow him.

"Just like following the pied piper," Joe Saunders, the other point man said, and urged his blue roan ahead with a kissing sound. Scraps of a song drifted back as he walked his horse slowly through the straggle of longhorns.

The herd had grown increasingly wary, the shadow of change making them restless. They rolled their eyes and glanced about suspiciously, tossing their heads. Nervousness spread rapidly through the herd and the bawling increased.

After Joe, the swing riders moved into position and the flank men followed after them. Most of the herd was moving, the dust rising under their hooves until the blue sky was obscured in dust. Now and then an animal would attempt to make a break from the moving mass of bawling cattle and a rider would swing his horse around and ease the runaway back into the herd. When the last of the herd passed by, Josh reined Shadow over to take the left drag position and Jimmy Letts moved his big bay into the middle position. Jeb Motts, on the dark gray he called Toad, brought up the drag on the right.

The longhorns, tall, leggy and slat sided, were all colors from brindle to black to red, roan, brown, clay, gray, and white. Some were solid colored, others spotted. Josh, although he'd been warned, hadn't anticipated the amount of blinding dust that rose up from the thousand of hoofs, nor had he realized how much noise the herds' hooves and their bellering and bawling would make. The noise he could adjust to, he thought, but he wasn't sure about the dust. He kept his hat pulled low and his eyes squinted nearly shut, but still they watered, half blinding him. He was glad for the blue bandana Lee had given him to tie around his nose and mouth.

"You're going to be riding in a lot of dust and dirt, tomorrow, and you're going to be needing this. Belle noticed you weren't wearing one and mentioned it to Mother." Lee's eyes twinkled above that little lopsided grin he had. " Funny she'd notice."

Josh felt his heart do a somersault inside his chest and his face go red. "Tell her I'm much obliged. Your mother, too," he added, "for the slicker."

Yesterday evening Mrs. Rawlins had sent Lee out to give him the yellow slicker he now had tied behind the cantle. "Mother prides herself on her hands having what they need. If she sees they're short, she takes care of it."

Mrs. Rawlins reminded him of Rosita, even though they didn't look at all alike, or talk alike, or anything, but in both of them he saw a sameness for which he had no name.

Charley gave the orders to push the herd along as rapidly as possible "We get them out of the home range," he said, "and they won't be hankering to turn back. After today, we'll slow them up some so they won't lose their weight. Mrs. Rawlins won't be seeing much profit if the herd's mainly hide and hoof and bone when we get there."

Josh could see little of the sun in the haze of dust, but he peered at it often, wishing it would move faster. He sure was looking forward to stopping and letting the dust settle for a while. Moisture from his mouth was causing the dust to crust over the blue bandana and several times he took it off and shook it, but he hated the clammy feel of it as he tied it back over his nose and mouth.

Around noon, they came to a creek and watered the herd, stringing them out along the creek bank and allowing time afterwards to graze. With the cattle settled, half of the men, Joe Saunders who rode left point, Slim Rafters, right swing, Lee Rawlins, left flank, and Jeb Motts who rode right drag and Jimmy Letts, who rode drag between Jeb and Josh, rode into camp for a bite to eat and a change of horses.

By the time the first shift was back, the dust had settled over the herd, well watered and now content to graze and the blue sky was clear except for a little haze. Josh had blown dust and dirt from his nose and spit out even more on the ground. He'd dismounted long enough to splash creek water over his face and with nothing but a dirty sleeve to wipe it dry, he'd left it to the small wind that had sprung up a few minutes before. Now that he could breathe again, he realized how hungry he was and agreed, with a grin, when the usually quiet Billy Redfeathers, riding up beside him on the way back to camp, said he was so hungry he could eat a raw skunk, stink and all.

Billy Redfeather was about his age, Josh guessed, short, skinny, and dark. He looked to be Indian and probably was with a name like Redfeather. Josh filled his tin plate and sat cross-legged on the ground along with Billy and the rest of the men. They had joked and talked among themselves as they turned their horses loose and tossed their saddles on fresh mounts, but now they turned their attention to their plates filled with thick stew and biscuits and ate quickly. Afterwards all but Josh rolled a smoke and then rose to drop their plate in the wreck pan and hurry back to their horse. Josh gulped the last of his coffee. Hector had set out a good-sized jar of lick and Josh had dosed his coffee well. The sweet warmth spreading through him made him think of Pete. He sure missed the man. He had been the best pa a boy could have ever had. Although he wished his own father had been around to raise him, at the same time he was glad that he'd had the chance to grow up as Pete's son.

When he first came into camp, he had spotted Mrs. Rawlins' wagon pulled up a short distance from the grub wagon, but neither she nor her daughters were to be seen. In a way he was grateful for that, although he sure did like looking at Belle Rawlins. A quick sight of her, before he got his heart reined in tight, nearly knocked the wind out him and never failed, quick sight or not, to cause a stirring, almost an ache, deep in the lower regions of his belly. Although he'd like a glimpse of her, he didn't really want her to see him. He didn't think he was too presentable, dirty as he was. He'd slapped his hat against his britches, shirt, and vest, knocking off some of the dirt and he'd swished coffee around in his mouth before swallowing and ran his tongue over his teeth searching out fine bits of grit. He'd run his fingers through his hair and brushed at his mustache, and knotted the blue neckerchief back around his neck, grateful that for a little while he could suck in air not filtered through it. He knew he'd never look any cleaner on this drive, not as long as he kept riding drag, so he guessed he wouldn't worry about it. Besides if Mrs. Rawlins kept true to her word and went to teaching him to read and write, Belle was bound to see him, plenty of times, dirt and all. Either she'd like him or she wouldn't, and the way she had looked at him back at the ranch, she sure hadn't acted like he was too hard on her eyes, so maybe a little dirt wouldn't spoil her view that much.

Chapter Fourteen

Belle had ridden her horse all morning, enjoying the ride with the sun warm on her shoulders and the light touch of a breeze on her face. At times she'd pushed back her hat to hang by its leather thong, and let the little wind finger her long, dark hair. Other times she jammed her hat back on her head, pulled the chin strap tight and put Silver through his paces from a trot to an easy lope to a dead run, and all the time she imagined Josh riding his buckskin beside her.

On the bank of a small stream, where she and Silver had drank their fill, she sat on the ground among a scattering of daisies and, while the big gray cropped the thick grasses, she pulled petals from the flowers and recited, "He loves me. He loves me not." Later, she slid off Silver and sat in the shade of a pink-flowering tamarisk, and imagined Josh's arms around her, her lips and every inch of her face covered with his kisses. Even in imagination, delicious shivers coursed through her body and she wondered what it would be like if he were actually kissing her. She scorned the idea of swooning and yet she knew, Joshua Ryder, had the power to make her swoon.

Back at the wagon, the sun high overhead, and the first shift of men coming in from the herd to eat, she looked for Josh when she and her mother and Kit walked over to the chuck wagon to fill their plates from the kettles Hector had hung over the fire, but he was not among them.

She wished they could eat with the men here like they did at home, so sometimes she could eat with Josh, but Mother insisted they take their plates back to their wagon.

"At home the men have a chance to wash their faces and maybe run a comb through their hair before they sit down with us. We still have time to wash up, but those amenities are scarce for the men, so I'm sure they will be more comfortable if we women aren't breathing down their necks."

Mother had smiled at Kit who'd looked bemused over being called a woman and she'd added, "or little girls either."

Mother also insisted that after the noon meal and again after supper, Belle and Kit were to get in the wagon, or if it was a warm, windless day, they could sit on the ground on the shady side of the wagon and go over the lessons she'd prepared for Kit. While they were still at the ranch, Mother had worked out the lessons for each day and had given Belle the responsibility of being Kit's teacher.

Mother was as big on education as her stepfather had been before her. William Collins, her mother's father had been killed by Mexicans in the battle at San Jacinto and dying had asked his comrade-in-arms to notify his wife. That man, Ben Startling had ended up marrying Grandmother Ruth and had taken them to his home in Beeville where he had begun a law practice.

"Although a lot of girls were not given the opportunity to be educated," Mother said of those years of her girlhood, "my stepfather insisted I go to school and even sent me to a boarding school.

"Belle." Kit's voice brought her back to the present. Her sister sat looking up at her a frown on her small, elfin face. "Is that obtuse?" she asked, placing her finger on one of the words Mother had assigned her to use in writing sentences.

"Yes," Belle said. "Do you know what that means?"

"Dumb or dull," Kit answered and bent back over her slate to write a sentence from the word. It was hard sometimes for Belle to keep her attention on Kit's lessons for the job was boring more often than not.

As Kit worked on her sentences, Belle kept her eye on the chuck wagon, visible from the back of their wagon. Josh and the rest of the hands would soon be coming in to eat and she didn't want to miss seeing even a glimpse of him.

Just thinking about Josh made her heart flutter and a hollow kind of feeling rise up in her stomach. To actually see him, caused her heart to give a queer little jump and her breath to nearly stop. How handsome he looked riding on that beautiful buckskin he called Shadow. She could see him now, his eyes, a dark chocolate brown, but looking black in the shadowed brim of his gray hat. His teeth, glimpsed beneath his black mustache when he smiled, were white and even. She loved his thick, curly black hair and imagined her fingers twirling around each curl. A fullness to his cheeks and jaws belied the long legs and slender build of his body. In her imagination, she traced her finger along the deep cleft, dividing his chin, starting at the bottom and moving up to his lips, her finger pausing there to be kissed.

She had never felt this kind of attraction to a man before. A boy really, probably not much older than she was—maybe a year or two, possibly three. She knew she often caught the eyes of boys and men. She had seen their approval of her face and figure in their faces. Sometimes the glances were bold and made her slightly uncomfortable, but more often than not, there was a quick, furtive, eyeing of her face, her breasts, her hips, often accompanied by a flush of red to their faces. She smiled inside at those glances, drawing her body up a little straighter and lifting her chin just a notch.

She had been attracted to some, but never had she felt this fluttering inside, this need for her eyes to seek him out to feast on his features. She thought she had been in love several times in her sixteen years. Now, she wondered if those boys had been in love with her and she had merely enjoyed their attention. None had brought on her this feeling of intense pleasure, this instant cocooning each time she saw him so her eyes saw only him and only he existed in her world. In her daydreams his strong, square-shaped hands, browned and hardened by sun and work, caressed her face and slipped up under her dark hair to touch her scalp and lift her long tresses to flow strand by strand through his fingers. His strong arms would pull her close, his lips seeking hers, warm and tasting of... How would they taste? Sometimes she thought she could almost die from not knowing. Even in her thoughts her skin felt that almost unbearable pleasure of his touch, and oh, how she wanted him to touch her.

Kit called her attention back to her and for a brief second she was certain her little sister had read her thoughts and she felt her cheeks flush. But Kit was only interested in showing her that her work was done so she could go outside and play.

"Watch for snakes and such," Belle reminded her as the little girl climbed down from the wagon. With Kit gone, Belle stretched out on her stomach on the bedding, her arms and hands propping up her face, and watched for a glimpse of Josh.

She turned once to swat at a fly buzzing around her and as she turned back she saw him riding toward the remuda on Shadow.

The remuda was out of her line of vision, but in her mind she watched him ride to the rope corral, unsaddle his buckskin and select another horse. When he rode back in sight, on a bay, Belle kept her eyes on him, watching as he dismounted and went over to fill his plate from the kettle set over the fire. She willed him to sit and eat where she could see him, but she knew he would join the other men gathered on the off side of the wagon.

With a quick glance in the mirror, Mother had brought along, she fluffed her hair and stepped out of the wagon. She couldn't go where the men were, but she could stand around outside so when Josh finished eating, maybe he would see her. Maybe he'd give her a little nod or touch the brim of his hat or something. She moved around the wagon and stood in the thin strip of midday shade it provided and pretended to watch for Kit and her mother. Mother had spotted wild onions growing among the grasses and she and Kit had gone to dig some for tonight's supper. The men never stayed long at any meal, especially at noontime, so she'd not have long to wait before she would see him walk over to his horse and ride out again to the herd.

CHAPTER FIFTEEN

The dust didn't seem as thick on this stretch of the drive and Josh could, at times, actually see Jeb who rode on the far side of the herd. Jimmy Letts on a light sorrel rode the middle drag and was closest to him. Sometimes they exchanged a few words as they met over a couple of cows whose minds had to be changed from a desire to quit the herd to being back in its company. The herd was still a little skittish and Charley had warned them all to be extra careful and not to make any noise or a sudden move that might spook them into a run.

Except for turning back an occasional herd quitter or pushing along a lazy one, there was nothing to do but ride along at a slow, steady walk. Josh found his mind wandering back to the years he'd spent with Pete. They had been happy years. Pete had been like a father and he would have been content to think of Pete as his father, if not for the redheaded man.

He thought, too, of his mother. She had been a loving mother putting a hand out to touch him and sometimes hugging him to her, often for no reason at all.

Some would question that she had been a good mother, because of how she had made her living, but as Pete said, "We don't know what shadows lay across her back trail. 'Til we do, we got no right to sit in judgment."

Somewhere back along that trail, she must have met Cole Slade. *But when and where?* That he was determined to one day know. When he faced the dirty, miserable scum, his pistol aimed at his chest, he would demand that the outlaw tell him why he had murdered his mother.

A brindle cow mooed and trotted off to the right. Josh rode around in front of her and turned her back to the herd and resumed his thoughts.

He looked down at his reata, coiled and tied to his saddle. He and Pete had talked about a lot of things in the making of the rope—things that didn't have a thing to do with roping. Besides the time Pete got mad and yelled at him so that he'd spilled out the story of visiting those two old "sportin' women" as Pete called them, they had talked of how when you loved someone you wanted to be with them all the time, day and night, so you got married. In that conversation, Josh had come to realize how much Pete had loved his wife and still missed her, even after some twenty years. The thought of a wife brought him around to Belle Rawlins. Just the thought of her raised some pretty interesting things, he thought, a grin stretching behind the dirt-covered bandana. Then he sobered feeling the shame of his thoughts paint his face red.

They crossed the Colorado and the Brazos rivers without incident. Both were low enough that even the wagons had no trouble fording them. Charley had informed them at chuck last night, that by the end of the day, tomorrow, they should be just out of Fort Worth. Here they would lay in a few more supplies and if anyone had a big reason to go into town, they could do so, but only in the daylight and only if there were enough men left to guard the herd. "You boys work it out," he said. "But don't more'n half of you go at one time. And don't none of you go courtin' trouble and that means drinking too much and losing whatever good sense you was born with. Keep an eye on the weather and if you see the sky getting even a little cloudy, you high-tail it right back here, for if these critters get to running, we'll need every hand."

Josh rode into town with Lee, Jeb, Snort, and Slim. He listened to them talk about the town and the attractions it held for them from pretty girls to apple pie, to whiskey and cards. Apple pie sounded especially appealing to Lee and he vowed to get a slice before they headed back to the herd.

Josh had heard Swede mention that he would be driving Mrs. Rawlins and her daughters into town. Lee said Belle wanted to ride her horse, but the sidesaddles were at home and her mother wouldn't let her ride into town, astride.

"She stomped off mad about that," Lee said grinning. "Of course it don't take much to make Belle stomping mad."

In Fort Worth, a town of wooden and log buildings on the Trinity River, Lee suggested they all have a drink first. "Get the dust washed out of our innards," he said with his lopsided grin. "It'll make the pie taste better," he added when Josh said he thought he was raring to get himself a slice of apple pie.

Josh had never had a drink and was apprehensive about what it might do to him. Pete never drank that he knew of, but he'd seen drunken men staggering around Indianola and Port Lavaca. On those infrequent trips he'd made with Pete, into Port Lavaca, he'd usually see Abe Wooton, a fairly young man, but already so seeped in drink that he could not manage more than a job swamping out saloons and was usually either staggering the streets or slumped up against the wall of a building, sound asleep, or more likely, Pete said, "dead drunk."

Josh sure hoped whiskey wouldn't do that to him. Besides he wasn't sure what a drink would cost. "I only have a few dollars," he said to Lee.

Lee grinned. "The dance'll be on me, this time. But when we get to Wichita and you get paid, it'll be your turn to pay the fiddler. Okay?"

"Okay." Josh said and tried to shrug off the apprehension that followed him into the dark, smoky room. Stepping from the bright sunlight, they stood for a second on the threshold and blinked their eyes until the room and its occupants came into focus. Long and narrow, a bar stretched across half of the room where several men stood drinking, booted feet resting on the low railing along the bottom. Four tables lined the other long wall and a card game was in progress at one of them. Josh looked quickly for the women who made their living in the upstairs rooms of saloons such as this one, but saw none. The tension drained out of him when he remembered there had been no second floor in this long building so low, he'd had to stoop to go through the door. Still he hoped after this drink, they could go get some steak and pie.

A man so short and heavy he looked almost square set the drinks in front of them. "Ya'all here with a herd?" he asked, raising a sleeved arm to mop sweat from his head, bald except for a ring of sandy hair.

"Yep," Lee said. "We're the Lazy R up from Victoria, heading on north to the city of Wichita in Kansas."

Inclining his head toward the men standing a few feet farther on down the bar, the bar man said, "These boys is from down around Corpus they tell me. With the Bar L brand."

Lee turned to acknowledge the men. "You having a good drive?" he asked.

"So far," said one of the men, his hat pushed back to expose curly reddish-brown hair. "The herd's pretty well trail broke now and moving along like they was going to a Sunday School picnic."

"Sure could change at any time though," a man with a face full of dark whiskers spoke up. "Get us a lightning storm or heavy rain, or the smell of wolves or Indians and we're gonna wish we was at a Sunday School picnic." He grinned. "'Specially for the grub. We got a cook that'd cause a priest to sin. Temperamental as hell and don't know no more about cookin' then a bull does about preaching. I've bitten into rocks that was easier to chew than his biscuits."

Lee laughed. "We've got a good one. He and his mother have cooked for us for years on the ranch. Reckon we couldn't find one any better than Hector."

"You'd better keep an eye peeled then," said a slightly built man, a black hat set over straw-colored hair, "or we'll come a sneakin' over after dark with ours all hogtied nice and pretty and leave our dumb bastard and make off with yours."

Lee took another swallow of whiskey and wiped a hand across his mouth. "You make off with our Hector," he said with a grin, "You'd better get him tied quick for if you give him any edge at all you're going to think you tangled with a longhorn straight out of the brush and full of wild-eyed indignation at being pulled out of his peaceful surroundings."

"He can fight good as he can cook, can he?" the dark-bearded man flashed a row of crooked teeth with his laugh.

"I'd say his cooking and fighting talents are about equal," Lee said.

One of them mentioned their cook making rattlesnake stew out of a big, five foot rattler that had crawled too close to the chuck wagon. "Hell, he'll cook anything," the puncher said. "Prairie dog, skunk… It's all meat to him."

"I've heard of eating rattlesnake and prairie dog," Lee said. "But skunk. I'd draw the line at eating a polecat."

The talk turned then to rattlesnakes and to the drive itself and Josh listening to it all, but not volunteering a word, swallowed the last of his whiskey. The first swallow had nearly choked him and he'd been grateful for the semi-darkness of the saloon and Lee's attention to the men from the Bar L herd to hide his watering eyes. The second swallow had been better. At least he'd known what to expect. The raw burning liquid seared his throat, but the warmth it spread through him was quite pleasant. With the second drink he experienced a deep welling of goodwill for everyone; the Bar L cowboys, Lee, and even the short squat, bar man with the sweaty balding head. Feeling a grin spread across his face, he leaned across Lee and told the Bar L cowboys about their first night out and how Hector, setting up the supper feed, had let down the table on his chuck box and mixed up and rolled out his biscuits. He was putting the biscuits in the Dutch oven when he heard a sound like a horse stomping his feet, shaking off flies. Said he looked, didn't see a horse anywhere, but he kept his ears fine-tuned and soon heard a kind of snuffling sound coming from the back of his wagon. He went easy like around the wagon and there his mule team was helping themselves to flour and whatnot. Hector been so eager to get supper started, he'd forgotten to picket his team.

The Bar L Cowboys laughed and one of them started a story about a cowboy who went down to river to wash his clothes and while he had them drying on a bush, took a little siesta. He woke thinking someone had set fire to his skin. He forgot most of his body wasn't used to being in the sun without clothes on. "Hoo boy," the man said grinning, "was that gent a mess. Even his poker was burned." Listening to the story Josh felt a deep sense of belonging as if he were a part of every man in this saloon.

At one of the card tables, two of the men threw in their cards and came to the bar. A black whiskered cowboy and a slightly build blond one took up their chairs and a long, lean-faced man still at the table, began shuffling the deck.

"I'm not much of a card player," Lee said. He had turned with his back to the bar to watch the card players and fishing paper and tobacco from his pockets began rolling a smoke. "I'm safe if we're playing for fun, but get something valuable at stake and I'm going to lose for certain sure."

A wonderful feeling of confidence rose up in Josh. Warmed by drink and full of good cheer, he felt as if there wasn't anything he couldn't do and do extremely well. He had done well the few times they'd played stud poker back at camp, using beans for chips and he recognized the card game the men had been playing as that same game. He fingered the three dollars he carried in his pocket and said to Lee, "I guess I'll give it a try."

"Ata boy," Lee said with a grin. "Give 'er hell. I'll bring you over another whiskey."

His whole being filled with this newfound confidence, Josh strolled across to the table. Two other men had joined the long-faced man and one chair remained. "Mind if I sit in for this one?" he asked.

The long-faced man paused in shuffling the cards and said, "Always room for one more. Sit yourself down."

He played well for a few hands and won a dollar and then two more as he put away another whiskey. He was five dollars ahead when he began to feel a loss of concentration and by the time he was out of money and stood up from the table, he was a little unsteady on his feet. He wanted to close his eyes, but every time he did, his head began to whirl. His legs didn't seem to work all that well either and he stumbled as he made his way back to the bar.

"I'm flat broke now," he said. "Reckon I'd better get back to the herd."

"Ah, hell," Lee said with a good natured grin, "don't go yet. Let's just find us a new watering hole. We can't spend all our time in one place. What'll the boys back at camp think?"

That Josh had lost all of his money and would be dependent on him, seemed of no account to Lee. "Don't sweat it, cowboy," he said grinning his lop-sided grin, "I told you I was paying for this dance. There's other tables in town and as long as I've got money we ain't broke."

"Okay, let's move on," Josh said. He tried to sound in good spirits, but the truth was his old enthusiasm was gone, trampled by whiskey and his beating at the card table, but Lee was in such good spirits, he couldn't protest.

Josh felt the floor move under his feet as he made for the door. Lee didn't seem in any better shape. With every step he lurched a little sideways, gained his balance, stood a second or two weaving on his feet and grinning at no one in particular. Finally they both made it to the door.

The bright rays of the sun blasted them as they stepped through the doorway and they raised hands to shield their eyes. Lee made a sudden sound and grabbing the back of Josh's shirt pulled him back inside the doorway. "Mother!" he hissed.

Josh looked past Lee to see the Rawlins wagon go by, Mrs. Rawlins sitting up on the seat with Swede. He wondered if the two girls were inside the wagon, or if Belle, upset over not being able to ride her horse, had stayed back at camp.

He watched the wagon all the way down the street, hoping to see Belle poke her head out of the back, but it disappeared on down the street with no sign of the girl.

"Whew that was close." Lee said. Although it sounded more like, "Whew *sat was shose.*"

"She son't want you in shloons?" Josh was surprised to notice that his own speech was similarly affected.

Lee pulled off his black felt hat and combed fingers through his dark hair before setting it back on his head. He frowned, grinned, and reeling on his feet ever so slightly, said in a voice so slurred, Josh wasn't sure but thought he said, "Got too damn much fire water in me go meeting my mother in social places." He lurched toward Josh and clapped a hand on his shoulder. "Come on Cowboy, let's go find us a 'nother one of them watering holes. One that's got some fun in it."

Snort and Jeb and Slim had left the first saloon soon after Josh sat down to the card game and in the next saloon, Lee and Josh found Snort and Jeb at the bar, but Slim, according to them, was sparking a waitress and was buying and drinking gallons of coffee just for the chance to chat with her.

"The rattlehead," Jeb said, tossing back a shot-glass of whiskey and wiping a hand across his mouth. "It ain't like he's gonna see her again. Less'n he's got some hair-brained idea to come back this way after the drive and whisk her off to live on some spot of dirt, no bigger'n my snot-rag, run a few cows, and turn hisself into a damn farmer."

"Yeash," Lee said batting his eyes as if a fog had drifted in making it hard to see. "A damn farmer. A genuine, certified damned farmer." Weaving a little as he squared himself around to eye the liver-spotted face of the old man behind the bar, he said, "Give this here cowboy and me a whiskey."

"Rye all right?" the man asked.

Lee laughed. "Hell, man. We don't care, 'long as its whiskey."

Several Bar L cowboys were also at the bar and soon they were trading stories, not only of the cook, as their other boys had done, but also of their trail boss, whom they considered to be top notch. With a good natured grin and in words that slurred almost beyond recognition, Lee expounded on Charley Whitcomb's talents, ending with, "O' Charley's the best damn trail boss to ever sit his butt on saddle leather."

Josh leaned around Lee to add his own estimation of the trail boss's talents, but the words froze on his lips as a young woman came out of the back room and strolled over to the bar. Smiling, she wove her way through the men at the bar, slipping her arms around each one and rubbing her body up close. Josh felt his insides knot up as she made her way slowly, man by man along the bar. As she drew near, Josh flashed a quick look at the door. His heart filled with dread. Would she approach him, expecting something he couldn't give her?

He had not even thought of looking for an upstairs in this saloon and now he jerked around so quickly that his head nearly burst. There were no stairs leading to anywhere, but he'd bet the wages he was going to get when they got the herd to Wichita that the door she'd come out of led not to the outside, but to a back room and a bed and she was bent on finding herself someone to fill it. A shiver passed through his body and his blue, chambray shirt seemed to be suddenly too small.

Lee, an eye on the advancing woman, her fingertips walking up a Bar L cowboy's sleeve, poked him with an elbow. "She ain't too bad looking, is she?"

Josh shook his head and a sudden ache in his jaws and sour taste in his mouth sent him hurrying to the door. Stumbling out into the sunlight, he turned down the alley beside it and bending over, heaved up the watery, foul smelling contents of his stomach.

Lee, each drink seeming to only make him happier, had followed him out and now said cheerfully, "Bring it up Cowboy and we'll go get us some more."

"Count me out." Josh straightened up and wiped his mouth on his shirtsleeve. " I need to go back to the herd."

"Aw," Lee sounded mournful, then brightened. "Let's get some grub in your belly. See if that won't make you feel better. Sides I'm still hank-hank-hank…" he stopped and grinned. "I'm still a needing some pie."

"I don't know if my stomach'll take pie," Josh said. "Maybe some corn-bread and beef steak, but I'm still broke."

"Hey, Cowboy," Lee said. "I told you the dance was on me, didn't I?" Grabbing Josh's arm he pulled him out from the alley and up on the boardwalk. Giving him a little shove, he said, cheerfully. "You be the lead critter and look for an eating place, 'cause I ain't making out sign too good."

CHAPTER SIXTEEN

They rode back to camp their bellies full of beefsteak and apple pie. The food had erased much of the effects of the whiskey on both of them, and Josh's thundering headache had eased to a dull ache. The sun was warm and they dozed as they rode along, their horses poking along often stopping to snatch up a mouth of grass before moving on again.

A low nicker from Shadow woke them both just before they arrived at the camp. Grateful for not having ridden sound asleep right up to the chuck wagon, the two, lifted their hats and combed through their hair with their fingers, and tried to blink their eyes into a semblance of alertness before easing their mounts into an easy lope.

Quickly they changed horses and rode out to relieve Billy and Jake who were among those who wanted to head into town for the late afternoon and early evening hours.

"Thought you boys had forgotten us," Jake said as Josh rode up. "Was afraid town's attractions were gonna be too much for you young fellows."

"It nearly was," Josh said, knowing a small cloud of shame weakened his grin.

As Josh watched the herd graze his thoughts went back to the young woman in the saloon who had moved among the men at the bar, openly soliciting. She had been sort of pretty with dark hair and a round face that had matched her plump little body dressed in a pink dress nipped tight at the waist. She had come close enough for him to see that she was not as young as he'd thought at first. He wondered if she had a home like his mother's little adobe hut, or if she lived in the back room as Angel and Birdy and Floss had lived in their upstairs rooms. He wondered if she had a child or two and if they played alone, or, if she wasn't as strict as his mother had been, could play with other children while they waited to return home.

Several mornings after their trip into Fort Worth, as they were catching up their horses from the remuda, Lee said, "Mother wants you to stop by this evening, if you're still serious about learning to read and write."

Astonished, Josh turned from watching Sugar catch up the sorrel he was to ride to stare at Lee. "Really?" He remembered she had mentioned it, but he had not given it much thought, expecting it to be more of a passing fancy than a reality.

Lee grinned. "Yep. Find someone lacking in schooling and unless you tell her a flat out no, there ain't no stopping her."

"Well," Josh said. "Well." Totally at loss for words and feeling his heart hammer at the thought of being in close proximity to Belle, he turned back to slip his bridle on the sorrel. "Okay," he said. "I'll stop by."

All day as he rode behind the herd, Josh could think of nothing but the impending meeting with Mrs. Rawlins. By the time the herd was settled on their bed ground and he was finished for the day, except for night guard, he was, as Pete used to say, as nervous as a long-tailed cat in a room full of rocking chairs.

He woofed down the biscuits and beans Hector had waiting for them and hurriedly drank a tin cup full of sweetened coffee, hardly mindful of the others eating around him. As he headed for the Rawlins wagon, he again dusted off his pants using his gloves as a brush. He had dunked his head in the creek where they had watered the herd before throwing them off the trail for the night, and scrubbed the dirt and dust from his curly hair. With water available, Charley had decided to stop a few hours early, and give the herd time to rest and eat their fill.

As a boy, Josh had taught himself to swim in the salty waters off Indianola, but there wasn't time for that now, even if there'd been no one to catch him and tease him about sprucing up for the ladies. On a trail herd, he'd learned soon enough, there was no such thing as privacy. Every hand had heard bout him losing at poker and throwing up outside the saloon. Lee had told the tale in such a good-natured way, calling him Cowboy as he told it, that his shame over his foolish actions had dissolved into just a slight sheepishness.

"Don't you worry, Cowboy," Jake said, a sparkle in his black eyes. "Ain't a one of us ever pitched down our first whiskeys without we was weaving around like a horse with the blind staggers. Even us old hands at drinking have on occasion heaved up our guts a time or two when we was courting a good time."

For several days after that they had called him Cowboy and some on seeing him, mimicked a staggering drunk walk, or if riding, would begin to weave in the saddle. To which Josh just grinned, knowing they were only teasing and liking him enough to tease him, which put a warmth in his belly, much like that first drink of whiskey.

"Mrs. Rawlins," Josh said, hat in hand, as he approached the wagon where she and both girls sat on a gray blanket in the shade of the wagon's canvas cover. "Lee said I was to come by if I was wanting to take some lessons."

"Of course." Mrs. Rawlins jumped to her feet and proceeded to rummage about in a wooden box set by the left back wheel. Belle and Kit smiled up at him and Belle said, eyes dancing, "Hello Cowboy."

Josh felt the heat rush to his face until he thought it must be glowing as bright as a sunset. Belle must have heard the whole story, upchucking behind the saloon and losing at poker, too. "Miss Belle," he managed and quickly shifted his gaze to her little sister. "Hello to you, too, Miss Kit," he said, adding a small smile.

"Oh, you don't have to call me Miss," the little girl said. "Just Kit is fine."

He nodded. "I'll remember that."

"Same here, Cowboy," Belle said, a wide grin parting her beautiful lips and shining out of her eyes as blue as the sun-warmed sky overhead.

"I'll remember that, too," he said, feeling the flush painting his face, deepen.

Warmed by his attention, Kit offered up a piece of printed light blue material that had been on her lap. "I'm embroidering the pockets on an apron to use for good when I get growed up."

"Grown," Mrs. Rawlins said gently, looking back over her shoulder from where she was pulling papers and several books out of the wooden box.

"Grown," Kit corrected herself and Josh suddenly realized that the way Mrs. Rawlins and her daughters spoke were somehow different than most of the men. Lee was well spoken too, but often lapsed into using the more common speech of the men. He missed the first few words of Kit explaining how the apron she was sewing on was to be put away for the day she married and started her own home. "I wanted to embroider cows on the pockets, but Mother thinks flowers are more suitable. What do you think?"

Josh bent to examine the material and said, "I like that blue color and I 'spect a man coming in off of looking at cows all day, would think a flower on his wife's apron kind of soothing for a change."

Kit brightened at that and smiled up at him as if he had invented the world and put every living creature in it. Her admiring eyes made him feel sort of like he did when the hands called him Cowboy, but those other eyes looking out of that small heart-shaped face with the small pointed chin all framed with a cloud of smoky dark hair, sure made him squirm and made him wish, almost but not quite, that he was back with the herd. He loved being near her, seeing her, even though it made him as nervous as a horse that's been spooked by a lobo or some other critter the horse knows has a liking for his flesh.

She had called him Cowboy so he knew she had heard the story, probably from Lee. He sure hoped Mrs. Rawlins hadn't heard it. Conscious of his hat in his hand and how his fingers were working the brim around and around, he thought to put it on, but then decided he couldn't, not with women present, so he kept on working it around and around with his fingers.

"So how did you like Fort Worth?" Belle asked, eyes teasing.

"Why, it was all right. There's an eating house there that makes real good apple pie."

"Oh, it does?" Belle stretched her words out around a grin and rolled her damnable beautiful blue eyes at him. Flustered, he went on telling her about the other buildings in the town. About the courthouse that set on a bank above the river and the livery stable where he'd left Shadow. She kept nodding and grinning at him and he kept rattling on. Only later did he remember what Lee had said about Belle not going into Fort Worth.

"Mother wouldn't let her ride her horse, so she sulked in camp all day, too damned stubborn to ride in the wagon."

If he'd had his senses about him, he'd have teased her about that, but all his senses had, for the moment, been rendered useless.

Mrs. Rawlins saved him from looking the complete fool. "You girls go on now," she said. "You can work on that embroidery later, Kit. Some of the clothes we washed this afternoon should be dry now. You and Belle can bring them in and fold them." She turned to Josh, "We washed a few things down at the creek and laid them over bushes to dry, and hoped the wind wouldn't come up and blow them all away."

She motioned to a place on the gray blanket for him to sit and with a small slate in hand, she sat down across from him on a small stool. "We'll start your lessons at the beginning with the alphabet."

As they sat there that sunny late afternoon, Mrs. Rawlins told him about the alphabet and how each letter made a particular sound or sounds. As he rose to go back to join the other hands around the chuck wagon and to wait his turn as nighthawk, she gave him a small book with letters and pictures to study.

"As time allows," she said, smiling, "you study this book and in a few days, we'll meet again for another lesson."

Chapter Seventeen

Rain caught them on the drive some fifteen miles short of the Red River and the herd grew stubborn and sulky. As the rain pelted down, Old Crook, the tall, slat-sided black and white spotted steer with the crooked horn who had made himself the leader, began to slant the herd off to the east. Once started, the long snake-like trail of cattle moved with a dogged determination through the driving rain and could not be persuaded to head north again.

Worried that the rain would ruin the small book Mrs. Rawlins had given him to study, Josh had slipped it into the pocket of his yellow slicker. He had been keeping it in his vest pocket and it had begun to show some wear and he was worried that he wouldn't be able to keep the book in as good a shape as when she'd loaned it to him. He was pleased with himself for thinking about the pocket of his slicker. Deep, roomy, and waterproof his slicker pocket was the ideal place, whatever the weather. He aimed to take the book back to Mrs. Rawlins in as good a shape as possible and he could thank the rain for giving him the idea for protecting the book, but that was all he'd thank it for.

Martha Rawlins had drawn pictures to go with the letters on the pages of the small bound book, and it wouldn't take much wear or weather to rub them out. In the evenings after chuck and before dark closed in so he couldn't see the pages, he studied the letters and their sounds. When it was his turn to watch the herd at night, he made the lessons into songs as he rode slowly from one end of the bed ground to the other, meeting and passing one of the other men who rode in the opposite direction, also singing, or, if it was Slim Rafters, talking in a low monotonous sing-song voice about what had happened that day or maybe last year when he worked for another cow outfit, or, he said, just anything that came into his mind.

"I ain't no singer and that's the gawd awful truth," he said when Jake teased him about flapping his jaws in useless talk when he might be edifying the whole herd with beautiful, uplifting tunes. "Them critters hear me a caterwalling and they's gonna spook sure as God made rain. No, boys, you'd best be damn glad I'm sticking to my speaking voice."

Tonight, Josh knew there would be no nighthawking, no singing, if this damn rain didn't let up. Sometimes it gave them hope by easing up some and just when they thought their miserable soaking existence was about to end, it would start to pour again and the herd kept its steady walk towards the east.

"You think these critter want to walk the steps of the capitol in Washington DC?" Jimmy Letts asked cheerfully as he and his blue roan swung along side Josh on Shadow.

It amazed Josh how Jimmy could be so cheerful in the middle of this pelting rain when not only were their hats soaked and dripping rain down their necks, but their stomachs had all but caved from hunger. The herd moving with the rain had kept all hands in the saddle and they had long since passed noon chuck. Josh found his thoughts dwelling on the hot biscuits and bacon he'd eaten at dawn more than on memorizing the words Mrs. Rawlins had assigned him at his last lessons. So he started thinking how the words would be spelled. Coffee. *What he wouldn't give for a sweetened cup of the hot, black brew.* Coffee, like cat and colt started with a c, although they sounded like they could start with a k just as easily. So he started with the sound of each part of it as Mrs. Rawlins had taught him and decided coffee must be spelled coffe.

Charley put more hours in the saddle than any one of them, always riding back and forth along the herd when he wasn't out scouting the trail ahead, looking for the best place to throw the herd off the trail, either to water and graze at midday or to bed down at nightfall. Now as he passed by Josh, he said, "Take another notch in your belt, son, for I reckon we missed noon chuck completely and supper's not looking too favorable. These critters are still hell-bent on keeping on moving so that means we keep moving, too." Josh acknowledged his words with a touch to the brim of his rain sodden hat.

What Josh hated worse about the rain, if it kept up, was that he would not be able to have his lesson with Mrs. Rawlins. She'd told him that when he thought he had learned the lesson she'd given him to stop by her wagon and she'd give him a new set. He had finished committing to memory all the words and their sounds that Mrs. Rawlins had written in the small bound book in his slicker pocket and he was eager to learn more.

One evening coming back from Mrs. Rawlins' wagon, Josh had asked Lee if his mother had ever taught any of the other hands to read and write.

"I don't remember anyone but you accepting her offer," Lee told him. "Most of the men are outdoor men with little use for schooling, but several, like Charlie, have had a good bit of education. Billy Redfeather is the only one I know of with no schooling at all." He grinned. " I remember when Mother asked him about it, he said the longest sentence I ever heard from him. I bet it used up his whole set of words for that month. He said, as I recall, 'I sure do thank you, Miz Rawlins, but I ain't planning on being inside a building long enough to fool with reading no paper. Long's I can read the sky and the wind and the tracks left behind by man and critter, that's all the readin' I need.'"

Josh thought that even if he'd not wanted her teaching, he would have said yes, just to be able to see Belle up close and hear her voice. Most of the time she was around the wagon when he was there for his lessons, but a few times she had been off riding her gray horse. Like Shadow, her horse was about half pet. He'd seen the gray gelding nuzzle her when she was standing in front of him and, if in a playful mood, bump his head gently against her back, exactly like Shadow did to him. He was sure both Shadow and Silver would give their all, if it was ever required of them. It seemed to him that Belle got a little reckless on horseback. Not that she ever abused her horse. No, that sure wasn't her style, but she sure loved to race that big gray gelding, running him flat out, her black hair streaming out behind. They made a pretty picture, there was no denying that, but it worried Mrs. Rawlins and it scared him some, too. Lee had talked to her about the dangers of riding so hard and fast, that her horse could step in a prairie dog hole or just stumble on uneven ground. She'd laughed and reaching up had gently pinched her brother's chin between her thumb and forefinger. "Don't be such a worry-wart," she'd said.

* * *

When the rain finally stopped and the clouds began breaking up and drifting off southward, it was late in the afternoon. The herd was easier to handle now, but still restless

"We'll push them 'til they're going due north again," Charley said, riding by to inform each hand and giving them the welcome news that Hector was brewing coffee and stirring up some biscuits and frying bacon, so half of the men could go into camp, wolf down some grub and hot coffee, catch a fresh horse and come on back to the herd. Not until the weather cleared completely would he attempt to throw the herd off the trail.

When Josh and the other men, the last to go in to camp, arrived for a hot meal, Hector had used the last of the dry wood he kept in the cooley under the wagon. "Good thing they's no more of you fellas," he said. "'Speck when it be dry again, some of you has best be rustling me up some more wood."

"Don't you worry none, Hector," Charley, who had waited to ride in with the last of the men, spoke around a mouthful of biscuit and bacon, "You keep this good grub a-coming and sure as Hell's hot, your cooley's gonna be stuffed plumb full, soon as the boys can round you up some."

Still going over his words in his head, Josh, putting his plate and cup back in the wreck pan, his stomach completely satisfied, said to Hector, "Do you know how to spell coffee?"

Hector frowned and shook his head. "I don't be learning spelling. I read coffee though." He pointed to a large tin. "See that say coffee. Arbuckle coffee. "

As Josh swung up on the bay he chosen to replace Shadow, he smiled to himself. He need add only another e to coffee and now he knew the word Arbuckle as well.

CHAPTER EIGHTEEN

When they reached the Red River, the rains had swollen it into a rushing, swirling torrent of rusty red.

"Sure can see how it got its name," Josh said as he and Lee sat on their mounts on the high, red-colored bluffs overlooking the river. "Look at that dirt. It's a wonder it grows grass."

Lee flashed his lopsided grin. "You're not thinking to take up farming here, are you?"

"No." A chuckle escaped Josh. He remembered how Jeb and Snort had ragged on Slim about spending his time in Fort Worth at one of the eating houses so he could talk to the waitress. Snort and Jeb had been certain he was thinking about marrying the girl and turning himself into a farmer. The next evening, after chuck, the ill effects of their Fort Worth visit worn off, they'd jumped Slim about it.

"You planning to come back this way after the herd's sold and marry up with that girl," Jeb asked. "Get yourself all nice and settled down. Use your wages to buy yourself a hoe and start scratching in the dirt. Maybe raise some corn and pumpkins and a half dozen young'uns?"

Slim laughed. "Hell no," he said. "I was just like looking and talking. It's a sight more fun to talk to and look at a pretty girl then to get all liquored up, like you dumb cow hands. When morning comes, I'm feeling just fine and got some good memories to dwell on while I'm following after this bunch of cows, instead of being all hung over with a head the size of the wreck pan and a taste in my mouth like panther piss."

That had hit the mark with both of the men for they had come out of their soogans the morning after Fort Worth with aching heads so sensitive to light and noise that, according to Snort, even the buzz of a bee put him in more pain than the time he got pitched off a bronc and broke three ribs.

The other men, with the exception of Josh and Lee, had heeded Charley's warning about drinking too much and had had a good time mocking those who hadn't.

When they'd arrived here on the Red, Charley had considered the options.

"We might be able to swim them across," he said, "but we run the risk of losing some and it puts us all in jeopardy. We'll have to raft the wagons across, any way you look at it and it'll take a day to build one." He paused for a moment fingering his drooping sand colored mustache, his eyes on the river. "Up river some six, seven miles there's some good grass and a stand of trees with a lot of dead stuff in it we can use for a raft. I reckon we'd best get them headed up there."

* * *

Charley was restless those days beside the Red and spent a lot of time looking at the water or riding off on his favorite horse, a big bay with black stockings he called Jigger. The raft for the wagons built, the men, when they weren't riding herd, spent the time playing poker and drinking so much coffee that Hector complained they'd run out before they reached Wichita.

Josh found little time to play poker with the men for Mrs. Rawlins had stepped up his lessons. The last two days had seen a jump in his progress and he was pleased with himself.

When he arrived for his lessons the morning of the last day they would be camped beside the river, Josh was disappointed to find that Belle had taken her horse out for a morning ride, but he had no more than finished his lessons, when she came riding back. A pleasant hollowness filled his belly as he watched her swing down from the saddle, a movement as graceful as a dance step, the fabric of her riding pants stretched attractively across her small bottom.

When she had unfastened the cinch and let the stirrup drop back, Josh reached past her, thinking to pull off the saddle for her.

She turned on him. "I can do that myself," she said.

He put up his hands and stepped back. He watched her lay the saddle and bridle back in under the wagon and drape both with the saddle blanket. Giving her horse a pat on the rump she sent him away from the wagon where a few minutes later, he was rolling in a patch of dirt.

"You don't need to hobble him?" Josh asked, knowing her answer, for Shadow would never need to be hobbled either, but he wanted to hear her voice, to have her look up at him.

She answered him, as he knew she would—her horse as gentle, as attached to her as Shadow was to him, but her words were so cropped and crisp, he wondered if in trying to take off Silver's saddle for her, he had offended her. Dismissing him as if he were no more than a pestering fly, she turned to her mother.

" I'm going to get water from the spring, Mother. I need to wash my hair and Kit ought to wash hers too." She paused and a small frown wrinkled her forehead. "If you're done with him," she said, acknowledging Josh with a slight nod in his direction, "maybe he can go along and carry two buckets, so I'd only have to make one trip."

Josh felt his face flush and his heart thump like a rabbit's hind foot.

Mrs. Rawlins smiled at her daughter. "Take Kit, too. She can carry those two smaller buckets that are back in under the seat." She called to her daughter and in a few seconds, Kit came from around the wagon, a book in hand.

The spring was a little under a mile from the camp. The girls followed a narrow, shallow trail to the spring, walking in single file, Kit in the lead and Josh bringing up the rear, his eyes feasting, unguarded, on Belle's small, trim back, long dark hair, and the movement of her hips and legs inside the riding pants.

The clear running spring lined with willows had a red colored mud bottom and any disturbance raised the mud to cloud and stain the water. Surprised at the sight of a small pool deep enough to dip in a bucket, if not to fill it full, Josh said, "Well, this is handy."

"Belle and I dug out the mud," Kit said, "so we wouldn't have to dip our water out with a spoon."

Belle laughed, a silver-toned sound to Josh's ears. "My sister is stretching it a bit, but it did take forever to fill a bucket the way it was."

Josh nodded. "It's pretty here," he said looking around.

Belle looked up at him and her eyes softened. "I love it here. It's like a little oasis in the middle of a desert."

Josh felt himself falling into those blue, blue eyes. "It is," he agreed.

Using Kit's smaller buckets to fill the larger ones, Josh squatted at the edge of the pool, dipped the smallest bucket in and handed it to Belle to pour the water into the larger pails and hand it back to him. Each time they exchanged buckets, Belle's small, sun-browned hand touched his, a fleeting sensation, like the quick brush of a bird's wing. Josh thought he could squat by this stream and fill buckets for Belle until there was nothing left but red mud, if she would keep brushing her hand against his.

When the buckets were filled, Belle surveyed them a moment and then shifted her eyes to where Kit, farther downstream, had piled a mound of red mud on the bank and was patting it into a cone shape.

"We might as well set a while," she said. "It's cool here and Kit's enjoying herself." Without waiting for a reply from him, she moved over to a small shade tree and sat down, patting the ground beside her.

He stood for a while, pretending he hadn't seen her invitation. The ground she'd patted was awful close to her.

"Come, on. Sit down. I don't bite." She grinned. "Unless I'm mad and then you had better watch out."

"I'll remember that," he said, as he eased down on the ground beside her, putting a good space between them.

"You're skittish as a wild horse," she said, and with a twinkle in her blue eyes, she scooted over until her riding pants just touched his brown, twill trousers and involuntarily he pulled away an inch or so.

Mockingly she said, "You don't have to be afraid of me. I'm not going to sit on your lap." Her words accompanied by the mental image of her sitting on his lap, swept away his breath, turning his bones to jelly, and filling his chest, his heart with such a force he could only describe it as love. The desire she raised within him made him want to pull her into his arms and kiss her beautiful full lips, her neck, her ears, everywhere there was skin to kiss and to whisper love words against the cloud of her dark hair. He knew to touch her, to hold her would be to fall into a world of softness. He loved the smell of her, and he imagined he could breathe her scent into every crevice of his being and still want more. In this moment, he knew without a doubt that he wanted her for his wife. This, he knew, was what Pete had felt for his Etta Jane.

"Where did you grow up?" Belle asked, interrupting his thoughts.

"Indianola and on a small ranch outside of Port Lavaca," he answered. He told her about Pete and about his mother. He told her that his mother had been killed, murdered, but not what she had been.

Sympathy clouded her clear blue eyes when he told her of his mother's death. He told her that the sheriff had his suspicions, but no proof, that the outlaw Cole Slade had killed her. He damned Cole Slade with a fresh anger, a fresh hate. How he wanted to ask Belle now to marry him, to make plans for a life together on Pete's small ranch. He'd taken very little of the money from the herd so he'd have that to buy a few head for a start and there were still plenty of longhorns back in the brush country. It wouldn't take long to build up a good-sized herd. The house was small, but he could build on more rooms. He wanted to tell her that and more, but Cole Slade stood square in the way of any future he might have with her.

"When you came to our ranch, you were looking for your father's grave," Belle said. A breeze, rising, blew a strand of dark hair across her beautiful mouth and he resisted the urge to lift the silky strand away and put his lips in its place.

"I was. But I wasn't having any luck and I don't know where else to look."

"I miss my father." Belle looked down at her hands entwined in her lap.

A cloud passed across the sun and Josh turned his eyes to the sky. "Lee told me about him. I'm sorry."

Belle gave him a quick look before ducking her head again.

More for conversation than anything, Josh said, "I hope it doesn't rain before we get the herd across tomorrow."

"I wouldn't care if it rained a week."

Her words surprised Josh. "A week?"

"Yes. Then we could come here every day and talk."

"Even in the pouring rain?"

"Even in the pouring rain," she said, an impish grin lighting her eyes. "We'd sit under this tree and let it rain."

He would like that, too, but he knew he would have to be with the herd if it started raining again.

He rose to his feet and stood looking down at her. "We'd better get this water back to your mother. She'll be wondering."

"I suppose so." Although, Josh knew she was perfectly able to get up herself, Belle reached up a hand. His heart thumping, he pulled her to her feet and they stood for a moment, just inches from each other, their eyes locking. Then Josh forced himself to pull away and walk over to the buckets they'd left on the creek bank.

CHAPTER NINETEEN

Martha Rawlins knew she might lose her daughter, if she said anything to discourage Belle's infatuation for Joshua Ryder, and she vowed to step up his education, so the boy would be able to read and write fairly well if this love-match led to marriage. They were both so young, but she and Oliver had been young, too. They had married with nothing, but a passion for each other that had burned bright the entire ten years of their marriage. Ten short years and two laughing sons, gone within days, victims of yellow fever. She had thought she could not live through that kind of grief, and yet she had.

She had loved James. Although not with the same love, the same passion she'd had for Oliver, but she had loved him. Loved him for his goodness, his love for her, shown in so many ways. He had been successful as had his family before him and the ranch she now owned, with the children, was the result of his parents' foresight and hard work as well as his own. But it had been Oliver, with the blue-blue eyes and tousled head of curly sandy hair that had sparked a passion she had never felt again, not even with James. She could not deny her daughter this same burning passion, even if, in the end, it brought her heartache.

Josh was a good boy and from these few weeks of working with him, she had found him to be very intelligent. She had no reason not to accept him. It was doubtful he had anything, but Belle would get her share of the ranch as long as she stayed and worked beside Lee. Kit, too, when she was grown would share in the ranch. She could see one of them living in the ranch house, the others building their own homes on the grounds nearby. She hoped they would acquire more land and livestock and live happy, prosperous lives. She could see Josh working the ranch. He had a way with horses and was doing his job well on this drive. Soon she would start Josh to work on ciphering numbers, for that would be helpful in running his and Belle's share of the ranch. Of course Belle could cipher numbers. In fact she was better at numbers than she was at reading. Kit was the reader of the two. Belle was too high-spirited to stay still long enough to read a book. Josh's calm demeanor might be just what Belle needed to curb her restlessness. She wondered how the two, if they did marry would handle the children. Belle, she was afraid, would be quite willing to have someone look after them for her, especially while they were very young. Not that she wouldn't love them, but babies would frustrate her need to be up and going somewhere, usually on horseback, and it would be trial for her to be heavy with child. She had no such worries about Kit. Even at her tender age, she was a solid, down to earth child, much like James had been. Kit would make a marvelous mother, but Belle, she wasn't so sure about Belle. She hoped if Belle and Josh married that they would want to stay on the ranch so she and Kit could help raise their children.

She had not been fooled, yesterday, by Belle's seemingly nonchalance about taking Josh along to carry more water. She remembered how she and Oliver had invented excuses to be alone and she smiled to herself. Maybe in Wichita, while they waited to sell the herd, the two would have a little more courting time.

* * *

The herd now well fed and rested in this interval of waiting for the Red to go down, moved out without protest, although some were skittish about crossing the river. Charley had brought all hands up closer to the front of the herd to help urge them across the water and they sat in their saddles and watched with amusement as Old Crook keep trying to turn back, but Jake and Joe, the two point men, swinging their coiled reatas and yelling finally convinced him and he plunged into the water, the rest of the herd following, some bellowing their protest, but all moving. They all had to swim the deepest part of the river, the herd a moving mass of heads and horns.

Josh and several others, including Snort, had tossed their boots in the chuck wagon to keep them dry. When his horse stumbled, Snort kicked loose from his stirrups and slid off into the water. His horse quickly gained his footing and began swimming. Snort grabbed on to a stirrup and his horse pulled him the rest of the way across. He told them later that swimming was a heck of a lot easier when you ain't got your boots on.

On the opposite bank, they shoved the lead cattle out away from the water to make room for those behind, so they wouldn't bunch up in the water and some drown.

They were soaked to the skin by the time the herd was across, but the air was warm and the sun would soon dry their clothes. Most had dry boots and they had all put their guns in the chuck wagon, which, along with Mrs. Rawlins' wagon, had been ferried across on a raft of logs they'd built while waiting for the water to go down.

Building the rafts, the men, Josh included, more at ease on a horse than swinging an ax, jumped at the chance to drag the logs by horseback to the building site. With only one ax in the whole outfit, they had taken turns chopping down the still standing dead trees and hacking the limbs off those and the ones nature had already fallen. Charley had come to inspect the work shortly after they'd started and sitting atop his bay gelding, cut his eyes over to the two trees they had already fallen. "You fella's doing all right, I see."

Jake, who'd been at work on the third tree, leaned on the ax and grinned up at the trail boss. " This ain't just real fun work, Charley. Had a beaver come along and we figured to sit back in the shade and let him do the job, even offered him double our pay, but he turned us down. Said we'd be wantin' him to herd cattle next. Said cowboys were the only creatures he knew who worked like a beaver is said to and he sure didn't have no hankerin' to do that."

"So that being busy as a beaver is just a made up story," Charley said.

"Or else we just found us a lazy one," Jake said and went back to swinging the axe.

When the raft was finished, they loaded the chuck wagon first, as it was the lightest.

"If we have trouble with it, we can fix it before we take Mrs. Rawlins' wagon across," Charley said.

They fastened ropes to the front and back of the raft and Josh and Lee and Billy swam their horses across, each holding a rope which they dallied around their saddle horns when they reached the other side. Slim, Jake, and Joe, still on the opposite bank, the hind ropes dallied around their saddle horns, began to let out slack as the horses on the other side moved forward. A little bump or two and the raft floated across, as Charley said, "Just as pretty as you please."

Although Mrs. Rawlins' wagon was bigger and heavier, it, too, floated over without incident.

Jeb Motts, a lean rangy fellow with two crooked front teeth, who rode drag with Josh, spoke up as they untied their ropes from the raft. "Sure too bad we ain't got no way of telling the next herd that we got a perfectly good raft they could use, if they wanted to come over and get it."

"Hell, Jeb," Snort Beers said. "We figured you was planning on putting your rope on it and toting it back across, so's you could just sit there on the back end of your carcass and when a herd came along you could charge 'em a ferry fee and make a heck of a lot more money then chasing after cows."

Jeb grinned at him. "If I had me a wife and a little house, I just might be content to sit on that there river bank and grow rich. But I ain't got neither and I don't hanker to live by my lonesome, so I'll leave that growing rich to you."

"Seems I'm partial to city life," Snort returned. "When I gets myself to Wichita, I just might quit this cowboying and set me up a sportin' house and get rich that-a-way."

Josh felt his face flush at Snort's words and was grateful when Charley rode up and said, "Come on, boys, quit your jawing and let's get these cows moving."

As they swung up on their horses to take their places alongside the herd, Lee called out, "Look! Over there on that hill. Is that a cross?"

"Sure looks it," Josh answered. "Suppose someone drowned crossing this river?"

"Could be someone got throwed off his horse, or snake bit," Jeb said. "I'll go take a look see." He reined the dark gray, he called Toad, around and headed at a canter up to the top of the small hill.

Around the chuck wagon that night, they talked of the cross on the hill and the man buried there. "He died last year," Jeb told them. "They cut down a small tree to make the cross and sliced off a front of the cross piece and burned in his name, which was Manny Martenson, and the date, but they didn't write how he died."

"I still bet he drowned," Jake said. "My horse nearly lost his footing twice crossing that damn river."

"Hell of a way to get a bath." Jeb took a swig of coffee and wiped the back of his hand across his mouth. "Real efficient, too. A fella can wash hisself and his duds at the same time. I betcha, tonight, we're some of the cleanest fellas in the territory. What do you reckon?"

"Cleaned my innards out, too," Slim said, grinning, and everyone laughed. Like Snort's horse, Slim's had lost his footing and gone down. Slim had kicked out of his stirrups and gone off the horse sideways, "grabbing on to nothing, but muddy water," he said, later. Jake seeing his predicament, swam his horse over in time to grab Slim by the back of his shirt and drag him through the water to the opposite bank.

"Bet I'll be pissing and shitting mud for a week," Slim added cheerfully. "But I shore as hell ain't complaining. If Jake here hadn't come along, you'd be a digging me a hole up there along side that other fella."

"If we could of found your carcass in that damn mud hole," Snort said.

A few minutes later, Josh swung up on Shadow and with Lee riding Ace they rode off to take their turn at night hawking. As Josh rode out to relieve Joe, a wolf howled off in the distance and Joe began softly singing, "Let sixteen gamblers come carry my coffin, let sixteen cowboys sing my last song..." Josh couldn't help but feel a shiver of apprehension. He had not given it a thought before, but they might not all make it to Wichita and back to Texas again.

The rain Belle had wanted while they were back along the Red came a week later, along with lightning and thunder. The herd, bedded for the night, lunged to their feet at the first crack of thunder and might have run, if Charley, anticipating the storm when the clouds began rolling in a few hours before, hadn't had all hands in the saddle, with most of them at the head of the herd to turn the leaders back into the herd until they started milling around. It took the run out of them, but it didn't stop them from wanting to move and as before, they headed east, walking with that same dogged determination. As the storm gathered in intensity, they could see only the dim shape of the herd until the lightning flashed, a brilliant white light that momentarily lit up the sky, the herd, and the surrounding prairie.

Josh, riding, Top, a big bay from the remuda, was grateful for his slicker as the rain poured down. He flinched at every flash of lightning and every clap of thunder booming out of the black sky. The lightning came so dangerously close that it sent blue lights dancing across the cattle's long horns, buzzed the tips of his horse's ears, and played eerily around his hat brim. It kept him on edge. Any minute he expected a bolt to strike him or his horse. They had left spurs and guns in the chuck wagon, so the only metal to draw the lightning's fire, were the horses' bits attached to the bridles with metal shanks. He was glad Shadow was with the remuda.

They rode all night in the rain, the lightning and thunder easing off sometime before dawn and the sky clearing with the sun.

The herd had drifted several miles off the main course of travel and Charley gave them orders to turn the herd until they were pointed due north before throwing them off the trail. It was late morning when they finally allowed the tired animals to rest and graze.

Without sleep or food and in the saddle for half of a day, a night, and close on to half of another day, Josh's eyes were gritty and his stomach felt as if it had caved into his backbone.

He rode his horse over to where Sugar had brought up the remuda and pulling the saddle and bridle, turned the bay loose.

"You going to get any sleep?" Josh asked the slightly built Mexican.

"*Sí*," Sugar grinned. "Like you, I eat and get sleep now."

Hector had bacon favored beans and biscuits, stewed apples, and gallons of hot coffee and the hands gulped it down like starving wolves. Josh glanced over at the Rawlins' wagon, wondering if he should go over and tell Mrs. Rawlins he was too sleepy for lessons today, but Lee seeing his glance, said, "She's a hard taskmaster, but even she won't expect you today. Tomorrow, though, if you aren't herding cows, you'd best get your scrawny hide over there and get on with your lessons." He grinned. "'Sides Belle's gone off riding. So your schoolin' won't be near the fun."

Josh answered his grin with one of his own. He had seen the girl ride off, putting her horse into an easy lope. He worried about her riding off

146

alone and wished Lee would go with her, but she wouldn't stand for it. In her view, she was as capable of looking after herself as any of the men and she always took a pistol along, stuffed in a saddlebag.

When they reached Indian Territory, five members of the Kiowa tribe came riding into camp while Hector was setting up for the midday meal. Charley invited them to eat and afterwards, they accepted smokes from some Charley had stored away in the wagon. Having heard that they enjoyed smoking and might be appeased if the hospitality was right, Charley had brought along extra tobacco, not only for the Indians, but also for the hands who were regular smokers on the chance that they'd run out of smoking material before they reached the end of the drive.

"Catch a man short who's been puffing on those things for days and months and years and he's gonna be on the prod when he runs out. Won't nobody be able to live with him and we'd probably have to tie him to the grub wagon at night to keep him from lifting someone else's makings and causing one heck of a fight."

"Anyone try to pilfer my makings would sure pay hell doing it," Jake said.

Charley nodded. "That's what I mean. Run short on cigarette makings and it could cause such a blow-up, we'd be liable to have two cowboys stove up from fist't cuffs or dead from lead poisoning. Either way they won't be any good for working a herd."

The Indians having eaten, their smokes now burned down to ashes, their leader, a long nosed individual with a wide thin mouth, named Short Eagle, announced by word and sign that they had come to collect a toll.

Charley argued with them a few minutes, during which time they reminded him that the buffalo were all but gone and that it had been the white buffalo hunters who had taken the great beast away and left them destitute. Charley reminded him that no one had owned the buffalo, that they should have registered a brand and stamped the critters with a hot iron to prove ownership. They laughed at that and Short Eagle, asked if he'd ever tried to brand a buffalo.

"Can't be much meaner'n a grown longhorn fresh popped out of the brush," Charley said.

Whereupon Short Eagle reminded Charley that according to the government, the Indian owned this land, although, he'd added scornfully, "Who own grass, sky, water? Where put brand?"

Charley told them the brand for sky and grass and water was on paper.

Short Eagle made a poofing sound of contempt and torn an imaginary paper in pieces and tossed it to the wind. "Where brand, now?" he asked.

Charley laughed and getting to his feet said, "Come on. We'll pick you out a couple of beeves and you can take them home."

The leader stopped him, "How many couple?"

"Two," Charley said, holding up two fingers.

Short Eagle held up four fingers.

Charley held up three. Short Eagle shook his head and held up four fingers.

Charley turned and motioned to Hector who brought over a box of Arbuckle coffee.

Taking the coffee, Charley held it out toward Short Eagle and raising three fingers, said, "Coffee and three beeves."

With one look at his companions, Short Eagle nodded toward Charley and held out his hands for the coffee.

Charley sent Josh and Lee to cut out a lame red cow and two small steers. "Jeb and Jimmy are sure gonna be glad when I tell them we're rid of Mildred here," Josh said as the two drove the animals over to where the Indians sat on their ponies, waiting. "We spend half our time making her keep up with the herd. She's a wily o' thing. Any o' bush or hump a-ground she thinks will hide her, she goes for it."

Jimmy had started calling her Mildred after a teacher he had in his one-room school house back home. "'Course we called her Miss Dunbar to her face. Somehow we learned what her front name was and started a little sing-song that went like this, "Mil-Dred Mil-Dred pretty as a pig turd." Jimmy had laughed. "'Course it didn't rhyme so good, but we loved it, anyway. On hindsight, I reckon she wasn't so bad. She had to be tough to keep some of us in line."

The Indians acted pleased with their transaction and as they rode off driving the cattle ahead of them, Lee and Josh watching, Lee said, "Charley allowed we'd be lucky if the Indians didn't get a few head. He says they've had a tough go of it, trying to live their old ways in a new world. He says these few head will keep them respecting us and not causing any mischief, and that maybe we did owe them a toll for crossing their land."

The Indians increased Josh's worry about Belle riding out and away from camp by herself. These particular men had been friendly, but he thought there might be others who were not so inclined.

CHAPTER TWENTY

Josh had just ridden in off night guard and was hoping to grab a little sleep when a stranger on a rawboned black gelding hailed the camp.

"You all light a spell," Hector said, greeting him. "I 'bout got the fixins ready for breakfast. Help youself to the coffee there."

"Much obliged. Name's Frank Walker." He poured himself a cup of coffee and nodded to Josh and the rest of the men who were raising up out of their bedrolls and peering at him in the semi-darkness of the early summer morning. "Just came down from Kansas. Worked for the Bar S down near the Rio Grande." He squatted on lean haunches and cautiously took a drink of the hot brew. "Took a herd up to Dodge City last year and instead of going back, decided to winter over. Did some looking around up there. Most near settled in Wichita." He shook his head and a wry grin touched his lips. "But I got homesick for Texas. Decided this spring to go back."

"Guess you crossed the South Canadian," Charley said.

He nodded. "Had to move on downstream some eight, ten miles from where I'd been fixing to cross. Had to scout out a part of the river clear of quicksand."

"So we're facing quicksand?" Charley frowned and lowered his coffee cup raised halfway to his lips. "We figured to be there tomorrow and maybe even get across for daylight's gone. Sure didn't figure on quicksand."

"Damn river's full of it." Frank Walker stopped and a look of surprise crossed his face. Josh turned quickly following the man's gaze and saw that Mrs. Rawlins, Belle, and Kit were coming to fill their plates, as they did every mealtime, then returning to their wagon to eat. Hector had offered to have a couple of the men bring their food to them, but Mrs. Rawlins had insisted they come and get their own. Josh had heard that she had said, "We aren't to be a nuisance on this drive. We don't need to be waited on."

Mrs. Rawlins noticing the extra man spoke a greeting to him.

"Ma'am." He leaned forward in a little bow as he swept off his black hat. "Name's Frank Walker. Didn't reckon to meet such lovely ladies on a trail drive."

Mrs. Rawlins smiled, "You just never can tell about us Texas women."

"No, ma'am," Frank Walker said. "I reckon not."

"He's headed back to Texas," Charley said. "He was with the Bar S down by the Rio Grande. They took a herd up to Kansas last year and he wintered there."

"So you're heading back to God's country." Mrs. Rawlins again favored him with a big smile.

"Yes, ma'am. I'm homesick as a little o' calf taken from his mama." He turned and smiled at Belle and then down at Kit's small, upturned face.

"My daughters," Mrs. Rawlins said. "Belle and Kit."

"So pleased to meet you ladies." Again the courtly bow, the hat already off, crushed against his chest, his fair hair falling forward against his handsome face. Frank Walker was full of charm. Where he had learned it riding behind the back end of a cowherd, Josh didn't know. Maybe he'd studied it in Dodge City and Wichita where he'd wintered. Somehow he didn't seem like no ordinary cowboy.

It made Josh's insides turn to see Belle smile up at the man and he wanted to push between the two, knock Frank Walker aside, take Belle's hand, and announce to the whole camp and that slick, smiling devil, that she was his girl, and as soon as they got back to Texas he was going to ask her to marry him, if she'd have him. But damn it! He couldn't ask her yet, not until he knew if Slade still lived. He sure wished that son of a bitch was dead. It'd sure save him a lot of grief.

He could imagine them living on Pete's place. He could see himself down at the corral or riding in from checking the cows and Belle standing at the door waiting for him to come into supper, her small, slender hands shading her eyes against the glare of the sun, low in the western sky. He could see them holding each other, kissing, even in the middle of the day, as he had seen Rosita and Miguel one sunny afternoon, when he'd stayed that week with them so Shadow would get used to being a horse. He had taken the then little Ramon out to tend to the goats and when he and Ramon walked back into the house, the two had broken apart, laughing, and, as Miguel left the house, they had exchanged a look, their eyes shining. Josh had felt warmed by that look and had never forgotten it. He had been too little then to know of love between a man and a woman but he knew it now. He knew he loved Belle and whatever it took to keep her, he would do. He wished they could have a chance to be alone. He thought often of that day they had gone to the spring for water, and wished they could again, but this time without Kit tagging along. Although it wasn't at all likely Mrs. Rawlins would allow that. As Old Man Shippley had once told him when a man hired a buggy to take a pretty woman for a ride. As they drove away, the old man had scowled, muttering, "Nice girls don't go about un-chaperoned with a man." Not familiar with the word, he asked what it meant. "It means without someone else along. Young folks can get into trouble when they goes off somewheres alone." Narrowing his eyes as he regarded Josh, he'd added. "You pick yourself a nice girl, boy. Don't go visiting no whores or other trash, either."

"Yes, sir," Josh had muttered ducking his head, his face on fire with anger and embarrassment. When he looked up Old Man Shippley was looking at him, his thick white brows drawn together in a quizzical frown. A customer had ridden in then and he'd gone to take the man's horse, thankful to escape any questioning.

As Mrs. Rawlins, Belle, and Kit filled their plates, Josh mentally urged them back to their wagon, but they lingered, Mrs. Rawlins questioning Frank Walker.

"Do you have folks back in Texas?" she asked.

"No ma'am, I ain't. Not anymore. My folks died and my sister up and moved back to Tennessee where her husband's from."

152

Josh felt a small tug of satisfaction at hearing the man say ain't. Mrs. Rawlins had leaped on his use of the word, like a chicken on a bug. Several other words, he'd used all his life, hadn't suited her either, but it was hard to remember not to say them.

After Mrs. Rawlins and the girls left, Charley asked Frank Walker about crossing the South Canadian.

"We turned at the Red last year and went west a hundred miles or so and then went up straight north to Dodge. When we reached that part of the Canadian, it was pretty low and we didn't have no trouble a-tall. But seeing as there was still some quicksand, our trail boss had us cut out a hundred head at a time and force them across, hollering and swatting them with our ropes. You keep a critter moving and it don't sink down. Anyways not so much, and those that get bogged down, you can pull out before the next bunch and saves some from drowning." He set down his coffee cup and reached in his shirt pocket for his papers and sack of Bull Durham tobacco. He talked as he rolled his cigarette. "Coming back, though, there was a good heavy rain somewheres on to the west. The clouds was dark and heavy-like. I figured to get into the down pour, but missed it by some few miles and only got a drop or two."

"That probably unsettled the river and got the quicksand stirred up," Charley said.

"Most likely."

Charley frowned and swallowing the last of his coffee, rose to his feet. "You fellas get the herd started and I'll go on ahead and see what kind of a situation we got there."

A few minutes later, they saw him ride away on Jigger, heading north.

As Josh walked away from the chuck wagon to get his horse, he heard Frank Walker offer to wash the dishes and help hitch the team. It was a considerate act, a thank you for the feed he'd just put away. Still, it irritated Josh.

* * *

The herd was still several miles from the South Canadian when Charley appeared on the horizon, riding toward them. "The river's down but the bottom's still soft." he told them. "Waded in myself and could feel the pull. Jigger, here," he leaned over and patted the bay horse's neck, "He didn't want to have nothing to do with it. We'll take 'em west a ways.

Walker says there's a small creek and good grazing some six, seven miles on. We'll bed down for the night and check out that part of the river in the morning."

As they turned the herd, Josh saw the chuck wagon bouncing over the prairie and behind it a rider on a black horse.

CHAPTER TWENTY-ONE

Josh seethed with anger when Frank Walker all but hovered over Belle when she and her mother and Kit came to the chuck wagon that evening to fill their plates.

Afterwards, as he and Lee walked over to the Rawlins' wagon, Lee said, "Mother is pleased with how fast you are learning to read." He glanced a sideways look at Josh. "You working so hard to impress her, or Belle?"

Josh grinned. "Maybe I just like being educated."

"Sure you do," Lee said returning his grin, "But I also think you're pretty damned smitten with my sister. And if you are, you'd better be stating your intentions for some other gent rides in here and ropes her right out from under your nose. Someone like that Walker fellow." Lee jerked his head toward the herd where Frank Walker was riding the first watch with Snort.

"I'll keep that in mind," Josh said. Walker did worry him. He had hoped the man would ride off after helping Hector with the cleaning up and getting the mules hitched. But, instead, he'd asked to ride along. "You ain't so far from Kansas now and I reckon some of you all will be riding back to Texas afterwards and I'd sure like the company. Never was much to be by my own self."

Josh sure hoped if Walker didn't know how to read or write that Mrs. Rawlins wouldn't take it upon herself to teach him. Not that there were that many days left. In three weeks or less, depending, they ought to be in Kansas.

"Hello, Josh. Lee." Belle, rounding the wagon, greeted them. It was a warm day and she had rolled her sleeves up on her softly rounded slender arms. Josh longed to run his hands over their smooth softness and he was aware that his eyes had lingered a second too long when looking up, he caught an impish grin and a dancing sparkle in her blue eyes. She turned to Kit who was up in the wagon and reached for the two small pails her sister handed down to her. She turned back to smile at Josh and her brother. "Kit and I are going to go look for berries. We're hoping to find enough for Hector to make a cobbler. He makes the best cobblers."

Mrs. Rawlins followed Kit out of the wagon, a book in her hand. "Remember Hector's resources are limited here on the trail," she said to her daughter, a twinkle in her eyes. "Hector has a big sweet tooth, though, nearly as big as Sugar's, so I suspect he'll do his best. He insisted we add more sorghum to what Charley and I thought would last us through the drive." She turned to Josh. "You ready for your lessons?"

"Yes, ma'am," he said.

"Oh, Mother!" A pert little pout formed on Belle's lips. "Why can't you dispense with that this time. It's such a lovely evening and you said, yourself, you have a beastly headache." She smiled up at Josh and Lee. "We'll take these two cowboys with us and you get some rest."

"I could use a nap." Mrs. Rawlins smiled. "I did have a headache earlier today. It's gone now, but I'm feeling a little tired."

* * *

From the open gap in the back of the wagon, Martha Rawlins watched her two daughters, her son, and Josh, whom she was certain would one day, soon, be her son-in-law, walk toward the creek that wound through a stand of small trees and bushes. She couldn't help but smile at her beautiful, brazen daughter's excuse to get Josh to go with them. She doubted if Belle had ever heard her complain about a headache, for she rarely ever had one and certainly never a beastly one.

She spent the rest of the early evening, reading, pausing often, with thoughts of her children, the dark headed ones she had now and the two little blond boys who had never had the chance to grow out of childhood.

Although her grief now slept, at times, the memories of those she had loved so dearly awoke within her, bringing tears and a longing to see them, to hold them again in her arms.

She would miss having children. Kit was still her little girl, but in a few years, she would be finding a husband and raising her own family. If Belle married Josh, perhaps they would have a house full of children, dark-headed little babies to grow like weeds in a garden patch. She smiled to herself imagining small boys and girls running to greet her. "MeMa! MeMa!" She would have them call her the name she had called her own grandmother. If possible, she would keep them on the ranch. Josh was no shirker and would work hard to keep the ranch going. He was a good boy and he and Lee seemed as comfortable with each other as brothers ought to be, but weren't always. Kit adored him. That was plain to see. He wasn't very old, just eighteen, Lee's age, only a little older than Belle's sixteen years, but he seemed to be very responsible. Even that time back in Fort Worth when he drank too much, Lee told her, it hadn't been a love for liquor but his lack of experience.

Well, Wichita would tell. With money in his pockets and the trail drive over, if he was going to kick over the traces and whoop it up, like she'd heard many a cowboy did at the end of a drive, he's do so then. She'd set Charley and Swede Davidson to watching the boy. If he lost his head too many times in the saloons or visited the fancy women, even once, she would do whatever it took to break up the romance, although Belle would probably do the breaking up. She would be furious and it was doubtful that she'd give him a second chance. Belle was strong willed and Josh would about have to walk on water to get back in her good graces. But Josh was a good boy, she knew that, so why was she worrying? It wasn't likely he'd go astray.

She mused some more on a union between Josh and her daughter, until she dozed off and dreamed of children and their sweet laughter echoing throughout the ranch house.

* * *

They walked across the prairie heading for the small creek lined with bushes and where Belle was sure they would find some kind of berries. Belle and Kit walked ahead, leaving Josh and their brother to bring up the rear. It had crossed Josh's mind that maybe Belle just wanted to be close to him, but she acted now as if he was of no more interest to her than just as another set of eyes and hands to find and pick berries.

"Hey!" Lee stopped near a small tree and knelt down, his hand parting a tangle of grasses. "A nest of turkey eggs."

"I hope they're still good," Belle said. She pulled up several handfuls of grass to line one of the pails and Lee carefully deposited the eggs. "Maybe Hector can make scrambled eggs, if we can find more."

"Makes my mouth water to think of it," Lee said.

Looking at the light tan, speckled eggs, Josh was conscious of Belle only inches away, her eyes shining, her lips parted in a soft smile. He loved her, but he had no right to court her, not until he knew if Cole Slade still lived. He drew back and a look of puzzlement crossed Belle's face.

They followed the creek, looking for berry bushes, but found none.

Disappointment showed in Belle's voice and then she brightened. "I was so hungry for Hector's cobbler, but maybe we can find more turkey eggs. Maybe some wild onions too. Let's spread out and search. Josh you and I can take this side of the creek and Lee and Kit can take this pail and try the other side."

"That's a good idea," Lee said as sober-faced as if he thought searching for turkey eggs was all Belle had in mind. Josh felt his face flush and his heart leap. She wa*nted to be alone with him.*

Lee jumped across the narrow creek and reaching for Kit's hand swung her across. He squinted up at the sun and said, "We'll meet back here in about a half an hour."

His heart aching with a desire he'd have to keep a tight rein on, Josh followed Belle through the brush and small trees growing along the river bank. She was silent except for reminding him to keep an eye out for a turkey's nest and exclaiming over one of the many flowers that grew among the grasses along the creek bank.

Josh, walking behind this girl and so aware of every movement, every tilt of her head, was unprepared when she stopped abruptly and his hands came up and curled without reasoned thought around her arms. All his promised restraint vanished as she turned in his arms and lifted her face to him. Whispering her name, his lips tasted her mouth, her cheeks, her eyelids, her hair. They drew apart and he remembered Cole Slade. He should not be doing this when he could not ask her to marry him.

"Do you love me, Josh, "she whispered.

"Oh, I do, Belle. I do." He could not lie to her, but maybe Slade was dead. Maybe.

"I heard you tell Mother you had a small ranch." Her fingertips traced his eyes, his mustache, his mouth, and the cleft in his chin.

"Yes. I sold the cattle and I have friends keeping an eye on the place for me."

"Mother wants us all to share in the Lazy R."

"Belle. We can't talk about this now. Wait until we get to Wichita." He glanced at the sun. "I think Lee and Kit will be here soon."

"I suppose," she said, a small pout belying the merry look in her eyes. "I'd much rather keep on kissing you, but I suppose we had better at least pretend to look for eggs."

They walked a little farther upstream and stopped to kiss again. When she pulled back, Belle said, " I'd love to see your place, Josh, but there's room on the ranch for us."

An unsettled feeling tightened his chest. *He had let it go way too far.* "Your mother might not approve of me," he said. "She might not want to give a part of her ranch to us if you married me."

"I think she will," Belle said smiling. "She will want me to be happy. But, let's not talk of it now. Let us save our lips for kissing." Then her arms went around his neck and her lips sought his and his senses so filled with this girl in his arms that he could do nothing but push aside all thought of Cole Slade.

Time slipped away until suddenly Josh remembered that Lee and Kit would soon be at their meeting place, waiting. "We have to go," he whispered against her cloud of dark hair.

"I know," she whispered back, and lifted her lips for one last kiss.

"Hello," Lee called a few seconds before he and Kit appeared around some brush growing along the bank of the small creek. "We've come empty-handed. No more turkey eggs to be found."

Josh felt his face flush with guilt.

"We didn't find any either," Belle said as serenely as if they had indeed been hunting for eggs. "Maybe Hector can so something with what we have." She sighed. "I do wish we could have found some berries."

"We'd better start back, anyway," Lee said. "I'll have to take watch before long."

At Belle's insistence, they climbed a small, grassy hill where they could see the camp and in the distance, the herd spread out over the prairie, moving slowly as they grazed.

"Oh, look at those cute little prairie dogs," Kit called pointing toward a small colony of animals. "Funny they're called dogs when they aren't dogs at all."

"They do look like dogs sitting up and begging," Belle said of the ones standing on their hind legs, their smaller front legs held up in front of them.

"They're so cute," Kit said. "I wish I could capture one and make a pet out of it."

"I'd as soon you got a mouse or a rat," Lee said. "I think they're all in the same family." He paused and then added, "Their holes can be dangerous. I've heard of horses stepping in one and breaking a leg. No, I wouldn't care if something came along and wiped them all out. Might keep from ruining a good horse, or keep a man from breaking his neck."

A shiver of alarm raced through Josh at Lee's words. He thought of how Belle loved to race her big gray across open land and turning to her, said, "If you see a bunch of prairie dogs, I want you to rein Silver in to a walk."

She laughed. "Oh, I will. Don't be a worry-wort, Josh." Happily, she twirled about, spreading her arms wide. "Remember that song that new man sang last night? The one about being buried out on the prairie where the coyotes howl and the wind blows free?" She ran on a few steps and turned back, her face flushed with joy belying the context of her next words. "If I die here in this prairie land, let me lie here with the wind blowing over my grave, the wild flowers blooming... Yes! And even the coyotes howling. To me, this is heaven!"

"That's foolish talk," Lee said, frowning.

"I don't care," Belle retorted. "I love it here and I wished I could live here forever."

"Just quit that dying talk," Lee said, his frown deepening.

The sweet, melodious song of the meadowlark, a small yellow and black bird they heard often on this open prairie land, rippled through the evening air and Belle still caught up in her fantasy of death, said. "And when I die and I'm buried out here, the meadowlark will come and sing over me, every day."

"Stop acting the silly fool," Lee growled.

Belle giggled and winked at Josh. "I should tell him, I guess, that I have no intention of dying."

Josh smiled. "I think he knows. But it is best not to talk of it."

"I know," Belle said, suddenly twirling around in a circle, her arms flung wide, "Oh, I'm so happy. Heaven could not be better than this."

"Just don't tempt fate, my sister," Lee said, his face matching his solemn voice.

* * *

Hector received the turkey eggs with a smile. "It too late for tonight's cookin'," he told them. "'Spect, though, I can fix somethin' up tonight so's they don't go bad and we could eat 'em tomorry evenin'."

True to his word, the next evening Hector had a sweet desert made from the turkey eggs, apples, raisins, a dessert the men all raved about and Mrs. Rawlins called "a taste of pure heaven."

Hector beamed at the compliments.

"Ma used to make a cake with apples and raisins," Billy said quietly.

"Didn't know Injuns ate cake," Frank Walker said, a small curl to his lip.

For a second no words were spoken and the only sounds were non-human ones, the call of a dove, the lowing of a couple of beeves in the herd, and nearby, the sound of a grazing horse, occasionally stomping a hoof to scatter flies.

"We Injuns eat most foods, don't eat us first," Billy said and a warning could be heard in the tone, if not in the words.

"My mother fell in love with Mexican food when she moved with my daddy to Texas," Jake spoke up. "She loved that firey taste. My daddy used to call her "Spitfire." He grinned. "She had some spitfire of a temper, all right. Harmless as a butterfly, but boy, her mouth could sure skin the hide off us boys."

Josh felt as if he'd been kicked in the gut at Frank's next words. "I hear them Mexican women can sure heat up in a hurry," he said. "If you know what I mean."

Jakes eyes flashed fire. "My Mama wasn't no Mexican," he said.

"Hey. I didn't mean nothing," Frank said quickly, his eyes going past Jake to where Sugar, who had just come in, was loading up his plate. The small, wirey Mexican man's dark eyes, hooded and unreadable were fastened on Frank Walker.

"So are we gonna brave that old quicksand, tomorrow?" Jimmy said, breaking the tension, his words directed at Charley.

"We're gonna give it a try anyway. Jake and I scouted up river a good five, six miles and Snort and Slim went down river. Reckon this spot is as good as any."

Josh saw a slight shiver pass through Jimmy and knew he was dreading the crossing.

Not being able to swim, Jimmy hated the river crossings.

Charley paused and took a swig of coffee before continuing. "We'll do like Frank here said the Bar S did and cut the herd into small bunches and take 'em across a bunch at a time, pushing 'em just as fast as we can. We don't want no stoppers, so you boys, keep swinging your reatas and yelling."

They talked about the crossing for some time. They had spent the day building the raft to ferry the chuck wagon and Mrs. Rawlins' wagon across as they had done on the Red. Jimmy mentioned the next rivers, the North Canadian and the Cimarron, still to cross before they would hit Kansas and the buyers at Wichita. "I hope they don't get no rain up that way, leastways 'till we're across," Jimmy said.

"Hell, Jimmy," Frank Walker said, looking up at the tall, thin man, "You'll never drown. Skinny as you are you'll just float on top like a stick broke off'en a tree. You ain't heavy enough to sink."

"I sure hopes so," Jimmy said with a wiry grin as he turned away to catch up a fresh horse from the remuda and take his turn at night herding.

Jake brought out his cards and all but Frank Walker either joined in the game, or sat to watch the others play.

"Reckon I'll stretch my legs some," Walker said, standing up and flipping the butt of his cigarette into the fire. Josh saw him look toward the Rawlins' wagon. Following his gaze, Josh saw Belle standing alone on the small knoll they had topped coming back yesterday evening. A small, solitary figure, her hat was off, her black hair loose about her shoulders. Frank Walker angled off towards the creek, but Josh couldn't help but think, he would swing around and come up beside Belle and, in a gentlemanly way, of course, escort her back to the wagon where he would flatter Mrs. Rawlins and somehow get her to thinking he was more of a gentleman than he really was.

Josh couldn't keep his mind on the cards until he saw Belle go back to the wagon alone and a little later, Frank Walker come back up from the creek. As darkness descended over the camp, Walker brought out his mouth harp, as he had done every evening since his arrival, and the men sang the songs familiar to them. Josh listened in gloomy silence. He could not shake the idea that Frank Walker had his eye on Belle.

The night was warm and the men slept on top of their bedrolls. Josh had trouble sleeping. Thoughts of Belle, her kisses, and her body pressed close to his, filled him with pleasure even as it filled him with hopelessness. Belle was expecting marriage as soon as they returned to Texas and he couldn't do that. He couldn't marry her until Slade was taken care of, one way or another. It wouldn't be fair to her, for he might not come back. Slade was a cold-blooded killer and had to be smart and as wily as an old wolf to have survived all these years. He shouldn't ask Belle to wait for him, but if he did, would she? Or would she start making eyes at that damnable good-looking Frank Walker?

CHAPTER TWENTY-TWO

The men ate their breakfast in the gray light of early morning, the sun creeping, as yet unseen, up on the edge of the eastern horizon. Choosing their mounts from the remuda, they rode out to where Josh and Slim rode slowly around the herd. No dew had fallen in the night and now most of the herd had quit the bed ground to graze on the dry grass.

"There can't be no stopping once we push them into the water," Charley had reminded them again as they wolfed down breakfast and prepared for the day. "We've got to keep 'em moving so they don't bog down." Pausing, he fingered his drooping mustache, pulling down on the ends as if to make them longer, a habit he had when mulling over something serious. Finally he spoke again. "It'll take all of us pushing each bunch to get 'em across. Swede," he turned to the man who drove Mrs. Rawlins' wagon. "You'd best catch up a horse and come with us. An extra rider sure won't hurt. We can't have no laggards, no hesitation. We'll start running 'em a ways back and take 'em down to the river as fast as they can go. I hope running 'em will take them halfway through before they know what they're into."

The herd was a good quarter mile back from the river and as they cut out the first bunch, Josh was glad he was riding Shadow for the buckskin was fast on his feet and could stop and start and turn back a cow seemingly with little effort. Josh also knew that if it came to swimming or stepping into quicksand, the buckskin wouldn't panic, but would follow without question, Josh's commands.

With yips and hollers and the swing of their coiled ropes, they got the first bunch cut from the herd and running as planned and there was no hesitation as the first group came to the river. They plunged in as if the very devil was pursuing them and as the waters deepened, began swimming. When the longhorns came out on the opposite bank, they were driven back away from the river to make room for the next bunch.

Half of the herd was brought over in two more bunches before they began to have trouble. The hooves of the cattle already across had stirred up the river bottom until it was a quagmire of quicksand and mud. After roping and pulling out a dozen bogged cattle, all coming out fighting mad and looking to raise some hell, and especially after Jeb's gray gelding got a horn raked across his chest, Charley decided to leave Sugar with the part of the herd already across and settled down to grazing and take the rest of the men and the remaining herd down river six or seven miles to where Sugar told them he had crossed with the remuda. Although the river was deeper there, he'd told them, it was narrower and relatively free of quicksand.

They were at the new crossing and were ready to push the first cut into the water when they heard the distant sound of a gunshot. Josh, riding in front of Jake, jerked around in his saddle to question the older man. "Could that be Sugar, letting us know there's trouble?"

Jake squinted and looked down river as if his dark eyes could penetrate the miles between them and the part of the herd they'd shoved across the river. The men were all with the remaining cattle, only Sugar was back with the herd across the river.

"It came from that direction, near as I could tell," Jake said.

Charley, at the head of the herd they were hazing toward the newly selected crossing, loped his horse back along side of the herd and motioned to each man he passed to follow him. They pulled their horses up in a circle and discussed the gunshot, they all agreed had come from somewhere down river.

"Sugar's got his gun," Jimmy said.

Charley, his face drawn up into a tight knot of worry, said, "I hope I'm glad he took it with him."

The men nodded. Sugar had insisted on taking his gun instead of putting it in the chuck wagon along with the rest of their guns.

"I only go once across," he'd said. "If I wrap it in a slicker, it not get wet."

"Could be he seen some wolves eyeing the cattle," Snort said.

"Some of us had better go investigate," Lee said.

Charley nodded. "Sugar wouldn't have chanced firing his gun, if he didn't have to, for fear of startin' the herd to running. Maybe a rattler got too close for comfort." He paused and pulled on his mustache. "Whoever goes had better get their gun first."

" I'll go," Frank Walker said.

Josh lifted his hand, "I'll go with him." *Walker would have to go back to the chuck wagon for his gun and the Rawlins' wagon and the chuck wagon were together back there waiting to cross the river. Walker would turn on the charm for Belle and probably made a big show of getting his gun.*

"Okay," Charley said. "You and Josh go get your guns. But don't neither one of you go to pulling some foolish stunt. You need help, you hightail it on back here, pronto."

* * *

Hector and Mrs. Rawlins with Belle and Kit were waiting anxiously at the wagons. The gunshot had come from just across the river close to where Sugar and the first part of the herd waited and they, too, were trying to think of a reasonable explanation.

Josh was surprised that Walker didn't jump in with an answer to Mrs. Rawlins' worried questions. In fact he didn't say anything or even cut his eyes at Belle standing beside her mother. Maybe, Josh thought, he had judged the man wrong.

Conscious of Belle's big eyes on him, Josh fought the urge to look at her as he spoke to her mother. "We going to see if Sugar needs help," He jerked his head toward Frank Walker. "Frank, here, and Charley, too, think he could of come upon a rattlesnake or maybe wolves stalking some of the cattle. There haven't been any more shots, so we're pretty sure he got whatever it was."

"Be careful," Mrs. Rawlins called after them.

Their horses balked at crossing the river, until they put the spurs to them. Josh wished he had Shadow under him and not the knot-headed roan he was riding. They had all changed horses several times between crossings and Shadow was with the remuda where he hoped they'd find Sugar and nothing more worrisome than a dead rattlesnake or wolf.

They crossed the river and on the opposite bank, put their horses into a lope. The herd paused in their grazing to watch them, a few skittish ones scattering.

Josh was startled to suddenly realize that some of the herd seemed to be missing. When he pointed it out to Walker, the man agreed. "Best draw your gun and keep it handy," he said, "I reckon what we've got here is some cow thieves."

As they topped a small ridge, they could see the remuda grazing, Sugar's chestnut, his saddle empty, grazed among them. They kicked their horses into a lope and rode down to the remuda, a knot of fear for the small Mexican cowboy tightening Josh's gut.

As they drew close to the horses, they saw Sugar sprawled some feet away, lying face down, dark blood staining the back of his shirt.

Josh leaped from his horse, knowing the man was dead, even as he turned him over. Sugar's eyes stared vacantly at the blue, cloudless sky overhead.

"The sons of bitches, " Walker said stepping down off his horse. "They shot him in the back."

Josh reached out and closed the dark eyes as he had done Pete's that early morning that now seemed so long ago, but the anger that surged through him, was not for Pete's death, for it had come natural and in its time, but for Sugar's and his mother's. Some rotten bastard had taken it upon himself to play the hand of fate, as if he were God and had the right to do so. He stood and looked out over the rolling prairie land and in his mind's eye Cole Slade left his mother's house and mounted the big bay tethered outside. Lately, he had tried to forget about the man, not wanting to leave Belle to take up a search that could last a year or better and one that might end in his own death. But looking down at Sugar, he knew that before he would ever be free to live a life with Belle, he'd have to find Slade and bring him to justice, one way or another, or die in the attempt.

"Here's another set of tracks," Frank said, bringing Josh back to the reality at hand. "The killer rode up to be sure he'd finished him off, I reckon."

"Do you think Sugar even saw him coming?" Josh asked, looking up into Walker's face. "And where is the missing part of the herd?"

"*Quien sabe?*" Frank Walker shrugged "But I'd put my money on cow thieves. See that spiral of dust off in the distance. Reckon that's our missing cows." He walked over and caught up the chestnut's reins and led the gelding over to where Sugar lay. "Let's get him up on his horse and you take him on back. I 'spect Charley'd want one of us to beat it back and let him know about Sugar."

"What'll you do?" Josh asked.

"I'll take a look for tracks. See where they lead and then I'll come on back and help you fellas get the wagons across. Charley'll want them wagons across 'for dark. Poor Sugar may have to wait awhile on his burying."

Josh was surprised that the man would show any concern for Sugar. He'd sure thought that Walker didn't care much for Mexicans. It still puzzled him that back at the wagons, Walker hadn't paid a lick of attention to Belle. He was beginning to think he had the man all wrong.

Sugar's chestnut snorted his fear but stood still, his hide quivering, as Frank lifted Sugar's slight frame and laid him on his stomach across the saddle and brought a rope up under the horse's belly and around Sugar's body so it wouldn't fall off.

Josh swung up in the saddle and reined his horse around to take the chestnut's reins from Walker. "Keep your eyes peeled and your gun handy," he said.

Walker nodded. "Don't worry," he said.

By the time Josh came in sight of the river, the cattle that had crossed upstream were arriving to mix with what was left of the first half of the herd. He pulled off his hat and waved it slowly overhead before riding down the incline toward them.

It was early dark when both wagons had been ferried across the river.

Snort and Joe had dug Sugar's grave up on a high rise of ground overlooking the river. Now too dark for Mrs. Rawlins to read from the

Bible, she held it against her chest, and recited several verses from memory.

Certain Frank Walker would be back as soon as it got too dark to read tracks, they'd began to worry as the night wore on and by sunrise when he hadn't returned, they were deeply concerned.

Billy offered to go look for him. "I can find him or no one can, " he said.

"Okay," Charley said. "Jake. Slim. You boys go with him. We'll wait here 'til you get back."

The sun was high overhead when Billy, Jake, and Slim rode back into camp. Frank Walker wasn't with them.

"You ain't gonna like what we seen, Charley," Jake said as he and Billy dismounted.

"Tracks show Walker's in with the thieves," Billy said. "Tracks show they took a couple hundred head while we was crossing the river."

"They figured we'd be too busy to miss 'em, and they figured right," Jake said. "Sugar must've saw 'em and was coming back to tell us when they shot him. Walker took pains to hide his tracks, but Billy, here," he added canting his head toward Billy, "can read them prints that big, black gelding left like he was readin' an open book. Showed me where plain as daylight, he joined up with 'em."

"He was looking for an outfit like ours. The son of a…" Lee stopped, conscious of the presence of his mother and sisters.

"He knew we'd have trouble here at this river," Jake said. "He's the one suggested we take the herd across in small bunches."

Charley looked towards Mrs. Rawlins. "What do you think, Martha? We'd be plum short-handed if we sent some of the boys to try to get those cows back."

"It's like spilt milk," Mrs. Rawlins said. "You could get some of it back in the jar, maybe. But most of it's lost. I expect that's the way it will be with those cattle. I can't risk the men's lives for something we might not get back anyway. No, we'll cut our losses and go on."

Chapter Twenty-Three

They moved on, the days now hot with a relentless sun beating down. The herd crossed the North Canadian and the Cimarron without incident and plodded on to the north. They would soon be leaving Indian Territory and entering Kansas.

A few clouds had begun to gather as Belle saddled Silver after supper.

"Don't go far," Martha Rawlins called to her daughter. "There's not a lot of daylight left."

"I won't Mother," Belle said, adding under her breath, "*Only far enough to see Josh.*" Lifting the reins, she clucked to Silver and cantered off toward a rise of small hills where she could look down on the grazing herd. Soon they would start to bed down. A little while ago she had seen Josh and Billy Redfeather ride out to take the first hours of watch.

The moon would be full tonight, so even if she had to wait until dark, she'd have no trouble telling the riders apart

Ever since the evening they had searched along that small creek for berries and had found the turkey eggs instead, she had ached to be with Josh. Seeing him at the wagon as he listened intently to her mother's lessons, just wasn't enough. She needed his kisses, his body pressed close to hers. Somehow, someway, she had to get him off alone.

She had thought about pretending to get herself lost, but Mother would send out every hand, the cattle be damned, and Jake or Slim or someone else would find her and the humiliation would be a little hard to take.

She could hardly wait to get to Wichita. There, when the herd was sold, maybe she could meet Josh downstairs in the boarding house or hotel or wherever they stayed and once in a while, they might sneak out in back for a few kisses. She was sure when they got to Wichita that Josh would ask her to marry him. If he did not ask, she would ask him. She wanted to be with him always, to be married as soon as possible. Maybe Mother would consent to a wedding in Wichita.

She watched the two riders circling the herd in opposite directions and little delicious shivers of anticipation coursed through her. She would ride around the herd, far enough away so they wouldn't be aware of her until she actually rode up to Josh and, by keeping Silver to a slow walk and the herd being used to Josh who would be singing or talking to them, they weren't likely to spook. They didn't spook when the men changed watches, so they shouldn't see her as anything more than another man. She'd find some brush or a gulch where she could wait unseen, until Billy passed by. She'd ride out to intercept Josh when he made his opposite loop around the herd.

She had to ride a little farther than she'd hoped to find a stand of brush big enough to hide herself and Silver. She waited until Billy rode by, remembering at the last minute to dismount and hold Silver's nose so he wouldn't nicker a greeting to Billy's horse.

Just as the rim of the moon showed, she heard Josh singing and in a few seconds, he caught sight of her riding toward him. His hand dropped to the gun at his side and stopped as he recognized her. "Belle," he said in a hoarse whisper. "What are you doing here?"

She urged Sliver closer. "I came to see you. To be alone with you." She smiled. "I came to give you some kisses. But," her smile deepened, "If you don't want them, I'll just go on back."

For an answer, he reined Shadow up close and slipped an arm around her. He nearly pulled her from the saddle as he kissed her full on the lips. She clung to him, wanting to climb in the saddle with him. To hold him tight and kiss him until she ran out of kisses, which she was sure she never would. Not with this man.

After much too short of a time, Josh sat her back in the saddle. "You have to go back now, Belle. You just can't be here. It late and your mother's probably worried." He cast a look at the sky. "It's clouding up and it might storm. It'll be dangerous for you out here if the herd starts to run."

"And for you," she said, surprised when a quick look showed her that the sky was fast filling with clouds.

"It's my job," he said.

She lowered her eyes and sucked in her bottom lip. Did she dare ask the question?

"What is it, Belle?" he asked.

She raised her eyes. "I know it's not for women to ask, but I don't know why we can't, the same as men." She paused but kept her gaze steady. " I have to know, Josh. Will you marry me?"

He looked at her gravely. "I would marry you today, if I could, but I can't. Not yet. I have a score to settle with a man named Cole Slade."

"Who?" She was confused. *Who was Cole Slade?*

"Slade was the man who murdered my mother. I have to find him and bring him to justice, one way or another. I can't marry you. I can't do anything, until Slade is dead or behind bars waiting to be hung."

"I kind of understand" Belle said. "But you may never find him and waste your life and mine in hunting him. Would your mother want you to avenge her death, and in doing so, maybe get yourself killed and break my heart?"

She saw the startled look on his face, followed by a frown, and knew she had half won him over. Given a little more time she would make him see that his mother would not want him to risk his life for an act already done. It was foolish. He could not bring his mother back to life.

"I don't know," he said slowly. "I'll think on it. But now you have to go, Belle. Please."

"One more kiss." Belle leaned forward into his arms. This time Josh pulled her from the saddle and held her for a space of time that couldn't she thought have been more than a second, but she wished could have lasted forever. Sitting her over again on Silver, his arms still holding hers, he said, "Now go, my darling. We'll make plans when we get to Wichita and I can talk to your mother."

172

Her heart sang. He had called her, *my darling*. She smiled at him, touched her fingers to her lips and blew him a kiss before reining Silver around. She rode, slowly out away from the herd, only vaguely aware of the faint rumbling of thunder.

Just before she rode down into a dry wash and out of sight of the herd, she pulled Silver to a stop and looked back, her eyes searching for her beloved on his buckskin horse. *He loved her! He wanted to marry her! He had called her, my darling!* She wanted to shout it to the skies. *Joshua Ryder loved her! Loved Belle Rawlins!* She whispered their names joined together: Joshua and Belle Ryder. Mr. and Mrs. Joshua Ryder.

Now conscious of the rising wind, the dark clouds shadowing the moon, the distant boom of thunder, and the streaks of lightning that followed, Belle called softly into the night, "I love you, Joshua Ryder." Then she reined Silver around and putting him into a long lope, headed back to camp.

Minutes later the sky exploded with a brilliant flash of light, followed by a sharp clap of thunder. Immediately, the clouds opened and poured out sheets of rain. She heard the cattle, the thousands of pounding hoof beats shaking the ground and in the lightning flashes, she could see through the pouring rain a dark mass, like a river, flowing by.

Praying for Josh's safety, Belle swung her horse out away from the thundering herd and leaning over his mane, urged him into a dead run, her happiness now turned to fear, not for herself, but for Josh. She had heard of men trampled in stampedes, their mounts stumbling, falling, tossing them beneath the herd's thundering hooves.

"Please, please God, keep him safe," she whispered, as she raced Silver into the night. Then her horse was falling and she was flying over his head. She felt a sharp jab of pain as she hit the ground.

Chapter Twenty-Four

Martha Rawlins heard the first sharp crack of thunder and immediately afterwards, felt the earth tremble under the hooves of the running herd. The first spatter of rain hit the canvas roof sheltering her and Kit and seconds later became a downpour.

"What is that, Mother?" Kit asked. "Why is our wagon shaking?"

"The herd's stampeding!" Martha moved quickly to the front of the wagon to peer out into the pouring rain. With the moon lost in the storm clouds, only the lightning flashes brought any visibility through the heavy sheet of rain.

Fear gripped her with a heavy hand. Where was Belle? Why had she let her go tonight? *Where was that girl!* And Lee! Lee was in danger riding after the herd trying with the other hands to stem the flow of their mindless running. She sent a prayer heavenward for Lee and Belle's safety. She hoped Belle had found shelter of some kind, but she knew there was little shelter in this open prairie land and the lightning was a danger in itself. Surely, at any minute she would hear the sound of Silver's hoof beats, now that the herd and its noise had passed on. She wished Belle had not insisted on going for a ride this evening. If Josh had not had early nighthawk duty, he would be here taking a lesson and Belle would have stayed here too, her eyes soaking up the boy like she couldn't get enough of him.

She tried not to think that Belle might have ridden toward the herd, hoping to catch a glimpse of Josh. She had ridden off in the opposite direction, she had watched her go, but she might have turned back as soon as she was out of sight. The herd was large and covered a lot of ground. If Belle had been anywhere near.... She shuddered. In their blind flight, the stampeding herd might swerve off in any direction. They could sweep Silver along swallowing him and Belle in their midst.

She was thankful, now, although she hadn't been then, that Belle had insisted on having Lucy sew her the riding outfit, half pants, half skirt so she could ride astride. It would keep her balanced on the horse and make it less likely that she would fall, if the herd did stampede in her direction.

Lucy had come to her that day, her black eyes wide with indignation, "Your daughter be wanting me to sew her up some sort of pants so's she can ride astraddle of her horse. It gonna have a skirt, sort of, she tell me, but what she draw on paper for me to make, look more like pants with big, wide legs. I tell her, it not be proper at all. She just laugh, Miz. Martha, and she say. 'We're going on a trail drive, Lucy, not to an afternoon tea. Mother won't let me help herd the cattle, but she says I can ride Silver all I want to and I want to race him with the wind. I know I could ride better, if I didn't have to perch up on one of those dumb, damn sidesaddles. Didn't the dimwit who invented them know we'd look like frogs on a lily pad?'" Lucy had laughed, her eyes twinkling. "So if you don't be minding, Miz. Martha, I'm gonna sew that girl the best damn riding pants that ever was."

Dressed in her new pants, Belle had begged for a regular saddle. "There's no sense having this outfit, if I still have to ride sidesaddle," she'd said. Silently pleased with her daughter and wishing she might trade in her sidesaddle, too, she'd bought the girl a small saddle. The pants had given Belle so much more freedom on the horse and she often raced the big gray gelding just as fast as the horse could go. She rode well, like Lee said, "As if glued to the saddle." Belle did love to ride. She hoped if she and Josh married that the babies would not come too fast or too many, so Belle could still ride now and then.

The herd was somewhere miles away by now, only the riders with them knowing where. The rain had eased and the lightning flashes were fewer and weaker. She was certain Belle would be here soon, soaking wet. She would have the girl strip to her skin and wrap her in a blanket and help her towel off her long, dark hair. She wished she could build a fire and fix them all a hot tea, but such was life on the trail.

The hours went by, achingly slow, the moon and stars emerging from the clouds. Martha grew chilled with apprehension.

"Where can Belle be, Mother?" Kit asked anxiously, waking from a fitful sleep and climbing over the wagon seat to sit beside her and stare out at the coming dawn.

Hector had built a fire out of the dry wood, he kept in the cowhide cooley under the wagon, and had brewed a pot of coffee. Coming up beside the wagon, he handed her and Kit each a cup, hers black like she liked it and Kit's thinned with water and heavily sweetened.

"I been a watchin' for Miss Belle. Can't figure why she don't be back. You be all right if I go take a look see?"

"Oh, Hector, I would be so grateful. We'll be fine. We'll go over and keep the fire up and the coffee hot and start a meal for when the boys get back. Swede's rifle is under the seat here. I'll take it along and if Belle comes back before you find her, I'll fire it three times."

"That be a good idea," Hector said. "I'll get me a rifle out of the chuck wagon and when I finds Miss Belle, I'll shoot three times, too." He took a few steps and turned back. "The rain will have done washed away her tracks, Miz Rawlins. I maybe be gone some time."

"I know, Hector. I know."

All throughout the night Martha had pleaded with God for Belle and Lee's safety. She had added prayers for the men, too, that none would be hurt or killed, especially Josh. If Belle would lose her Josh, it would break her heart as surely as losing Oliver had broken hers. The cattle were of little consequence to her now. If they all fell over a cliff and drowned in a river of quicksand, it would not matter to her, as long as the men and her children were safe.

She kept her prayers silent so Kit would not know of her fears and her pleading words for mercy echoed over and over inside her head. Even as she pleaded, she knew it would do no good. She had pleaded for her two little boys and for Oliver, but to no avail. She had pleaded with the Lord for James, too, praying he would seek a doctor's attention before it was too late, but the Lord had not listened to her then, either.

She remembered the scripture about the rain falling on the just and the unjust. God would give them no promises but, he would give eternal life. *"In my Father's house are many mansions,"* Jesus said. *"And where I am there you shall be also."* She could ask for their safety but she knew that God could take them just as He had taken Oliver and her two little boys, and James. God was not a safety net to catch you or those you loved. But He would take us to Him, when we left this world.

She found flour and Hector's sour dough starter and some salted beef he'd earlier set to soaking. She mixed the biscuits and set them in a Dutch oven and set it in the coals with more piled on the lid. She rinsed the soaked meat in two more batches of fresh water and rolled the pieces in flour before dropping them in skillet grease. When the meat was done, she added flour to the grease and then water, stirring until the brown gravy was smooth and bubbling. As she finished dropping a lid over the gravy to keep it warm, she looked up to see some of the men coming into camp, Lee in the lead riding a red roan.

"Lee!" Martha Rawlins ran to her son and as he swung down out of the saddle, grabbed him and hugged him. "Oh, my dear, I'm so glad you are safe."

"Did you see Belle?" Kit asked, looking up at her brother, her small face pinched with worry. "She went for a ride on Silver and she didn't come back."

"What!" Lee drew back from his mother's arms and quickly she told him about Belle and that Hector had gone to find her.

"Half of us came in to get fresh horses. I'll turn this one loose and saddle Ace and we'll go look for her. Don't worry, Mother, I'm..." A shot rang out interrupting him. They froze listening for two more. Two more shots to say that Hector had found her. But there was only that single shot. Not three shots, but one. One shot had killed Sugar. They had heard no more. Cold with shock, she stared up at Lee, too numb to even cry.

Not one of the men hesitated or reached for the coffee, but mounting fresh horses started off at a canter. Billy rode in the lead his eyes on the rain soaked ground following the prints left by Hector's horse.

Charley had gone with them, insisting that Lee stay with his mother and sister. "You're needed here," he said.

Martha was glad Josh hadn't come in with them, but was one of the men staying with the herd. If something had gone horribly wrong she didn't want Josh to find her.

A half an hour later, the three back at the camp, heard another gunshot and they turned to each other, wondering and afraid.

"Maybe that's a signal from Hector," Lee said. "He probably thinks we'll have someone searching by now and the shot will pinpoint the direction." He stuck a small splinter of wood into the fire and lit his cigarette. "Belle could have fallen off Silver and broken her leg, or..." He shook his head. "I don't know. We'll just have to wait."

A tear sliding down her cheek, Kit said, "Maybe Silver got hurt and they can't leave him."

Martha drew her daughter close, her mouth dry with fear.

* * *

They found Hector sitting beside a slicker covered mound, his horse, ground tied, grazing nearby. As they drew close they saw that Belle lay beneath the slicker, covered but for her crown of long black hair.

The men dismounted and Hector his eyes swimming in tears, said, "She's gone. I always be 'fraid she gonna do that, runnin' that pony like she do. He step in a prairie dog hole or something, break his leg and she fall. Pretty sure her neck be broken." He half turned to look to where the big silver gray gelding lay. "When Sugar killed, the one shot told us of trouble, but we don't know what trouble." He sighed and ran a hand across his face. "I fire one shot to warn Miz. Martha and to put Miss Belle's horse out of his misery."

"We heard a second shot," Swede said.

"Thought you'd be tracking me now. It being daylight and the rain stopped. Figured the herd be stopped and too tired to run some more. Knowed Miz. Martha terrible anxious and needing to know, even this awful news. Might be you'd get here faster, if I was to let you know the direction." He rose to his feet. "I be carrying her back to camp, if that be all right."

"Hell, yes, Hector," Charley said, his voice harsh, rough. He knelt beside the still form and wrapped the slicker all the way around Belle's slender body and gathering her in his arms rose and handed her up to Hector now mounted on his horse. Tenderly, Hector took the slight body in his arms and lifting the reins, nudged his horse with his heels and rode off, the men following behind. Billy had pulled Belle's bridle and saddle off the dead horse. Charley looped the bridle over his saddle horn and carried Belle's small saddle straddled across his thigh.

CHAPTER TWENTY-FIVE

"We're still two days drive from Wichita, Martha. It's summer and the weather shows no sign of cooling down. There will be problems." Charley was putting into words what they all knew, even Mrs. Rawlins, herself, but she was having a hard time dealing with the thought of burying her child out here on the prairie. She had suggested hurrying on ahead with her wagon and getting Belle to Wichita, where her body could be preserved so she could take her back to Texas to be buried in the family plot in Victoria.

Josh wished for that, too. Not only for her mother's sake, but for his own. If Mrs. Rawlins would keep him on, he'd stay at the ranch and Belle would not be so far away.

"What about Slade?" said a voice inside his head. He pushed the thought aside. Someday he would deal with Slade, if he were still alive, but now it was all he could do to deal with Belle's death. Grief and guilt battered him until he felt doubled over in pain, although he still stood upright. Tears threatened. Tears, he feared if started would never end. Tears that lodged in his throat choking him and shutting off his breath so he had to pull in gulps of air to breathe. And guilt. Guilt rode him hard. He should have sent her back immediately instead of holding her, kissing her. They had only spent a few minutes together, but those few minutes might have cost her her life.

When the men who had gone in to get fresh horses and grab a bite to eat had not come back to the herd to relieve them, and hearing what had sounded like the second faint gunshot, he had been elected to leave the herd and see what was happening.

He'd arrived only a few minutes ahead of the men coming back with Belle in Hector's arms. The shock had torn a hole in his heart that bled with a raw, burning pain.

They sat outside Mrs. Rawlins' wagon. Someone had pulled a chair out of her wagon and she sat on it while he and Charley and Lee squatted on their heels in the wet grass. Kit stood, leaning on her mother, her small face and her mother's both drawn tight with grief.

After Mrs. Rawlins asked Charley to help them make a decision, she turned to Josh. "Belle loved you. She would want you to have a say, too."

"Yes, ma'am," Josh said. "I loved her, too. I wanted to marry her. I…" His voice broke and tears stung his eyes.

Now, listening to Mrs. Rawlins and Lee talk about taking the wagon and going on ahead and hearing Charley's obvious doubts about it, he remembered the day they found the turkey eggs. He could see Belle standing on the small hill, her arms spread wide, declaring her delight in the vast prairie land. She had brought up the song Frank Walker had sang the night before about a dead cowboy not wanting to be buried on the prairie and she had run ahead a few steps before turning back to look at them, smiling, her eyes sparkling. "If I should die here," she'd said, "let me lie here with the wind blowing over my grave, the wild flowers blooming… Yes! And even the coyotes howling. To me, this is heaven!"

Should he mention that day to her mother?

As they talked, the idea that Belle should be buried here grew stronger until he could not hold his words any longer. Motioning to Lee he got up and walked some distance away and when he turned to face him, Lee said, "I know what you are about to say. You're thinking of the day we found the turkey eggs." Josh nodded and went on to explain his thoughts.

"I think you're right, Josh. I'll talk to Mother."

* * *

Several hands took turns digging Belle's grave, going deeper than they would have any other grave, the others rode back to a small tree lined stream they had passed yesterday, to cut a tree and fashion a frame with cross pieces for Belle's body to lie in state. They would bury her at sunset.

Jake and Charley set the frame in the shade of the wagon and folded a blanket over it.

Tenderly, Charley lifted Belle's body out of the wagon and laid her on the blanket. Martha Rawlins had washed her daughter's face and brushed out her long dark hair. She kept her daughter dressed in her riding clothes, knowing that would be Belle's preference, and pulled a blanket over the lower half of Belle's body, so she appeared to be simply sleeping. Asking Lee to bring Silver's bridle to her, she laid it across Belle's chest, lifting the small still hands over it. "Perhaps," she said, the glitter of tears in her eyes, "She and Silver will meet or have already met in heaven."

Faces grim, hats in hand, the men nodded to the family as they filed past Belle's body. Josh had started to go with the men, but Mrs. Rawlins had held him back to stand with her and Lee and Kit. Kit had gathered an armful of wild flowers and had placed the bouquet atop her sister's hands folded over the bridle. As the men filed past, Mrs. Rawlins clinging to her remaining children, began to sob softly.

Josh fought his own tears as he looked for the last time on that beautiful face, it's vibrant glow paled into a sleeping stillness that would never wake again.

When they had all passed by, Martha Rawlins fell to her knees beside Belle's bier, harsh sobs racking her body. Lee brought over her chair and helped his mother up off the ground. She stayed with Belle's body through the rest of the afternoon.

As the sun began to sink below the horizon, Charley carried Belle's blanket wrapped body, and led the way to the small rise of ground where the grave waited. Behind them, Mrs. Rawlins walked between Lee and Kit, her hands clinging to theirs. Josh followed with the rest of the men.

At the graveside, Charley read the Lord's Prayer from Mrs. Rawlins' Bible and Jake, in his deep bass voice, sang a song he had learned as a child, "Rock of Ages, cleft for me…."

Josh fought back his own tears until the grave was filled, but as they turned from the grave, Josh stumbled towards a brush filled draw where, out of sight of the others, he dropped to the ground and gave way to hot bitter tears.

Chapter Twenty-Six

Charley rode ahead as they neared Wichita and came back with the news that several other herds now occupied the range nearest the town and they would have to swing the cattle west five or six miles for grazing ground to hold them until he could arrange for a buyer.

As he had done in Fort Worth, Charley allowed the men to go in shifts into town. Each rider was paid half of his earnings, the rest to be collected when the cattle were sold.

"Pick out a man you can deal with," Charley said as he handed out the gold pieces. "Just remember he's back here with the herd waiting his turn."

Mrs. Rawlins and Kit took a room in the Palmer House, a hotel on main street, but Lee, as was expected of him, stayed with the herd.

Josh had no desire to see the town. Thoughts of Belle followed him day and night. Often he dreamed of her and woke in his bedroll, sick with longing. The musical sound of her voice and her infectious laughter sometimes came to his ear and almost, he would turn expecting to see her and the jolt of his loss would hit, leaving him sick with a hollow emptiness that twisted his gut and brought the tears he had to fight hard to suppress. He thought often of Mrs. Rawlins, knowing she had to be enduring terrible pain. He knew Lee and Kit were suffering, too, for they had loved their sister, but he figured Mrs. Rawlins' pain had to be almost more than she could bear.

"You'd better go, Josh," Charley said, when he heard Slim and Billy urging him to go on the second shift into town. "Get a bath and a haircut anyway. It'll do you good."

So Josh saddled Shadow and rode into Wichita. He got a haircut and for a few seconds toyed with the idea of letting his mustache go along with his week old beard, but decided against it. On the day they found the turkey eggs, Belle had pulled back from his embrace to trace her finger tips over his mustache and on down over his lips to the cleft in his chin.

"You are such a beautiful man," she'd said, smiling sweetly.

Slim and Billy bought new clothes and so he did, too, his pants more faded and ragged than he'd noticed before. Afterwards they met up with Jake, Snort, and Jimmy and the six of them took in a series of saloons, buying a drink and moving on to the next one.

Standing at each bar with the men, some strangers, and some he had ridden up the trail with, Josh felt an odd detachment from even these men he knew, and thoughts of Cole Slade returned. Downing his fourth drink, but feeling as cold sober as when he'd started, he told the men he was going to get a bite to eat and go on back to the herd. They offered to go with him, but he shook his head.

"You fellas don't need to play nursemaid to me. I appreciate it, though." His quick glance took in Slim and Billy at the bar with him and Jake and Snort deep in a poker game, the others watching. He wouldn't see them again after the herd was sold, for in these past few hours he had come to a decision. "*So long, fellas,*" he said inside his head. "*You were good to work with and I won't ever forget you.*"

His stomach full of steak and potatoes, he decided on a piece of apple pie. He knew he was dragging his feet, trying to work up the courage to pay a visit to Mrs. Rawlins. He wasn't coming back into town anymore. He'd stay with the herd and when Charley got the cattle sold, he'd draw the rest of his pay and head back to Texas. He'd stay at Pete's for a while and practice his gun handling and then take up Slade's trail. The lawmen couldn't seem to find him, but maybe another outlaw could. He'd grow a beard and build up a reputation with talk. Along the border towns he'd let it be known that Cole Slade was his hero and that he was looking to join up with the outlaw. He figured flattery might catch Slade faster than outspoken revenge.

He hated to tell Belle's mother he was leaving. He had come to think as much of her as he had of Rosita. Both women were warm and accepting and each had made him feel good about himself. He had loved Belle, still loved who she had been, but he had also liked knowing that married to Belle, Martha Rawlins would be his mother-in-law. Kit was a sweet child, too, and he would miss her, and Lee. Lee had been a good friend, almost a brother. He would have loved being in the Rawlins family. If his trails ever took him anywhere near the Lazy R, he would stop in and see them, if he wasn't wanted by then for being with Cole Slade.

It worried him that he might have to participate in some of the Slade's robberies, but if he needed too, he would do what he had to, short of killing someone. If any killing had to be done, he hoped Cole Slade would be the one looking down his gun barrel.

* * *

"Are you sure that's what you want to do?" Mrs. Rawlins asked. In a gown, black as a crow's wing, she sat in a high-backed rose-colored chair a book spread open on her lap.

Josh had dreaded this goodbye visit, but she soon put him at ease. He explained about Pete and the small spread he had left to him and he thanked her for teaching him to read and write. In response, Martha Rawlins took two books and a slate from a small trunk and handed them to him. "These will help you improve on what you already know," she said with soft smile.

"No," she said firmly laying a hand on his arm when he started to protest. "It gives me pleasure to give these to you."

"Thank you ma'am." Josh said. He had to fight tears and looked quickly down at the books in his hands before he could speak. "I will study these on the trail home and after I get to Pete's place."

"You would make me proud if you would do so." A helpless expression came over her face, and fresh tears welled up and spilled down her cheeks. She reached out her arms and held him in a tight embrace, her face pressed against his chest. A few of his own tears fell, despite his effort to hold them back.

When she let him go and stepped back, her eyes still awash with tears, he murmured, "Thank you Mrs. Rawlins. I'll remember Belle and all of you for the rest of my life."

He turned to leave, but she caught him by the arm. "Wait, please. Let me pour you a glass of fresh water. If you will stay with me a little longer, I promise we will talk of other things. Lee and Kit will be here soon. They went over to the mercantile to buy Kit a new bonnet. Her old one is so faded and worn."

He sat down in the chair she indicated and at first their talk was stilted. She asked him about Pete's place and about Pete. He told her about the Pinõs family who had been more than neighbors and who now looked after the place.

She told him about Oliver, her first love, and the two little boys. Then she told him about James Rawlins and how he had become someone she had learned to love. "You will, too, Josh. You'll remember Belle always, but you will find someone new. Someone, I hope, you will love as much as you loved Belle."

"Right now, I can't imagine it," Josh told her.

She nodded, "I know." She reminded him of the search for his father that had brought him to the Lazy R ranch. "Will you continue that search, or let it be, a mystery of the past?"

" I don't know where else to look. I've kind of given up hope of ever finding out anything about him."

"If you do find him or his grave and learn from those who knew him that he is not one you would chose for a father, will it bother you?"

"I don't know," Josh felt a frown furrow his brow. He had never given that a thought.

"If you do," she said, "Don't let it eat at you. Remember he was once a child, and all children are born with a clean slate. Whoever he is now, or was, is often determined by what is written on that slate, especially while he was growing into manhood."

Josh nodded. "Pete once told me that if we live long enough, most of us will acquire a shadowed past. Some things we're not too proud of. He said we all ride a shadowed trail."

She smiled. "How true. I would have liked to have met that man. He did a good job finishing the raising your mother started, I can tell you that."

Josh looked down at his hands. "Pete told me once that a scrub horse throws a scrub foal. If my father isn't any good..." he left the rest unsaid.

Her face grave, she leaned toward him. "Pete might have been right about horses, but people aren't horses."

There was a commotion at the door and Lee and Kit came in, Kit, wearing the new bonnet. Mrs. Rawlins made over it a few moments before Kit turned to Josh. "Do you like it?" she asked, a worried expression on her small, solemn face and in her hazel eyes fringed with long, dark lashes.

For an instant, her face was Belle's and a hard knot rose in his chest. He had never noticed before how much they looked alike. Except for the eyes, Kit might be the image of Belle at eleven. He wondered if Kit would still look like Belle when she was grown. "I always was partial to blue," he said.

She smiled at him, a small, sweet smile and turned back to her mother.

They talked of many things, Wichita and the crowded streets full of cattle buyers and cowboys and those who hoped to gain from them, of the ranch back in Texas, and of someone who reported seeing a lone buffalo a few miles outside of town. Later, Lee walked with Josh downstairs and they rode out to the herd together.

CHAPTER TWENTY-SEVEN

Josh turned Shadow south towards Texas, Top following behind on a lead rope. Josh had purchased the big bay from Mrs. Rawlins to spell Shadow on their journey.

The days were long, filled with his memories of Belle. The nights, as darkness pressed in around him, were, at first, intolerable and if not for the comforting sound of the horses moving around in the night, he might not have slept at all his first weeks on the trail. Loneliness, too, dogged his trail back to Texas. He missed the men he had ridden with and Mrs. Rawlins and Kit and Lee. He even missed Hector. They had, for a time, been his family and he wished he could forget Cole Slade and ride on to the Lazy R and wait for them. He was sure Mrs. Rawlins would hire him on again. Although he wanted to find Slade and avenge his mother, at the same time he hoped the man had already been apprehended and had either been hanged or was waiting to be hung. And if he was, there was no doubt but what he'd return to the Lazy R, at least for a while. Someday, he'd go back to Pete's, build up a herd and hire Miguel and Rosita's boys to ride for him.

He often thought of Belle's words the night she'd ridden out to see him and he knew that even if he found Slade, he might mess up and Slade would kill him.

"Would your mother want you to avenge her death, and in doing so, maybe get yourself killed and break my heart? she'd said. "Would she want you to hunt for a man you may never find and in doing so ruin your life and mine?" He had loved seeing that earnest side of her, a side he had not had a glimpse of before.

How he ached for the girl. He saw the wisdom of her words and for her he would have turned his back on Slade, but she was gone, and Slade, if he wasn't already dead, needed to be before he brought pain and death to any other little Mexican girl. For those young girls, if not for his mother, he must hunt down Slade. Belle could not have argued against that.

He stood for a long time at Belle's prairie grave, his senses filled with the memory of her. Charley had made a wooden cross from a board off the chuck wagon and had carved her name with his knife. As soon as they had reached Wichita, Mrs. Rawlins had ordered two tombstones, one to bring back to this lonely prairie grave and the other for the cemetery in Victoria where Mrs. Rawlins had buried two husbands and two sons.

The lettering on each tombstone was etched in his memory. The first to be set here, read: *Here Lies Our Love, Belle Lorraine Rawlins, age 16.* The one to be placed above an empty grave in the Victoria cemetery, read: *Our daughter, Belle Lorraine Rawlins, Born September 17, 1859—Died June 4, 1875. Her mortal remains in a prairie grave, her soul with the angels.*

As he had promised Mrs. Rawlins, he got out the books each evening and practiced writing words and figuring numbers. It had a soothing effect on him and passed away the lonely evenings. He always allowed an hour of daylight each night to practice and as he rode through the days, he went over in his head, the lessons he'd given himself the night before.

His thoughts turned to who his father might have been as he neared Victoria, but he'd waste no more time searching, at least until Slade was dead or behind bars. He stopped at a feed store next to a livery stable to buy grain for the horses and was tying the sacks behind the cantle when he spotted an old bay horse rounding a corner of the livery stable.

A sudden hammering started up in his chest as his eyes swept over the old bay with the four black stockings. Even without seeing the white spot on the horse's forehead, nearly covered by a long black forelock, he knew it was Cole Slade's horse. The one Slade rode the night his mother was murdered. He finished tying the grain sacks and walked over to the old horse and reaching up, pushed aside the coarse, black mane to expose a thick, white backward J. He turned to the old man who had come up beside him "Where'd you get this horse?"

The old man spat out a stream of tobacco juice before answering. "Outlaw name of Cole Slade left him some five, six years back. Traded him in the middle of the night for a young sorrel belonging to a customer." The old man paused, spat another brown stream, and wiped his mouth on a dirty sleeve. "The sheriff and his men got here in time to shoot one of the men. Didn't kill him though and he spilled his guts. Said he rode for Slade." The old man peered at Josh. "You ever hear of Slade?"

"Yeah," Josh said.

The man nodded toward the bay. "Boss's little daughter made a big, old pet out of him. Wasn't worth much, wind broke like he was. Reckon it's been the best life he's ever had."

Before he left town, Josh rode out to the cemetery. He walked among the tombstones until he located the massive stones for Mrs. Rawlins' husbands and the two smaller stones for her sons, both etched with winged cherubs. Mrs. Rawlins had told him Belle's stone would be next to the little boys' and he imagined it there, tears blurring his eyes. In his walk through the cemetery, he'd noted a number of unmarked graves. Now, lifting his eyes to sweep the cemetery, he wondered which one held his father's bones, if indeed his father was even buried here.

* * *

Pete's place looked the same as when he'd left it. As if the owner was merely gone for the day. Miguel had kept the place in good repair, probably grazing his sheep and goats on the grass to keep it from becoming overgrown. He pushed open the door and stepped inside. He remembered the first time he'd seen this room and had to grin a little at the boy who had stuffed cornbread in his mouth and washed it down with the dipper full of water. The pail was empty now, turned upside down, the dipper still hanging from its nail.

Tomorrow he would ride over to the Pinõs and tell them he was back, but for how long, he couldn't be sure. He pushed open the door to the room where he and Pete had slept all through his growing up years. Pete's bed was still covered with a tarp. He dropped his bedroll on the rawhide sling bed he'd used and went back to start a fire in the stove for coffee. The Pinòs had left a stack of kindling on the top of a filled wood box.

He walked down to the creek for a bucket of fresh water and cooked his first decent meal since he'd left Kansas from supplies he'd picked up before leaving Victoria. It tasted good after weeks of beans and bacon. That evening he sat out on the porch, his chair tipped back against the wall, and watched the stars pop out one by one and the bats and nighthawks swoop and glide through the darkening sky.

Stretched out on his bed, he faced a sleepless night until he got up and took his bedroll out to the porch. Listening to a soft wind sigh through the branches of the old live oak, he soon slept.

"Hello the house," Josh called as he rode up to the door of the Pinòs adobe. Miguel stepped out of the shadowed doorway. "*Buenos dias,*" the Mexican said. Then a smile wreathed his face. "Josh," he said. "You are home."

"Yes," Josh answered. "I'm home."

As he swung down from Shadow, Rosita appeared in the doorway behind her husband.

"Josh!" she exclaimed and ran to meet him, clasping him in her arms. "Oh, bless the saints that bring you."

Josh looked over Rosita's dark head, barely reaching his chest, and grinned at Miguel.

The Pinòs boys suddenly appeared. Ramon and Gordo, recognized Josh at once, but the two younger boys, Manuel, and little Pete hung back at first and gazed at him shyly out of solemn black eyes.

Rosita hustled them out of the hot sun and over to the shaded side of the adobe. They sat on the ground, the boys crowded close to Josh and listened, wide-eyed, as he talked about the trail drive.

The Pinòs were surprised to learn that Mrs. Rawlins and her daughters had accompanied the herd and Rosita's dark eyes grew wide in surprise when he told them that Belle had ridden astride wearing something more like pants than skirts. He did not dwell long on memories of Belle, afraid that his emotion would give him away and they would be sad at the pain he still carried, although it had softened some and did not now plague him every second of every minute of every hour of every day. Later, he would tell them about Belle.

He tried to keep the talk light-hearted and told about building rafts to float the wagons across the rivers and about Jake's tale of trying to get a beaver to help cut down the trees. He told about the quicksand and pulling out the steers bogged down in the mess and how then the thanks they got was a mad steer on the prod bent on hooking a horn in your horse's side. He told about Sugar, betrayed by Frank Walker. He told about Mrs. Rawlins teaching him to read and write, and although, he had planned to wait to tell them about Belle, Rosita changed that plan.

"Something it make you very sad," she said, her dark eyes looked into his and he told it all, the words spilling out of him, words ragged from holding back tears. "We were going to be married and maybe live here on Pete's place. I wanted to bring her to meet you."

"Poor Josh," Rosita murmured and catching his hands in her small ones, rose to kiss his forehead. It was all he could do to keep from falling into her arms and sobbing his heart out.

Later, the three older boys sent to carry water and bring in wood and Rosita fixing their meal, Miguel asked, "You have plans, now?"

Little Pete sat on his father's lap, his big, dark eyes intently watching Josh's face.

"I'll stay here for a while." Josh said, hating it that he was lying by omission to Miguel. But he knew that to tell Miguel he was bent on hunting down his mother's killer would not set well with him. "If I can't settle down, I may go pick up odd jobs and go with another herd next spring.

"Where do you go, 'til it spring?" Miguel asked.

"South, I guess. Maybe along the border." He looked at Miguel. "If I go you wouldn't mind looking after things a while longer would you?"

"For you, Josh, never."

"Thanks," he said, emotion tightened his throat. "I'd appreciate it."

"We are glad you try to stay with us awhile."

"I'll try but I feel restless. I'm not sure I can stay long."

"No worry, Josh. You are young. We wait. See if time not bring you back."

Josh stayed for the evening meal and then rode back over to Pete's place. That night he tried again to sleep in his old bed, but the house seemed to close in around him and he took his bedroll back to the porch. What little sleep he did get that night was full of dreams of Belle and he woke with his face wet with tears.

Knowing Pete's old long barreled, single action Colt wouldn't be the best gun if it came to a showdown with Slade, Josh rode into Port Lavaca and bought a new six shot Smith & Wesson with a six inch barrel, a Henry rifle, and so much ammunition that the clerk behind the counter asked if he was going to start a small war and then laughed nervously. Probably, Josh thought, afraid he'd challenged an outlaw. Afterwards he went to the newspaper office and bought the current issue and several back copies.

For two months he lived at Pete's and divided his time between practicing with his gun and improving his spelling, reading, and ciphering. He studied the newspapers, each article word by word, and when he had all the words figured out, he read the article first silently and then aloud. While he worked on his education, he was aware of Martha Rawlins beside him, still teaching. "That is a "b" sound, Josh," she would say. "You learn the sounds of letters and you can figure out almost any word." When he practiced drawing and shooting, a figure with long yellow curls and a black hat stood in front of his gun and sneered.

"You are maybe going to shoot your way to the border?" Miguel asked one day after a week of hearing the distant gunfire. "There are some banditos about, I'm most certain, and some rattlesnakes, too, but I'm wondering if you are thinking of maybe going to a war."

"I like shooting," Josh said light-heartedly as he worked up what he hoped was a disarming smile. "It takes the kinks out and for all that noise, I sleep better."

The lies had grown easier now. Rosita often insisted he come for dinner, sending Ramon or Gordo with Manuel tagging along to invite him. The boys were very interested in his gun and getting Rosita and Miguel's permission he often allowed the boys to shoot at the targets he set up for them. He set up tins, emptied of their contents for the boys and small pieces of wood. He also used those small targets for himself, alternating with a log, propped to the height of a tall man. To keep it upright, he roped it to the old, unused snubbing post in the corral. Shadow and Top tethered on fresh grass everyday, some distance away, were only corralled at night. He had cut the dead tree down and limbed it before dragging it out of the hills behind Top and propping it up. He had at first thought to tack a piece of burlap on it at the height of a man's chest, but decided against it. Miguel would question such a target and maybe did wonder, but as yet hadn't voiced his concerns. To throw off suspicion, Josh had riddled the log with bullets from top to bottom, but the most bullets went into the log at chest height to a man.

A week before he'd decided to leave, a storm blew in with high winds and rain. He spent the next week clearing the debris and making repairs to the house and the shed. The shed had suffered the most damage in the wind and Josh borrowed Miguel's donkey and cart to haul the lumber he needed from Port Lavaca. The Pinõs adobe had withstood the storm with little damage.

"You hear about Indianola?" the man asked, taking the money Josh handed him for the lumber.

"No," Josh said. "They catch this wind and rain, too?"

"Had a hell of a storm, they did. A real rip-snorter of cyclone. Some, I hear, calls them hurricanes. Anyhow, it came roaring in off the water and knocked buildings flat and killed a whole lot of people. Some, they tell me, got swept out to sea and drowned. Some bodies they won't never find. Guess it's a real mess. And smell…" He took a breath and stepped back, staggering a little as if his nostrils had suddenly been assailed with the odor of decaying death. "Man. It's got to be powerful bad."

Josh handed him his money and he stuck it in the wooden till and came around the counter. "I'll help you load," he said.

On the way back to the place, he still thought of as Pete's, Josh thoughts were on Indianola. He wondered if his mother's adobe still stood and the saloon where Angel and Birdy had once lived and after them the two women who had terrified and embarrassed him, especially the blond Myra who had grabbed him through his pants.

He shook his head at the memory, a small chuckle escaping him. As Pete would have said, she was a ring-tailed tooter. When he set out to find Slade, which would be soon, he would go to Indianola first and see if anything was left of his mother's small adobe and the saloon.

While he worked on the shed he realized that if he did find Slade and the outlaw killed him or they killed each other, it wouldn't be fair to the Pinõs to keep looking after this place for him. Probably they wouldn't even know it, if he did get killed. Without Belle, he doubted if he'd settle down any time soon and maybe never, so the best thing to do would be to turn Pete's place over to Miguel and Rosita.

His mind made up and the repairs done, Josh rode Shadow into Port Lavaca and at the courthouse, signed the papers that would give Pete's place to the Pinõs. It made him feel good to think of Miguel and Rosita's boys having extra land for their families and he knew Pete would be just as pleased.

The next morning he dug up the cattle money from under the corner of the house, stuffed it into a saddle bag, and rode Shadow over to the Pinõs, with the legal ownership paper to Pete's land. He knew neither Miguel nor Rosita could read, but they would take it on good faith, that what he said was true.

" I'm going down to the border and look around, maybe stay, maybe not, but I don't want to hang on to Pete's place. Ramon will soon be needing a place of his own, especially, he grinned at the dark-eyed boy, if he finds himself a wife."

Ramon, ducked his head and squirmed a little, before looking back up at Josh, a wide, teasing smile on his lips and in his eyes. "Sure. Fall come, I turn twelve. I get a wife now, real soon."

Josh laughed. "Well, maybe not soon, but someday, *Quein sabe?*" He had begun to use some Mexican words now, especially around the Pinõs. He hoped his mother wouldn't mind and he thought she wouldn't. She would have liked Miguel and Rosita.

"You are still restless?" Miguel said, his dark eyes shadowed with doubt as if he did not believe that restlessness was the whole story.

"You will come back?" Rosita said and in her eyes he read the same worry. "We will miss you. The boys will miss you." She put out her arm and drew Little Pete next to her side. "We ask the Madonna to bless you." Suddenly she turned and sent Ramon back into the adobe. He came out a few minutes later with a cloth sack which Rosita handed to Josh.

"Some tortillas and a sweet cake for your journey," she said. "We pray you find what you seek."

Miguel walked with him to where Shadow stood waiting. He ran a hand along the horse's jawbone and patted his neck. "If you ever come back to these parts, even if just passing through, you will stop. No?"

"*Si amigo.*" Josh swung up into the saddle. A feeling of loss so overpowering it made a knot in his gut, he touched fingertips to his hat brim and reining Shadow around, put the buckskin into a long, easy lope.

Chapter Twenty-Eight

The October sun was closing in on midday when Josh, astride Shadow and leading Top, rode into what was left of Indianola. He could hardly believe the devastation that lay before him. Most of the buildings were gone and those that still stood, it was evident, had taken a beating. He rode to where the adobe and the saloon once stood and saw nothing there but scattered debris. Memories of his mother crowded his senses. He remembered the warmth of her body when she held him to her, her thick black hair falling over him, a curtain of comfort against his loneliness and his jealously of the men who came at all hours and took her from him. He smiled, now, at those memories, but it was a bitter smile and he knew it.

Reining Shadow, to the right, he rode down to the water's edge where he had so often played, his only companions the sun and the sand and the sea. He swung down from Shadow and dropping the reins on the ground, sat on a sandy bank.

He could almost see the solitary child he had been playing in the waves lapping at the sandy shore, while the gulls cried, wheeling through the sky overhead, and the heron stalked the marsh grass in search of prey, and the shorebirds skittered along, leaving tiny tracks in the sand. Some debris still littered the shoreline, but the sea was calm, peaceful. It was hard to imagine how it must have looked last month when it had to have risen in angry, gray swells, ten, fifteen, twenty feet, or more to break over the town, bringing death and destruction. He could not remember seeing the two long piers that stretched out into the sea so empty of vessels. Ships used to dock there every day and he imagined would again, but the docks, too, had taken a beating in the storm. He could see workers making repairs and hear the pounding of their hammers.

He visited the graveyard before leaving Indianola. His mother was somewhere here among the dead in an unmarked grave.

He was astonished at the number of fresh graves in the cemetery. Row after row of dirt mounds told of the death the hurricane had brought to Indianola. At one of the graves, a woman knelt weeping, and he felt a stab of pity.

* * *

He made Seadrift by nightfall and camped along the upper end of the bay. A little over a week later, he was in Brownsville.

The saloons seemed to him to be the likeliest place to hear rumors of Cole Slade, so he headed for the nearest one. Coming into the saloon out of the bright sunlight, it took a moment for his eyes to adjust to the dim, smoky darkness of the big room.

"What'll it be, young fella?" the barkeep, a freckled faced, balding man asked as Josh stepped up to the long bar stretched across the north end of the room.

"Whiskey," Josh said.

A laugh turned his attention to the two tables across the room where some men were playing cards. One of the table had only two players and neither one seemed to be taking the game seriously, judging by their relaxed looks and the friendly banter that went on between them. It reminded Josh of the evening poker games he and the other hands had played on the drive.

"Here you go, cowboy," the barkeep said and as Josh slid a coin across the counter he brought the glass of whiskey to his lips. He still wasn't much of a whiskey drinker, but he had learned to swallow it without gasping and he did enjoy the soothing warmth of it in his belly and the way two or three could soften memories.

"Hey! Where'n the hell did you get that ace?" demanded one of card players, at the two-man table, a lanky fella, his hat tipped back from his long, horse-like face.

"Hell, man. From my boot. Where else?" The shorter, round-faced individual said, grinning.

Josh looked back at the barkeep with raised eyebrows.

"Don't pay them no mind," the freckle-faced barkeep said. "Those two jaw each other all the time."

"They don't never play for money, just for fun," the man beside Josh said. "Me and Lem here," he indicated the man next to him. "we ride for the MK over west of here with them two knot-heads."

"You looking' for work?" the man called Lem said. "We just finished roundup, but the o'man'll have us popping the wild ones out of the brush all winter long. Likely we could use another hand."

"I wouldn't mind, but I'm heading to Laredo," Josh said. In his mind, he added, *"Or wherever I have to go to find Cole Slade."*

"Been there to Laredo oncet," Lem said. He ordered another whiskey from the barkeep and turned back to Josh. "Ever been on a trail drive?"

Josh nodded. "Went with a herd up to Wichita for the Lazy R out of Victoria."

A tall man who had recently entered the saloon spoke up. "Heard women folks went along. That true?"

Again Josh nodded. The image of Belle sitting astride her gray gelding, hat pushed back off her dark hair, cut through him like a knife. "Mrs. Rawlins and her daughters."

"Heard Mrs. Rawlins died on the way."

"No," Josh said. "It wasn't her."

"No one died then?" the tall man said.

"Two did. Mrs. Rawlins' daughter, Belle, in a fall from her horse and our horse wrangler got shot by outlaws who took off with a couple hundred head."

Explaining to the tall man, Josh had trouble keeping his voice level and unemotional and he was relieved when Lem said, "I ain't never been on a drive. But Bert, that tall drink of water over there playing cards, went to Dodge City, Kansas with a herd in '73. Said he ate a lot of dust and had to swim his horse across more damn rivers than he ever wants to see again in his life. Said he went naked, so's he didn't get his clothes all wet and take a chill."

The tall man laughed. "That must have been some sight."

Lem grinned and turned to face the card players across the room. "Hey, Bert," he said. "Have you had a bath since you went a'swimming on that cattle drive?"

"Got rained on a time or two since then, as I recall," Bert answered good naturedly, "But ain't had no formal bath. But, hell, it's only been what? Two years?"

Lem laughed and turning back to the bar, downed his drink and asked for another.

The tall cowboy beside Josh scooted his empty glass across the bar and said, "Hit me again, too, barkeep." Hunched over the bar, the tall man moved his drink in small circles and then said. "I rode for an outfit over by Beesville the last two years. Drew my pay and figured I'd head down to see Mexico for I started on back north."

"Been over there oncet or twicet," Lem said. "Met me a gal there. She was a purty little thing, but her pa wasn't too keen on me, so I left while I still had my hide." He paused and squinted at the tall cowboy. "You say you gonna be heading north?"

"Yeah. Don't mind Texas in the winter, but it's too blamed hot here in the summer. Heard some fellas been gathering themselves a herd to drive to Montana, come spring."

"Don't rightly know where Montana is," Lem said. "'cepting it's a hell of a long ways from here."

"Yeah," the man agreed. "Heard they got mountains up there and I sure am hankering to see mountains again."

"Some places in Texas got mountains."

"None like them I left back in Vermont."

"Vermont," Lem said. "Where in the hell's Vermont?"

The tall man laughed. "It's a heck of a long ways away and I'd go back, but mostly they got farms and I ain't no farmer. 'Sides it's too blamed tame for my blood. Don't have no one left back there, anyway." He paused and looked into his drink a while and finally said, "Yeah, I think I'll try Montana."

His sudden melancholy mood seemed to settle over the room like a thick blanket of fog. Josh not wanting to close off the conversation in case he could lead them to talk of Cole Slade, if they even knew of him or his reputation, said, "Did you fellas catch any of that storm that about wiped out Indianola last month?"

"Heard tell that was the granddaddy of storms," the barkeep said. "Killed hundreds, I guess. We got some of the tail end of it and lost some signboards and ripped off a few roofs, but far as I know, nobody died."

"We've a fella works with us had folks there," Lem said. "Went to see if they was alive or dead and came back, still not knowing. Some folks is just gone, swept out to sea, they say."

"Heard they had two outlaws, one name of Bill Taylor, in the jail there. Had to turn 'em loose when the water got up into their cells." The man spoke from behind Josh and he turned to see that Bert, the lanky, horse-faced man, and his companion had left the card table for a drink at the bar. "Heard they went wading out into the streets, stole some horses and hightailed it" Bert took a swallow of his drink and added, "He was damned lucky that storm came when it did, or sure as hell, the way I heard it, he'd of been dancing from a crossbeam in the town square."

"Them scaffoldings they build in towns sure does seem cold to me," Lem said. "Me I'd rather, if I was going to have to do some dancing, take my do-se-does from the shady branches of a cottonwood."

"Crossbeams or cottonwoods, don't matter, you're still dead," his horse-faced companion said.

"Yeah," Lem answered good-naturedly, "But I'd get to die more graceful like."

"Speaking of outlaws, you fellas ever heard of Cole Slade?" Josh said.

"Sure have." the horse-faced man tossed back a half glass of whiskey and slid the empty toward the barkeep. "Heard he's one mean son of a bitch. Steals little Mexican girls right out of their villages and they ain't never heard from again."

"He's one lucky bastard," Lem added. "Been terrorizing folks along the border for years, and God only knows where else."

Josh finding he had had a few more drinks than he had the capacity for, suddenly found his tongue loosened. "Well his luck is about to change," he said, feeling the anger rise up in him until it felt as if it had become his voice. "He killed my mother when I was eight years old. Killed her one night when I was playing outside and I went in and found her."

"Ain't never heard of him foolin' with no white women," Lem said and then added, "I ain't meaning nothing by my asking, but you got dark hair and all. Was your mama a Mexican?"

Josh saw the others give Lem a swift, dark look. Lem, he was sure, was one of those always asking one too many questions and never looking to see if it was the acceptable thing to do. Asking if his mother was Mexican, or Indian, or Negro could in some men raise a fighting anger that could and maybe would get Lem killed someday.

"Yes, she was." At Lem's words the small buzz from his latest drink loosened its hold and left him stone cold sober. Even Lem wouldn't ask her occupation. And if he did, Josh was prepared to lie just as his mother may have done about the redheaded man.

But the cowboy only said, "Thought so. He's hell on them young, Mexican fillies."

An uneasy silence now filled the room. Everyone had turned their attention to studying their drinks and the four men playing a serious game of poker at one of the tables.

Finally Bert asked if anyone was game for another round of stud-poker and the silence lifted.

The freckle-faced barkeep swiping the counter in front of Josh said, cautiously, softly, "You go hunting for Cole Slade and you're liable to end up dead. I'd be careful if I was you."

Josh nodded. "I know he's dangerous."

"Like a wild boar crossed with a water moccasin," the barkeep said.

Josh stayed a few more minutes and then said, "Well, I guess I better be heading on." He looked into their faces and saw them nod, wishing him well, he knew, but not taking any bets. In a way, he felt as if he were again taking leave of those men he had ridden with on the trail to Kansas. These cowboys had different names and different faces, but they were as alike as Jake, or Slim, or any of the others Lazy R hands.

The sun now behind the saloon, shaded the horses standing at the hitching rail. Shadow gave a soft little nicker as Josh approached. Although there was no kick left in the drinks he'd consumed, he did feel slightly dull and a little off as if his arms and legs moved at a slower pace. If he met Cole Slade now and challenged him, he thought ruefully, the killer would be able to add him to his tally. With a short laugh, he swung up on Shadow. Not all lessons were learned in books. Liquor and a quick arm didn't go together. At least not for him.

As he cantered Shadow down the streets of Brownsville, his eye caught the sign of the newspaper office and he pulled Shadow to a stop. A few minutes later, a newspaper rolled up and stuffed in his rifle scabbard, alongside his Henry, he rode out of town. He had his reading material for the few hours of light left in the day.

CHAPTER TWENTY-NINE

Cole Slade eyed the little bitch crouched against the trunk of a mesquite, glaring at him out of the one eye that wasn't swollen shut. As soon as he had let her go, she had jumped to her feet and before he could grab her, was up against the tree ready to fight some more.

He'd sure figured her to be younger than she was. She must be sixteen, eighteen, but small, so small, he had thought her a lot younger when he snatched her up from among those other bitches in that back alley. They had all ran after him, screaming their Mexican lingo shit.

He hadn't realized she was so damned good looking and when he got her back here to camp, Buck and Runt got so excited they about shit their britches waiting for their turn with her. The stupid assholes got their pleasure just once, he got his again when they was done and he got to plant a slug in her. One more for Nettie," he always said.

He had loved his sister as much as he'd hated his ma and pa. He didn't ever remember his ma feeding or dressing him. All he remembered about her was her wicked mouth and hard eyes. "You little bastard," was about the only name she ever had for him and she'd had a backhand that had knocked him flat on his back more'n once.

Pa liked it when Ma got all het up and slapped 'em around. Didn't matter none if it was him or Nettie. Pa'd get a gleam in his weak, watery eyes, and throw in his advice, his words slurred with booze. His "Don't take no shit off'n that snot-nosed brat, Myrtle." sounded more like "Shon't shake no shit off'n that shot-nosed brat, Smyrtle."

Pa had come home from the Mexican War crippled up with a leg shot all to hell. "Dirty, god-dammed Mexican shit-ass sonsabitches," he'd ranted nearly every morning after he'd pulled himself out of bed and staggered around, falling over his cane, as drunk in the morning as he was at night, the bottle having gone to bed with him.

His earliest memories were of sleeping with Nettie. Her arms holding him close. Four years older, she was the one who fed him from whatever scraps she could scrape out of the pots and pans when the old bastard and the old bitch got done eating. He'd wondered some since he'd growed up if Nettie had gone hungry sometimes, so he could eat. Nettie had been simple-headed. He could still see her almond-shaped eyes and round moon-like face. She treated him like she was his ma and he was her little boy, kissing his cuts and bruises and combing the tangles, real gentle, out of his long curly hair. She used to love to comb his hair and afterwards play with it awhile. She'd wrap his curls around her fingers or pull 'em straight and watch them bounce back when she let go. He still kept his hair long for Nettie, although it wasn't as curly as back when he was a boy.

Nettie was thirteen when a bunch of Mexicans showed up wanting liquor and food. Seeing Nettie was what she was, he guessed they figured she wouldn't know no difference so, with a gun held on him and his ma and pa, they took turns with Nettie, one coming out from behind the bushes buttoning his pants and another going in.

Nettie's cries had seared him worse than fire and choked him up with such a rage, he'd damned near exploded, and he would have torn right in to them bastards, if Ma hadn't griped his arms so hard it left a dark, purple bruise. "You little shit. You gonna get us all killed," she'd hissed through her snags of yellowed teeth.

When the bastards left, he had run to the bushes, to Nettie. She was on her stomach, crying big, gulping, strangled sounds that scared him shitless for he was sure she was gonna die. He'd sat by her, patting her back, and crying some hisself. Finally, she stopped, humped her back up, and got up on her knees and then on to her feet. The way she'd looked down at him shaking her head, her face and her eyes red from crying, cut a ragged hole in his gut. "Oh, Cole. Those mens hurt me. Hurt me awful."

He had taken her hand and led her back to the house.

Ma had acted like it was Nettie's fault and told her she'd better not be growing a big belly 'cause they sure as hell didn't want no half-wit Mexican bastard to raise.

But Nettie did grow a big belly and sometimes sleeping beside her he'd accidently feel the little bastard move around inside her like it was looking for a way to get out. If it had knowed what was good for it, it'd stayed put. One day Nettie doubled over like she had the bellyache real bad and started crying and wailing, even after Ma slapped her across the face and told her to shut the hell up. Ma had to almost drag her into her and Pa's room, she was carrying on so.

That room was the only other room 'sides the main one where the stove was and where they ate and where he and Nettie slept on a blanket on the floor. He'd covered his ears trying to shut out Nettie's awful screams, but they just kept a coming, the sound ripping through his gut like a saw-toothed knife. He'd wanted to run into the woods so he couldn't hear no more, but he couldn't get his damn feet to move any farther than outside the door where'd he slumped down and stuffed fingers in his ears.

Pa, either coming or going to the outhouse, had fallen over in a patch of weeds and was snoring to wake the dead. If he'd of knowed what was happening to Nettie, right then he'd just a kept on snoring. Pa didn't give a damn about Nettie, or him either.

The sudden silence that fell over the house scared him damned near as much as Nettie's screaming. He scrambled back inside and stood looking at that door to Ma and Pa's room, wondering what the silence meant, when Ma came out holding a pale-skinned, wet, bloody thing that had looked to him like a skinned squirrel. The thing lay in his Ma's hands, still as death, and then it gave a great wail of a cry that made his skin crawl like a thousand lice was feasting on it. Ma glared at that bloody little scrap, raised her big hand and put it over its nose and mouth. It squirmed a little and went still.

She'd given him the limp, bloody thing to bury. Afterwards, he'd scrubbed his hands in the dirt trying to get rid of the feel of it. When he got back to the house, he'd pushed open the door to his folk's room, the room where Nettie had birthed the thing.

He was gonna tell his ma he'd done what she asked, but his ma was bending over the bed, over Nettie who was on her back and being real still. Ma'd jerked up right quick and said, "Ya sister's done died. Lost too must blood, I reckon." For a long time afterwards, he'd dreamed of Ma covering his mouth and nose with her big hand.

For weeks he'd climbed the hill back of their house to sit on Nettie's grave, his nine-year-old tears watering the ground above her. There he had promised to find those Mexicans bastards, just as soon as he got big enough, and kill ever' last one of them.

He figured he'd run off from home and steal himself a horse and a gun, but he had to be some older, maybe twelve or thirteen.

"Soon's I get big enough, Nettie," he always told her. "I'm gonna kill them sonsabitchin' Mexicans for you."

He had killed a good share of them. Not any of those men, for he never found them, and finally he'd stopped looking. Now, he took their young girls, girls no older than Nettie, some from villages, some from outlying dwellings where they herded sheep and goats. He'd snatch the girls right from under their noses and he done to them what the bastards had did to Nettie. Then he put a bullet in their heads.

He looked again at the girl hunched down by that mesquite tree, ready to run or fight, he wasn't sure which. Either way she was dead meat.

She reminded him a little of that other girl. He'd had no trouble with that one. She had struggled, but not hard. Fear had kept her still. That is 'til he raised up off of her and then the little bitch pulled a knife and stabbed him right in the gut. She had escaped him for going on nine years, but in the end he'd found her. The cunning little shit had fooled him by staying still under those old people's bodies. When he found out she was still living, he and Lester went back to that old sheep farm figuring to kill her after they got a little pleasure out of her. So he and Lester, and come to think of it, Mace was riding with them then, too. Old Mace, gut shot two years later after a robbery that had gone bad, and crying like a sick calf. A bullet between the eyes shut that bastard up.

Anyway... Goddamn, but he got sidetracked in his thinking these days. Anyway, they went back to that old sheep farm to finish the girl off, but she wasn't there. They found a water jug and footprints going into the

Rio, but none coming out on the other side. Lester and Mace both bet him she'd drowned. They rode up and down the river, hunting, but never did find no body. They was still of the opinion she'd drowned, but something told him she'd made it across. Still if she was a-foot in that Texas land north of the Rio, she wasn't goin' to make it anyway. Three, four days and she'd be buzzard bait. They'd waited a couple of days at the adobe, just in case she came back, but she never did. Funny how he had kind of watched for her those nine years, even knowing she was certain to be dead. And then he hadn't even been thinking about her that day in Indianola.

He'd come to town to look over the bank. He always liked to try and figure on the best time of day and in what direction they ought to go to make their get-a-way. He couldn't do that now, ride into town in broad daylight. Folks knowed him too well now. But that had been back eleven, twelve years ago. Before he got to be famous. Before he got to be a legend.

That evening, darkness just gathering, he was in that saloon standing off by hisself at the far end of the bar when she came down those stairs in the back, said something to the bartender and left out the door to the street. He'd knowed it was her, the added years hadn't fatten her up, but it'd sure shaped her out, otherwise she looked exactly like that little shit of a wildcat who'd jammed a knife in his gut near on to nine years before.

He'd followed her out and saw her go into that old adobe out back so he went around and got his horse, so's when he was done with her, he'd not have to come back out to the street and take the chance of being seen, 'specially if he had some of her blood on him.

She'd knowed him right off. Funny, but she'd not put up no fight, just let him knock her around and didn't let out more'n a weak little whimper or grunt. She was real desperate about getting that damn broom outside the door. He finally he took it away and snapped it into. She'd cried then, a little bit. He'd sure enjoyed giving that knife back to her, plunging it in real deep. Odd that just before she died, she'd pulled herself up into kind of a ball around that knife in her gut, like she was protecting it or something.

That day he and the boys had gone to that old sheep farm looking for her, he'd found the knife under the bed and he'd knowed it was the same one she'd stabbed him with. Must of rolled over and pulled it out from under the bed when he got up to fasten his pants back up.

It'd sure given him pleasure, that knife in his hand and seeing hisself cut that little bitch into pieces, but she hadn't been there and so he'd taken the knife with him, buying a scabbard to carry it in until he found her. He bet the sheriff had sure wondered why a skinning knife was sticking out of the whore's belly.

She'd been a tough little bitch, all right, like this girl now crouched before him. Even knocking her around hadn't taken the fight out of her. Backed up against a mesquite tree, she was glaring at him like a cornered cougar, her black eyes shooting mad. In a minute she was going to make her move so he might as well force her.

He took two steps and was commencing on his third when she jumped up and took off running. "Oh, what the hell," he said aloud. His gun slipped easy into his hand and the bullet in her back dropped her like a sack of spuds. She didn't move as he nudged her with the toe of his boot and for a minute he watched the blood seep around the bullet hole in the back of her yella dress.

When he raised his eyes from the dead girl, he saw Buck and Runt looking at him. The only one wasn't paying him no mind was the old nigger he'd picked up to cook his grub.

"Why'd you do that?" Buck said. "We ain't done got our turn."

Both the big, ugly-faced, bucktoothed idiot and the short, stocky one acted like he'd just pissed in their boots. "Hell, next week we'll go up towards Laredo and pick us up another one. Right now, one of ya get your horse and drag her off a good ways, so we don't get no stink. I 'spect to be here a few days and I don't want my air a stinking, ya savvy?"

He shook his head watching them both go for their horses. One never did nothing without the other one was along. Buck was big as a bear, but so dim-witted, he weren't no threat, even if he was mad. Runt was no bigger'n a pint jar of liquor and just as stupid as Buck. He given 'em both their names, had never even asked their real ones. They was too stupid to need names.

Cole turned to the old nigger he'd called Whitehead, 'cause his wooly old head was as white as a patch of cotton. Like Buck and Runt, he hadn't got the old nigger's name neither. 'Sides the names he gave 'em was easier to remember. "Get some grub rustled up, pronto," he demanded. "I'm hungry as a starved coyote."

Whitehead dropped an armload of dried sticks down beside the cold ashes of the campfire. "I sure will, boss. I surely will."

As the old black man moved about his business of starting a fire, Slade walked over to his bedroll and lying down, leaned against his saddle and rolled a smoke. It had suddenly occurred to him that when he shot that little bitch a few minutes ago that he had forgotten to say that the bullet was for Nettie. It shamed him some that he'd forgotten. Maybe he was getting too old for this business. The last time he'd let Runt and Buck go into town to raise a little hell, they'd run on to a kid who was asking about him. Said the kid was wanting to throw in with him. Some snot-nosed kid with big dreams of being an outlaw good as he was. Maybe he should find that kid and teach him all he knowed and start up a new legend.

Hell, he hadn't been more'n thirteen when Jeb Drake took him in. He'd got the smallpox when he was eleven and passed it on to his pa and ma. He got up one morning, feeling better, but they was in their bed, stone cold. He hid out in the brush near town, 'till the scabs fell off, sneaking into houses at night to steal whatever he could find to eat. Later, he got a mopping up job in a saloon for grub and a place to sleep on the floor in the small storage room in back. Drunks was all the time makin' fun of him. Called him pox-boy and scar-face and pulling on his long, blond curls, saying they wished they had a sweetheart with hair like that, or put a mask on you, boy, and with that long hair, you'd be fun to play with. The jabs never failed to make Cole mad and he'd tear into them, swinging both fists, but they'd just laugh some more. He was skinny and real short in those days. Never did get his growth til he was past fifteen. The men would grab a holt of him and hold him out away from them, laughing at his arms swinging wild but never hitting 'em.

One day Jeb Drake was in the saloon sittin' in a corner at a poker table when a couple of cowboys got to poking' fun at him. He tossed down his chips and pushing back from the table said, "Come on over here, boy."

Drake'd looked at him with his hooded blue eyes, his fingers smoothing his big handlebar mustache, for what seemed forever and Cole felt his knees start to shake a little 'cause he'd sure heard of Jeb Drake and he figured he was fixin' to shoot him or something. Which, if he'd knowed what the something was, he'd had just a leave of got shot.

To cover up the fear a tearin' him a new butt hole, he'd said, "What ya want, Mister? I ain't so big, but I'm big enough to give them two smart sonofabitches a taste of my fist, if you was to help me a little."

Jeb Drake grinned and said with a wave of his hand that took in the entire place, "You over fond of this here pisshole?"

"No, I ain't," Cole had answered him. "I hate this sonofabitching, damned old pisshole."

Jeb Drake chuckled again and Cole had felt his hackles rise, certain, he was going to be ragged on again.

"You sound to me like a boy could be trained to bite the heads off'n rattlesnakes and poke the eyes out of a catamount. Am I right?"

"I'd sure try," Cole had answered him.

Again Jeb Drake had chuckled. "Well, gather up your bedroll, boy. 'cause you and me, we's ridin' together."

"I ain't got me no bedroll," Cole had told him. "Ain't got no horse to ride, neither."

"Well, boy. This is your lucky day." Jeb Drake again let out a small chuckle. " 'Cause I'm gonna get you both."

Riding away from that saloon on the horse Drake gave him, he'd been excited as hell. He just knowed he was going to learn gunslinging and whatever other business there was to know about being a real outlaw. Drake showed him how to hold a gun and how to draw it smooth from a holster and he told him about keepin' a watch on the fella's eyes ya was fixin' to shoot or who was fixin' to fill ya hide full o' lead.

"His eyes gonna tell you what his hand's aiming to do." Good advice as far as it went, but Jeb Drake had been too far away to read Cole's eyes, when he shot him.

He'd learned to hate Jeb Drake from his first night with Drake's gang. He was feeling real good, eating supper and drinking coffee, just like a man, 'til it came time to turn in. That's when he found out that Jeb Drake was more interested in his young, hairless body than he was in teaching him to be an outlaw. It took several years, but his body hair finally came on and Drake quit leading him off into the brush and made him a full-fledged member of his gang.

By then hate was jammed so tight in his craw, it took everything he had to keep it from spillin' over in a rage that would of got hisself killed. Instead, he'd watched and waited for the day he could blow the bastard into hell.

His chance came one day when they was to hold up a stage and the law had got wind of it and they was riding inside it, just waiting. They opened fire and killed Lefty and Cal right off. Jeb Drake threw down his guns right away seein as he was caught by the short hairs and he was going to be laying there on the ground with o' Lefty and Cal, growing cold if he didn't start surrendering. But Drake always kept an ace up his sleeve. He always left one or two of his men back behind a rock or a bush or a tree or something, expecting if caught in a trap that he'd have a better chance of getting rescued.

Cole grinned to himself remembering how, he and Lester had been the ones hiding and how they'd raised up and fired from the bushes they was hiding behind. Lester's shot brought down a lawman and his had nailed Drake. He'd taken a moment to savor the sight of that bastard in a heap on the ground and then he'd yelled at Lester, "Drake's down! We'd better ride!" Lead flying all around them, they'd lit out on their horses just a tearing up the ground getting out o'there. Neither one of them got even so much as a scratch. Eventually, he and Lester picked up Mace and after that little Mexican bitch knifed him, he'd added two more men to his gang. Like Lester and Mace, they were more followers than leaders and he'd had no trouble moving into the position of ramrod and Cole Slade's outfit soon become one to reckon with. Every Mexican and every lawman this side of the Rio Bravo wanted his hide.

Some of the things he'd heard about hisself was that he was like trying to shoot a ghost, one minute there and the next gone. It was said that no matter how wide the loop was they throwed to catch him, they always drew back a slack rope. Oh, they might get one or two of his men, and often did, but Cole Slade was too slick, too slippery, too canny to be caught. But he was getting slower. His lightning fast draw had slowed some, thanks to that rheumatis that was makin' his hands stiff and growing knots on his knuckles. He didn't ride as well now either, not with his bum hip, 'specially when it was cold. Last winter his bones had ached so much, he'd left the three he was riding with, all young fellas, and found himself a rundown boardin' house. He'd kept his hair up under a gray hat and put away his black one, grew a beard and kept to hisself. He'd just been out a few weeks now, long enough to pick up Runt and Buck and the old nigger. Buck and Runt were the next thing to worthless, hardly worth the bullets it'd take to get rid of them.

Hell. Maybe he'd have 'em go find that kid and bring him back to camp and if he panned out okay, he'd keep him and go ahead and waste the two bullets it'd take to send both them dumb bastards to Hell.

CHAPTER THIRTY

In the saloons and Mexican cantinas, Josh began using Rivers for his last name. Slade might have known his mother's name or the one she went by anyway. Ryder wouldn't be all that common a name for a Mexican woman and might stick in Slade's head, especially of he'd had a grudge of some kind against her.

In every saloon and cantina, Josh always turned the talk around to Slade. He was careful with his drinks and managed to get by with only a few, knowing he'd better be cold sober if he ever met up with Slade.

The Mexicans had a real fear of the man, they called the *amarillo-cabello Diablo*, the yellow-haired devil. The first Mexican to verify the story he'd first heard in the saloon in Brownsville, was nursing a bottle in a cantina on Mexico's side of the border when the bartender pointed him out and Josh went over and pulled up a chair beside him.

"He steal our girl children and we no see them again," the Mexican said. "He steal my Rosa. Her mama she weep many tears." A gaunt man of undetermined age, every time he took a long pull on the bottle, he'd set it down carefully as if not certain where the table ended, and staring at Josh with mournful eyes would continue on with his tale. "He swoop down. He take. No one catch him. He move like the wind and no one sees. He like the ghost. He strike and he vanish."

Another man told him that his sister's daughter had been stolen in such a manner and the rest of her daughters now did not go outside the casa unescorted.

"Our children we see no more," one man said, although none of his daughters had disappeared. "We think they die or get sold away to be slaves. That's what we think."

In those cantinas along the border, Cole Slade was the devil incarnate. The evil ghost riding the winds.

On the Texas side of the Rio Grande, the talk in saloons was of a man living a charmed life. His co-horts may be killed and often were, but he escaped without a scratch. In those Texas saloons, Cole Slade had taken on something of a legend. Some, like the two in the last saloon, had bragged about knowing him and Josh had been a little skeptical. Both men appeared to have hardly a full brain between them. It didn't seem possible that Slade could have lasted this long with idiots like those two in his gang, but Josh went ahead anyway and let them know that he was itching to join up with this border legend and learn to be a great outlaw.

The short one, his voice high-pitched and eager, was about to tell Josh all about Slade, but the other one with the buck teeth had hissed, "You wanna get your balls cut off?"

The short one got a scared look in his eyes and threw down another shot of whiskey. A short time later, the two, casting quick looks at Josh, left the saloon.

Sure now that he had found some of Slade's men, albeit using the term "men" loosely, Josh made camp a couple of miles from town and rode in each evening, hoping the two would return.

As Josh Rivers, Josh had spent five months riding the border from Brownsville to El Paso. It was February now. Next month on the fifth he'd turn nineteen.

Belle still haunted his memories and he knew he would never forget her, but the ache in his chest and gut was not so strong now, at least most of the time.

Ten days had passed since Josh had met the men in the saloon who claimed to have known Slade and there was still no sign of them, so he guessed they had moved on. Sometimes he felt as if his hunt for Slade would be as elusive as his search for his father had been. The only difference was that no one had ever heard of his father, but plenty had heard of Slade.

If they weren't here tonight, Josh decided as he pulled Shadow up in front of the hitching post and dismounted, he'd move on.

Thinking about taking a drink in this rundown, dirty saloon he had been in every night since he'd met the two half-wits, was enough to turn his stomach. He hated drinking with the down and out men that frequented this rat hole of a saloon. This hunting a killer was lonesome business and he longed to visit the saloons where the cowboys would be lined up to the bar or playing a little poker, joking and jawing each other good-naturedly. He was often struck with a feeling of homesickness for those days of the cattle drive. He wondered if the men had all gone back to the Rawlins' ranch and he wondered how Mrs. Rawlins and Lee and little Kit were getting along.

With a sigh, he stepped around the hitching rail and headed for the ramshackle saloon set at the far end of the street. It looked, Josh thought, like it had been dropped into place from high above and had missed its mark. Not only was it out of line with the other buildings, but was set at an odd angle as well. A hard packed dirt path ran up to the sagging doors. Josh pushed them open and stepped into the seedy den of dirt and flies, cheap whiskey, and slopped over spittoons. Josh had purposely taken on the lost, scruffy, dirty look of those who lived on the edge of humanity. His hair curled now about his collar and he'd grown a beard to match his thick, dark mustache.

He was surprised to find them waiting for him. They came rushing over, both anxious to be the bearer of their good news. Offering him a drink, they motioned him over to a table in the far corner of the room.

"You two sure as hell look familiar," he said, seating himself in a chair scarred with dents and cigarette burns, two spokes missing from the chair's back. "Did I see you here the other night?"

"Don't 'member us, huh?" the short one grinned, his eagerness to spill whatever news he had was evident in the wiggling of his body which reminded Josh of a dog wanting to be petted.

Josh felt a rise of excitement. He was certain, now, that these two knew where Slade was and were about to tell him.

"Nine, maybe ten days ago we was here," the buck-toothed one said. He set down three glasses and handed the short one the bottle of rye whiskey he was holding. "You was in here, talkin' about meetin' up with Slade. 'member?"

"Yeah, I kind of remember," Josh said. "But hey, fellas, I was probably pretty pie-eyed at the time."

"So you ain't hankerin' to meet the greatest outlaw ever did get born?" The shorter one said, pausing in his studied effort to pour an even amount into each glass.

"I didn't say that," Josh said, and as soon as his glass was filled to the short one's satisfaction, he downed the whiskey in one smooth swallow.

The short one and the buck-toothed one both picked up their glasses and downed their own drinks as if showing Josh that they could drink, too. The buck-toothed one scrubbed a dirty hand around over his mouth and whiskered chin and waited while the short one refilled their glasses.

This time Josh let his drink set. "Sure is fine of you fellas to buy me drinks," Josh said. "But, say, you ain't telling me..." he opened his eyes as if wide with wonder and then closed them in a half squint. "Naw, you're funnin' me. You don't know Cole Slade."

The short one did his dog wiggle again and grinned like he'd won the pile in a poker game.

"We sure do. And it ain't us that bought this here bottle of whiskey we's drinking. Cole Slade did it."

Josh felt his heart give a little leap. "Why'd he do that?"

The short one shook his head and looked at Josh like he thought his brains were in his hind-end and turned to his companion. "Tell him, Buck," he said, grinning.

Buck shot a wary glance around before leaning in toward Josh and lowering his voice said, "We told him about you and he says if we was to see you again to bring you out to his camp."

So here it is, Josh thought.

"Where's he camped?" he asked.

"Close," the one named Buck said.

"Yeah," the short one could hardly contain his excitement. "Real close." He jerked his head toward the west side of the saloon. "He's just back up in them hills. If'n we leave soon's this here bottle's gone, we ought to be there 'bout sunup."

"Tonight?" Josh said. "Why not wait until morning?" *What had he gotten himself into? Would Slade see through his charade and kill him on the spot? Well, he'd stuck his neck into the noose this far, he might as well see it to the end, whatever that might be.*

"Cole don't like Runt and me to be a-coming into his camp when folks might be up and about to see us," Buck said.

Josh nodded. "So we'll go now?"

"The bottle ain't empty yet," the short one Buck had called Runt said.

"Well you two go ahead and drink my share," Josh said. "If I ain't going to get me any shut-eye, I ain't drinking no more." He grinned at the two men across from him. "Too much whiskey makes me so damn sleepy, I can't stay upright on a horse." He let his grin stretch wider. "I don't reckon you fellas got a buckboard I can lay down in and sleep all the way to Slade's camp."

Runt laughed. "We sure as hell ain't. We're going to be riding in rough country. A buckboard'd get shook to pieces."

"Don't reckon he was serious, Runt," Buck said, frowning. "You swallow every goddamn thing you're told."

"Don't neither," Runt retorted glaring at Buck.

"Well, gentlemen," Josh said. "When you're ready to go, you'll find me sleeping on a pile of hay at the livery stable. I sleep light and my horse'll be saddled and ready to go."

Riding back to the livery stable, Josh decided he'd leave Shadow and take Top. He would be riding into a dangerous situation and he'd sure hate to expose Shadow to it. He'd pay the man for a month of Shadow's keep and tell him that if he wasn't back in six weeks, he wouldn't be coming back at all and Shadow would be his.

Emotion tightening his throat, he pulled his saddle and bridle from Shadow and transferred them to Top. It worried him to leave the buckskin, but he really had no choice. For a brief moment he'd toyed with the idea of having the owner contact Mrs. Rawlins, if he didn't return. But the Lazy R was at least a hundred miles north and some east. No one was going to travel a couple hundred miles for a horse. Besides there was no guarantee the man would honor his wishes. He'd just have to come back that was all there was to it. He'd sure give it a good try, anyway.

"Reckon you think a lot of him." The liveryman had come up beside him while he stood with his arm around Shadow's neck, his hand rubbing his forehead up under his forelock and down along his jawbone.

"I've had him since I was eight years old."

"Well, I reckon I don't have to worry none about you not coming back for him then."

"No. I'll be back, unless I'm dead and can't," Josh said. He jerked his head toward the hay piled in the corner of the barn. "Some fellas are coming for me tonight. Mind if I wait here and maybe catch a little shuteye?"

"No. I'd charge you rent if it was all night." The man laughed. "Won't charge a man for just waiting, even if he sleeps a bit while he waits."

"Thanks," Josh said and moved back in under the sheltering roof of the hay barn and laid down on his back in the hay, placing his hat over his face. He dozed fitfully. A lot of questions roamed around in his head. Questions he had no answers for. Although he knew he might have to kill Slade, he hoped that somehow he'd get the drop on him and bring him hogtied into the sheriff for the law and the hangman's noose to do the job of getting rid of him. It might be hard to actually kill a man, but if he had to, he guessed he could.

A little before dark, Josh got up and went over to Top. Shadow trailed along behind him and nosed him in the back as he hooked the stirrup up over the saddle horn and tightened the cinch. He can't possibly know he's being left behind, Josh thought as he led Top over to the gate. He had to give Shadow a little swat with his hat to keep him from following them out of the gate.

No more than a half hour later, the two men appeared. The liveryman had gone home for the night and Josh was glad he wasn't here to see the two men, for odd as they were, they'd stick in the man's head like burrs to a saddle blanket. Runt was drunk, there was no doubt about that, but Buck appeared to be sober.

"Well, sum-bitch," Runt said, around a stupid looking grin. He weaved back and forth in his saddle a few seconds, his hand gripping the saddle horn and said the same words over again, "Well, sum-bitch." It was then that Josh saw the man's hands were tied to the horn and another rope passed under the horse's belly was tied around each boot.

"You ready to ride, Rivers," Buck said.

"Ready," Josh answered. "But is your pal there going to make it?"

"Oh, yeah. He's tied on good and tight. We'll have to stop every little while and untie him and let him get down to piss, but he'll be all right. By morning, he'll be his old self."

"Whatever that is," Josh muttered and reined Top around to follow after the two men both mounted on dark bays. Josh heard Shadow whinny and looked back to see the buckskin standing by the gate.

CHAPTER THIRTY-ONE

An hour after they rode away from the livery stable, a quarter moon rose in the dark star-studded sky and Buck called a halt.

"Get down off'n your horse," he said to Josh. "I've gotta tie this here bandana over your eyes, so you don't see nothing, til we gets there. And I'm leading your horse, 'case you get a wild-ass idea you ain't happy with us after all. And don't go to peeking, or I gotta tie your hands in back of you." He nodded toward the holster at Josh's hip. "I gotta take that pistol, too."

The blindfold disoriented him, so after a while he wasn't sure in what direction they were traveling. He could tell by the feel of the horse under him when they were on flat ground and when they began climbing. They rode for hours, stopping now and then for Buck to untie Runt. He could hear the man and smell the stink of his urine. Those times he let Josh get down too, but cautioned him about removing the blindfold.

"You don't want me takin' you to Cole Slade with no holes in your hide, you best mind like I say," Buck said the first time he allowed Josh to dismount, and repeated himself every time afterwards.

Even with the blindfold over his eyes, Josh could tell when it was daylight. Shortly after the sun came up, Josh was startled to hear a man's voice call out, "That you, Runt? Buck?"

"Yeah, Whitehead," Buck answered, "It's us."

They started to climb some more and then moved along on flat ground. Josh knew they were close to Slade's camp when Top whinnied and a horse answered.

The horses stopped and Runt said, "We brung him, Boss."

A sudden fear gripped his belly and sent his heart to racing as Josh waited the few seconds it took for Buck to maneuver his horse around Top and jerk off the blindfold.

Josh blinked and stared down at the man. Cole Slade sat near a fire that put off little smoke, drinking from a tin cup. An old black man, bent over the fire was turning slices of bacon sizzling in a fry pan.

"Just in time for breakfast," Slade said. He nodded at Buck. "Give him back his gun and take his horse for him." He looked up at Josh. "Ya got hobbles for that nag?"

Josh nodded. His brain was spinning with the knowledge that less then six feet away, sat the man who had murdered his mother, and his gun, back in its holster, hung heavy at his side. He had heard that Slade was about forty, but he looked much older. His eyes, a pale blue, were set in a wrinkled, leathery looking face, pitted and scarred. Except for a heavy mustache, a shade darker than his long, greasy looking blond, wavy hair, his face was clean-shaven and revealed a deep cleft in the middle of his chin. When he stood, Josh noticed a slight stoop to his shoulders, and that he seemed to favor his right leg.

"So ya been looking to join up with my outfit, huh?" Slade said.

"I reckon there ain't none better'n you to ride with," Josh said, staring bold-eyed at the man. He figured Slade would expect him to be a little big for his britches, but not too tough, so Slade would be more amused than angry. If he wanted to bring this man down and live to tell the tale, he'd have to be good at his game.

"What all'd ya hear 'bout me?" Slade asked.

Josh grinned. "Heard you could disappear like a ghost. Heard you was like a fox, wily and cunning. Heard you knocked over a bank once and took five thousand dollars. Heard you've robbed a stage and got away with a strong box full of gold, even with lawmen riding inside. Heard you got a lightning fast draw and a good aim." He let his eyes beam with admiration and saw the man puff just a little with pride.

"And ya want to join me?"

" Yes sir. I heard you was the best they is or ever gonna be and I want to learn the best from you and then prove them wrong and do better." He paused and risked a slight smile at the man. "Figured you learned from the bottom up and didn't have no teacher. If you'd had a teacher as good as you when you was young as me, maybe ain't nobody could be better. Not even me."

Cole Slade laughed. "Well, guess I could learn ya all right, but first we'll tie on the feed bag and then we'll see what ya know. Ya real good at shooting a gun?"

"I've been a-practicing," Josh answered.

"Well, kid," Slade said. "I reckon ya can shoot a gun all right, maybe practice 'til ya real good, but ya gotta learn some finer points about the man who'll be looking down a gun barrel with a gun of his own. We'll start ya lessons right after we eat." He turned to the old black man. "Bring this here young fella some grub and throw a good bit of sweetenin' in his coffee." He turned to Josh. "Ya like it sweet?"

Josh nodded, his eyes on the old man hobbling around the fire, fixing the plates.

"Looks to me like your cook's lame," Josh said. "Reckon I could get my own."

"Reckon you won't." Slade turned cold eyes on Josh.

Josh shrugged and sat down on the ground beside Slade.

After the old colored man served him and Slade, Runt and Buck stepped up and began filling their plates.

So, Josh thought, the old black man doesn't have to wait on them. That privilege was Slade's, and, at least for now, his.

All through the morning hours, Cole Slade had him draw and holster his gun and draw again. Josh pretended to be slower than he really was and once even dropped his gun which made Slade yell, "Damn it to hell, Kid! Watch it! Ya tryin' to kill me?"

Odd, Josh thought, that he called him Kid and never even asked for his name.

In the afternoon, Slade tied a piece of buckskin to an old mesquite tree and drew a bulls-eye with a piece of charcoal. Again Josh pretended to be slightly inept, gradually allowing himself to improve.

As the sun disappeared, Whitehead called that grub was ready, Slade slapped Josh on the back and said "Ya sure improving there, Kid, but the hell of it is, we'll be out of ammunition a-fore ya get real good." He frowned and shook his head. "Ya say ya been practicing? Shit Kid ya ain't never gonna get good as me at this rate."

"Sorry," Josh said and hung his head a second before straightening it and letting a ray of hope shine in his eyes. "I am getting some better though, don't you think?"

"Yeah," Slade said. "Some."

They spent three days in camp and now Josh seemed suddenly to have caught on to the art of gunplay. Runt and Buck laid around the camp, drinking and playing cards with each other. Josh rarely ever talked to them for Slade monopolized him almost completely. If he wasn't teaching him to shoot he was talking about bank jobs or stage holdups.

* * *

The morning of the third day, Josh woke to an all but empty camp. Slade and Runt and Buck were not in their bedrolls and when he rose to his feet he saw his bay gelding a little ways out from camp, moving slow in his hobbles, his tail swishing flies as he grazed, but the other horses were gone. He looked for Whitehead and saw him approaching the campfire with an armload of broken sticks.

Josh rolled up his bed as he always did and stashed it next to his saddle and bridle and after going behind a bush to do his business came back into camp. "Where's everybody," he asked.

"They be gone a few days," Whitehead said.

"Why?"

Whitehead shrugged, but declined to answer.

"So what do we do?"

"Wait."

Later, as Josh was eating a breakfast of bacon and biscuits and hot coffee, he said, "They left before breakfast?"

"He do that sometimes." Whitehead said, refilling Josh's cup.

"When do you expect them back?"

"Can't say," the old man answered. "When they is done, I guess."

"Done doing what?"

The old man shrugged.

The evening of the fifth day, Slade and his two men rode into camp with a sack of grub, more ammunition, and a young girl riding astride in front of Slade, his arm pinning her to him, her dress hiked up above her bare legs. She was Mexican and looked no older than twelve. Josh's heart leaped up in his throat. Everywhere he'd gone he'd heard that Slade took young Mexican girls, but he hadn't given any thought to him getting one while he was trying to bring the man down. *What did he do now?*

"Look what I brung ya, Kid," Cole Slade said, grinning down at him. He handed the girl down to Runt who had dismounted and had held out his arms for her. Josh cringed as the simple bastard pulled her up tight against him and when she tied to twist free, bent an arm back until Josh was certain it would snap. The girl screamed in pain and tears trailed through the dirt on her small face.

Slade swung down from his long-legged gray and took the girl from Runt. His hand gripping the girl's arm, he said with mock severity, "Had to buy more grub, 'cause ya ate up what we had. Had to get ya more shells 'cause ya shot up what we had. We was leaving to come back here when I happened to remember ya was sitting back at camp probably lonesome as hell. So to top it off, I brung ya this here little bitch to play with. Ya get to try her first. Runt and Buck and me, we'll wait our turns."

Josh shook his head. "I...I," he stammered. "I never... Isn't she awful young?"

Slade laughed. "Young is good. Best there is. Ya don't want to start on an old worn out whore." With the hand not holding on to the girl, he poked a finger at Josh and squinted one eye as if sighting down a gun barrel and clucked his tongue. "Ya ain't never had none before, have ya?"

"No," Josh shook his head.

"How old are you boy? Eighteen? Nineteen? Hell that's old enough." Sudden anger flashed in his eyes and his jaw tightened. "You ain't funny are ya? Ya ain't likin' boys better'n women. Ya ain't one of them kind, is ya?"

"No, I ain't," Josh said sounding, he hoped, angry and disgusted, for in Slade's eyes he'd read instant death.

Buck and Runt stood looking at him, hardly able to contain

themselves, Runt doing his dog wiggle again. He could almost read their minds. *If he didn't like her, then they were closer to having her for themselves.*

"Maybe ya just ain't tough enough for us, Kid. I make the rules around here and if ya don't like 'em and don't like what I provide for ya, then ya can take your sorry ass and hit the road."

"No. No." Josh felt a chill race up his spine. *And how far would he get before Slade sent a bullet through his back.* "I want to stay. To learn from you."

"Then take her," Slade snarled and thurst the girl at him. She staggered and stumbled and Josh leaped forward and caught her. She struggled for a moment and then grew still.

Josh swallowed the gorge that rose up in his throat. *What could he do to save this little thing trapped in this camp of evil?* Held against him he could feel her heart beating, a rapid thumping that spoke of terror. "All right," he said. "But can I take my bedroll and go out a ways. I don't aim to have my first time be before no audience."

Slade laughed, his humor returning with Josh's acceptance of his gift. "Sure, but don't let her go for a minute or she'll run and if we can't catch her we'll have to shoot her and I'll have to go to the trouble of getting ya another one."

"I won't," Josh said.

Holding the girl firmly by her small, slender arm, his bedroll tucked under the other, he lead the girl away until they were some distance from the camp and, where, bent down, they were hidden by rocks and scrub bushes. "Don't be scared," he whispered as they walked away. "I'm not going to hurt you."

She gave no sign that she heard and her body stiff from fear did not relax in the slightest. Was she deaf? Then he realized she did not understand his words. Searching in his head for the few Mexican words and phrases he'd learned from the Pinõs, he said, "No *espantar. Comprender?*"

She looked at him then, hope dawning in her dark eyes and started to speak.

He hushed her with a quick hand to her mouth. "I no *comprender*," he said. *"gastar tiempo,"* he added which he hoped she understood as having no time to waste on words he wouldn't understand, anyway.

He flopped his bedroll down on the ground and drew her down beside him. At this action, her eyes grew frightened again and she trembled and tried to draw away from him. "*Amigo*," he said, tapping his own chest. "No *espantar*."

She quieted and again hope flared up in her black eyes.

He searched for words to tell her what she must do. "*Grito*," he said, and made a sobbing motion. "*Ruidoso,*" he added, hoping it was the right word for loud. She caught on and began to wail so loudly that for a second it unnerved him. He let her cry a few more seconds and then clapped a hand over his own mouth. Her crying stopped as abruptly. He grinned at her and, for a second, so overwhelmed was he in his delight in her, his eyes stung with a quick, unshed tears.

She looked at him, startled and then smiled a smile small and weak, but it was a smile.

Now what? He thought. She waited ready to do whatever he directed. Her fear of him now replaced with trust. How would he save her from Slade and those other two brutes? Maybe, just maybe, if he asked Slade to let him have her for his own, he would let her be. He looked at the girl again and said, *"Grito."* Again the girl began to wail, her eyes watching him and again he let her go a few seconds and then clapped his hand over his mouth. And as before she stopped as abruptly. Now he decided she must scream, but what was the word for it? He shook his head, thinking hard, but the word escaped him. Finally, he looked at the girl, opened his mouth and screamed in silence. She almost laughed. "*Chillido,*" she said and screamed a scream that, even expecting it, nearly curdled his blood. Again he shut her off by putting his hand over his own mouth and she stopped just as quickly as before. He waited a few minutes, hoping the right amount of time had passed so Slade wouldn't get suspicious, then he leaned forward and gripping the girl's small arms, looked intently into her face. "We go back now," he said, gesturing back toward camp, the Mexican words eluding him. She drew back, fear rising up in her eyes. *Good, she understood.* "You. Me." He pointed to her, and then to himself. "We go *espaldo hombres perverso*." He figured he'd said it wrong until she repeated his words. "*Hombres perverso*," she said.

"*Si*, wicked," he said. "Men wicked."

She pointed in the direction of the camp, turned and jabbed a pointed finger in the opposite direction and looked up at him questioningly.

He shook his head, gave her a hard frown, and made a motion with his arms like running and then touched his gun. Pointing his finger like a gun and making a clicking sound, he clutched his breast and briefly closed his eyes. Fear filled her small face and she ducked her head, but not before he saw the tears.

He waited a few minutes and then touched her arm. As soon as she looked up at him, he let his face look mean, angry. Be scared. Be *espantar*. Me *perverso*. We...what was the word for fool? We *tonto*... Was that fool or foolish. Trick! Trick! That was the word he needed. *"Treta!"* That was it. *"Treta perverso hombres."*

She nodded, her eyes on him dark and anxious. Now if she could just understand that she had to fight him. Not enough to get away, but as if she hated him. Hoping this would work, he reached for her hand and placed it on his arm. She looked down at his hand and watched as he curled his fingers over hers tightening her grip on his arm. She understood and gripped as hard as she could, frowning and gritting her small white teeth. He jerked back, his face twisted, in what he hoped looked like anger and fear. Then he reached out and gripped her arm. She pulled back, hate and anger clouding her small face.

"Bueno," he said, smiling. *"Bueno."*

"Comprender," she said solemnly.

He stood up and motioned her to her feet. The bedroll back under one arm and a tight grip on the girl's, he yanked her along as she pretended to pull back and fight him.

Slade was watching for him. Actually, except for Whitehead, all three watched and as they drank their coffee they had imagined, he was sure, the goings on behind the bushes and had taken some pleasure from their imagining.

"Took you awhile," Slade said. "How's it feel to be a man."

Josh let his grin grow wide and his eyes shine with enthusiasm. "You sure knowed what to get to please me, all right. This little sweetheart is pure pleasure." He paused and added wryly, "After you get her to quit fighting, that is. She sure as hell didn't like it at first." He grinned down at the girl he still gripped by the arm and dropping his bedroll, pulled her up tight against him. She fought, like he hoped she would. Swinging her little fists and trying to kick him with her bare feet.

Slade stood up and before Josh could figure out what he meant to do, he'd slapped the girl's small face, leaving angry red marks. She stopped fighting and began to cry.

"Ya bein' too soft with her, Kid," Slade said. "Ya gotta teach her some respect or she'll go to fighting ya ever chance she gets."

Josh swallowed a surge of anger and grinned at Slade. "I guess I was. But damn, she's such a pleasureable little thing. I sure thank you, for getting her for me." He looked at the girl and loosened his hold. She slumped to his feet. "Looks like you took the fight out of her, all right. Reckon she'll be real enjoyable now."

"Don't ya be getting no ideas, Kid. We ain't keeping her. You'd best get that in ya head right now. Ya got the rest of this day and tonight to fool with her, then we is turning the bitch into buzzard bait."

Even though Slade's words hit him like a fist slammed into his belly, Josh hoped he kept his fear for the girl out of his face. He had to decide on a plan to save her and if he came up with something it had better include a way out for him, too. He watched Slade roll a smoke and wondered if he could actually kill the man. Buck and Runt would need killing, too, and possibly Whitehead. The old colored man might have a weapon concealed somewhere in the food sacks. His legs were crippled, but his arms weren't. He could still shoot a big hole in a man.

He looked at the girl still slumped at his feet and then at Slade. Forcing eagerness into his voice, he said, "Can I have her all night tonight in my bedroll?"

Slade hawked up some phlegm and turned his head to spit. "If ya want to, Kid. But that's it. I'm ready to move on and I ain't takin' long no extra baggage."

Josh hoped the leering grin on his face looked genuine. "But I get to have her all to myself 'til then?"

"Til the sun comes up," Slade said, pulling the makings of a cigarette from his shirt pocket. "We all get her then and I get rid of her, afterwards."

Slade took a long pull off of his cigarette and looked at Josh through narrowed eyes, cold as a snake's. Smoke curled out of his nose and mouth. Fear crawled up Josh's spine. He could only hope it didn't show in his eyes.

Finally Slade spoke, "I'm thinkin' we might do us a bank job."

Relief was a flood and Josh stammered, "A...a b...bank job?"

"Yeah. Ya's a good-lookin' fella that talks good. Shave off ya beard and trim up ya mustache and knock some of the dust off ya clothes and smile a little and ya ain't gonna cause no suspicion. Ya tell 'em ya wants to start doing business with 'em. I got fifty dollars in gold coins left. Ya takes it and ya tells 'em ya wants to put that in their bank and then ya hesitate, like ya ain't sure, and say ya'll come back in tomorra." Slade dropped his burned down cigarette and ground it under his heel. "While ya there, ya look it over good. Knowin' the layout of a bank sure can cut down on surprises."

"Where is that bank you want me to look over."

"Ain't sure yet. But ya go ahead get that beard shaved off and keep ya self clean shaven, 'cept for that mustache...makes ya look older and more like ya ain't just a drifter, til I do decide which one."

Feigning a casual attitude and hoping for the right touch of humor, Josh stroked his full, dark beard and grinned. "Been growing this chin fur long enough to get fond of it, but I reckon I can let it go for a good cause."

Slade chuckled. "I reckon ya better." He turned to look at Whitehead who was busy hustling up the evening meal over the small campfire. "Grub ready?"

Whitehead jerked to attention and his head bobbed up and down several times. "Yes'm Boss," he said.

Slade turned back to Josh and with a gesture toward a small mesquite tree, said, "Tie the little bitch over there while we puts on the feed bag."

"Can I feed her?" Josh asked

Slade shrugged. "Up to you, kid. If anything's left after we eat, but it's a pure waste of grub."

Runt who had come up to get his share of food, although knowing he'd have to wait until Whitehead served Slade and Josh, gave a snort of a laugh. "'Speck a fed bitch's is gonna buck a spell longer'n one that's half starved," he said, with a wink at Josh.

230

Josh flashed him a grin, but thankfully didn't have to say anything. This hellhole of vipers was more than he could stomach. He was going to have to get away from here and take the girl. There was no way he could shoot it out with three, maybe four, if the old colored man was at all loyal to this gang of cutthroats, but he'd have to figure out something and soon.

He tied the girl to the mesquite tree, trying to look like he was jerking the ropes tight, but only drawing them snug enough to keep her from getting away and bringing disaster down on herself and possibly him, too, but not so tight as to cause her extra discomfort. She kept her eyes on him, large and fearful, but he could give her no reassurance.

"Whyn't we buy some good grub whiles we was at it?" Buck grumbled as he spooned beans on to his plate. "My belly's plumb sick of beans."

"'Cause that's what ya bought, ya dumb shit," Slade snarled. "I sent ya in to buy us some grub and whatta ya buy? Beans! Ya stupid-ass shit." He laughed. Josh thought his moods as changeable as the wind. "Maybe we'll head on down to Mexico tomorra and get us some tortillas and fry bread." He turned to look at Josh. "Ya ever been to Mexico, kid?"

Josh looked up from his plate, so conscious of the girl he could hardly choke down his food. "I crossed the Rio a time or two, but never stayed long."

"I hate a damned Mexican, but I sure like tortillas and fry bread."

"They're good eating all right," Josh said. He jerked his head toward the girl. "Reckon I'll feed her now. Sure don't want the little honey to get too weak to be any fun."

Slade grinned. "Go to it, Kid."

Josh untied the girl's hands so she could feed herself. She took only a few bites of the beans and then pushed the plate away. He offered her coffee from his cup. She drank it, making a small face and handing the cup back to him, began making signs, pointing to her legs. He took the rope from around her and pulled her to her feet. She made a motion as if pulling up her dress and squatting, and made a hissing sound.

He turned to Slade and jerked his head toward the bushes. "She's gotta piss," he said.

Slade nodded. Josh led her over behind a bush where she squatted again and passed so much water that Josh wondered how she had kept from bursting.

"Get her tied back up, Kid," Slade said coming up behind them. "I want to go over the plans for tomorrow."

By the time they had drained the coffee pot and Slade was sure Josh understood his plans for tomorrow, he jerked his head toward the girl and said with a grin. "All right, Kid, go get her. Reckon you want your damned privacy, too."

Josh grinned. "I think until I get used to it, it's the only way I can."

CHAPTER THIRTY-TWO

Something about the kid bothered Slade, but damned if he could put a finger on it. When Buck and Runt brought him into camp, he'd felt a kind of tickling at the back of his brain, like he knowed something about the kid. He sure did remind him of someone, but who, he just couldn't figure.

Waiting here for Buck and Runt to get back with the kid, he'd let his head fill up with a bunch of dreams of the two of them raising hell together. Just the two of them, like they was father and son. He'd built up those imaginary pictures so much that he wasn't aware that he'd been expecting a boy with yella hair and blue eyes. A light-skinned boy that looked a lot like him. At first glance he thought the kid was a half breed Ingun or a Mex. He had questioned him about his folks. The kid said he didn't know about his ma on account of she died when he was a baby, but he seen a lock of her hair his pa kept in a locket. It was dark, but she couldn't of been no Mexican or Indian, though, he knew that for damned sure, cause his pa hated both like poison. Said he sure 'membered the strapping he got when he was just little and his pa coming out of a saloon, caught him playing with a Mexican boy. Said his old man had fire red hair and a temper to match.

It bothered him that the girl didn't fight the kid anymore than she did. The kid was a good looker, though, and young. Maybe she was beginning to like it. Well tomorra the little bitch'd be dead and then he'd study the kid some more. See if he should keep him on or feed him a chunk of lead.

He had hoped to learn the kid the ropes so he could carry on the legend. He had hoped he'd come to be like a son, but he was afraid the kid was too soft. Hell, he was young, though. He'd harden up, given some time.

Hard to believe he hadn't never had a woman. He'd had plenty by the time he was the kid's age. He sure bet the kid would make up for lost time, now. He was eager as a hound dog when he drug that little Mex girl off into the bushes a while ago. Hell, he was probably just worrin' over nothin'.

Runt and Buck was nearly asleep when the kid came out of the bushes with the girl and she was blubbering away like most of 'em did. Irritating as hell, too.

He rose up on his elbow. "Make that little bitch quit crying, Kid, or I'll get up and slap the shit out of her for ya."

The kid laughed, jerked the girl to him and told her to shut up in Mex talk. The little bitch stopped immediately. The kid winked at Slade. "Getting pretty damned good, ain't I?" he said.

Slade chuckled. A warm feeling washed over him as he lay back down. The kid was going to be all right after all. Tomorra, he'd get rid of the two idiots and it'd just be him and the kid from now on. Maybe he'd have the kid shoot 'em. He bet the kid had never killed anyone before and he'd best get that job under his belt before they did a job together. Two splitting the money from a job was a hell of a lot better than four. 'Course he'd toss the old nigger enough for chawing tobacco.

* * *

The girl lay close to him all night and Josh thought she even slept some. She was scared, but she was a brave little thing. Hell, he was scared, too. One wrong move, one stupid mistake and Slade would not hesitate to put a bullet in him. Out back of the bushes the girl had gotten sick and had thrown up her meager supper and that had started her to crying. He'd tried to tell her that Slade might hit her again if she kept it up, but she either didn't understand or she was losing hope and fear was getting the best of her.

He'd decided the best plan and the only one he could think of was to ask Slade for one more time with the girl. He might even offer to shoot her for Slade when they were all done with her. That should put to rest any doubts he might have. Then they'd stay in the bushes until Slade got to worrying and came looking for them. When he got close, he'd shoot him and then the two idiots, if they didn't run for their horses and hightail it out of there. He'd have to shoot Whitehead, too, if he decided to take up the cause.

The sky was pink with the coming sunrise when Josh woke. The girl stirred beside him and opened her eyes. He rose up on an elbow and looked across to the campfire where Slade sat. Whitehead was bending over him, giving him a shave as he did every morning.

Buck and Runt were sitting on the ground playing cards again. The two played the same card game over and over. Buck gathering up his cards, looked over at Josh and then up at Slade. "When's Runt and me getting the girl?"

Josh's heart knocked against his chest. "Cole," he said forcing his breath to come out a little overeager. "I sure got the hankering for one more taste of the little sweetheart, 'fore I give her up to you and Buck and Runt." He grinned at Slade. "Hells bells, Cole, I think you done got me plumb spoiled for living a pure existence ever again."

Slade, evidently in good humor, part of it maybe a good night's sleep, but part of it too, he was sure because he was going to have the pleasure of the girl, grinned back at him. "Okay, I'll let you go one more time, but let's put it off awhile." He inclined his head toward where Buck and Runt had abandoned their card game in favor of leering at the girl, and lowered his voice.

"They is so damned eager they can hardly keep their pants fastened up. Ya get all shaved up nice and we'll tell 'em I decided I'm gonna let ya marry this little ol' senorita."

Knowing each move he made, each word he uttered, was like walking a narrow ledge over a canyon that could fall away into eternity, Josh drew back as if shocked and said, "Hey. I ain't ready to get married."

Again Slade laughed. "Don't worry. I'm just gonna be funnin' with those two idiots." He stood up and took the razor Whitehead had just dried and folded back into its handle. "The o' nigger here will cut ya hair and trim away that beard so's he can give ya a clean shave."

"I'll get my razor from my war bag and get missy here tied up so's she won't be a trying to hightail it outta here." Josh showed Slade a grinning open face which he hoped said, *"Hey, ain't this gonna be fun."*

Whitehead welding the razor had just cut off a chunk of Josh's hair when Buck came walking over, his face a study in bewilderment.

"It ain't true, is it, that you gonna get hitched to that little gal over there?" he asked.

"Sure thing," Josh said, grinning. "That's why I'm getting all slicked up here."

"But she's a Mex," Buck protested.

"Hey," Josh turned his head carefully, well aware of the razor in Whitehead's hand. "You don't go to talking 'bout my bride to be, that-a-way. If Cole and I say she's white then she's white, and I sure as hell aim to shoot any man that says different."

"You ain't given her to us, like you promised?" Buck whined.

"Hell, no. I ain't sharing my bride with you bastards."

"Well, tell this ol' nigger to hurry up," Buck said crossly. "'Cause Runt and I's hungry as hell and if we ain't gonna have no good time then we's gonna eat."

As Whitehead limped around to cut the other side of his hair, Josh said, "They don't ever talk directly to you, do they?"

"Slade don't 'low it. I be his nigger and ain't nobody else's, less he say so."

"I see," Josh said.

When Whitehead finished shaving him and had wiped off his razor and handed it back to him, he said, "You be knowing Slade when you come here?"

"No. Never met him before. Why?"

"No mind," Whitehead said and went back to the campfire.

"That mustache looks good trimmed up like that," Slade said as Josh walked back over to sit and wait for Whitehead to serve him and Slade their breakfast. "That o' nigger's got ya looking plumb respectable." He jerked his head toward the girl tied to the mesquite tree and grinning at the two sullen faced men sitting on the other side of the campfire, said "Reckon I can get ya two to go hunt down a preacher man so's the kid and this here little darlin' can get wed?"

Runt mumbled something and Buck, who was the bolder of the two, said, "You gonna get us a new one, then?"

"No Buck, ya done had all the womenfolk ya's gonna get from me," Slade said.

"Shit, Cole," Buck whined. He jerked his head toward Josh. "Hell, if'n we'd of known it was gonna be like that, we'd of stayed in town."

Slowly Slade got to his feet. "Go get ya horses," he said.

Both men stared at Slade, slack-jawed. Josh knew they had heard the ice in Slade's voice and even dumb as they were, they knew they were in trouble. Fear popped them up from the ground, Runt spilling his coffee.

"C-Cole," Runt stammered. "We's... We's ain't... We's ain't bitchin' none. We's don't need us no woman. We's fine."

"Yeah," Buck said. "We's just disappointed. That's all. You the boss. What you say goes."

"Well, I say, get ya goddamned horses and get out of here."

"Please Cole," Runt was blubbering now. "Don't be mad. We's sorry."

"Yeah, Cole," Buck said, his eyes round and wide with fear. "We's dumb shits. We is just running off at the mouth. Don't mean no nothing by it. We is just talking. That's all."

Slade looked over at Josh, a hint of a grin in his eyes. "What do ya say, Kid. Should I send 'em packin' or not?"

Josh, not sure how to answer, decided to sit the fence. "You're the boss, Cole. Whatever you think is fine by me."

Cole turned back to the two men. "Ah, hell," he said grinning. "I was just a funnin' ya. The kid here ain't gonna marry the little bitch. Fact is he's turning her over to ya to do with as ya want."

Runt sent Josh a puzzled look. "You ain't funnin' us?"

Josh forced a grin. His plan to kill Slade and the others and save both the girl and himself had evaporated "Nope," he said. "I ain't funnin' you a-tall."

They both turned to Slade, obviously bewildered at this turn of events. "Ain't you gonna be first, Cole?" Buck asked.

"Yeah," Runt said. "Ain't we's last, like always?"

"Naw," Slade said, "Ya two ignorant bastards go ahead."

At Slade's words the two leaped around the campfire and headed for the girl.

Seeing them coming, the girl looked at Josh, her eyes wide with terror.

"I'll be damned," Slade said. "The little bitch is looking to ya to be saved. Ya done spoiled her, Kid."

Josh fought against the anger and the cold fear that clutched at his gut as the two fell on the girl and began yanking at her clothes. They weren't even going to untie her. She was doomed to live a few minutes of hell and then Slade would shoot her.

"Untie her!" Slade barked. "Take her away so's we don't have to see you bastards goin' at her."

Buck and Runt both stopped at Slade's command and with fumbling fingers began untying the girl. Josh saw her look once more at him and then as if she knew no help was forth coming from him, began kicking and screaming.

Slade frowned as the girl kept screaming. "Damn it," Slade roared. "One of ya two shit-heads shut that bitch up!"

Buck jerked his eyes from the ropes, looked at Slade and then brought around a hard, solid fist to her chin. Her head snapped back and she crumpled, unconscious, against the tree.

"That sure shut her up," Runt crowed. "Come on Buck. Come on." Now content to let Buck free the girl, he stayed on his knees, wiggling his body in anticipated excitement.

As Buck worked feverishly at the last knot, Josh took a step back from Slade and slowly eased his hand to his gun, but Slade, his eyes still on the two trying to get the girl untied, said soft and slow, "Shoot the idiots, Kid."

Startled, Josh jerked his eyes to the two men and the small, unconscious girl under the mesquite tree. "What!" he said.

"I said kill them. We don't need 'em. From now on it's gonna be just us, Kid."

"Now?" Josh said, his brain seemed to have deserted him and only a dull, stupidity remained. "Buck? Runt?"

Slade nodded. "The bitch, too."

Josh pulled his gun from its holster and looked again at Slade.

"Now," Slade said.

Knowing he had no choice, Josh raised his gun, aimed and fired, one shot, two. Runt toppled over sideways and Buck fell forward on top of the unconscious girl.

"Good shots," Slade said. "I'm proud of ya Kid. Now get the bitch."

"Ah,' Josh said. "I don't like killing a little girl."

"Hell, Kid. She's just a Mex. Here, I'll do it." As Slade raised his gun, Josh jerked his own gun up and fired. Slade's gun spun out of his hand and a red stain blossomed on his shirt, just above the wrist. Slade swung around, his face twisted with rage. "Ya sneakin' bastard," he roared.

Josh raised his gun, hesitated. This was his only chance to kill Slade. He was unarmed, his gun hand hanging limp. It would be no contest. Just one bullet would do it and a snake was a snake and given the chance would kill him and the girl, too.

"Can't do it, can ya, Kid," Slade sneered, his confidence growing in the wake of Josh's reluctance to pull the trigger. He took a step forward and Josh took a step back, stumbling. Slade leaped at him and grabbed the gun. As they fell to the ground, Josh's finger tightened on the trigger and the gun went off. Slade swore and released his hold on the gun and Josh rolled away from Slade and fired again. The bullet whistled harmlessly pass Slade's head.

Josh leaped to his feet. He had two bullets left, he'd better not waste them. His eyes swept the ground where Slade's gun had spun out of his hand. *It was gone!* His eyes darted to where Buck and Runt lay, Buck's body across the girl's still form. *Where was Slade's gun!*

Slade, on his feet, was barreling toward him, rage twisting his face. Josh raised his gun, but before he could squeeze the trigger, he heard a shot and Slade fell face forward to the ground, blood seeping up through a hole in the back of his shirt.

Josh jerked his eyes from Slade's body to see Whitehead with a gun in his hand, the barrel pointing downward. The old black man looked at Josh. "He was one of them humans needin' killin'. Thought it be best if I was to do it. Hate to see a boy have to kill his own pa."

Josh stared at Whitehead. *What was the man talking about?*

The girl whimpered. Josh hurried over and pulled Buck's dead body off of her and kneeling untied the last knot holding her to the tree. She fell into his arms, sobbing.

Chapter Thirty-Three

The girl sat huddled on the ground chewing the cold biscuit Whitehead had handed her. She had quit crying aloud, but silent tears still slid down her small bruised and swollen face.

"That child 'bout to the end of her rope," Whitehead said "You best tell her it be all right, now."

With Josh seeing, now, what Whitehead saw, a child pushed nearly to the limit of her endurance, he squatted in front of her. "No *bueno?*"

She shook her head, tears dropping on the half eaten biscuit. The fingers of her other hand pulled at her torn and bloodied dress. The blood startled him, before he realized it was Buck and Runt's blood. He rose and walked over to where his war bag lay beside his saddle and pulled out his extra shirt.

Again kneeling in front of her, he held out the shirt "This *bueno.*" Giving a little tug to the skirt of her dress, he said, what he hoped was bad, *"Malo."*

Her head slumped forward to her chest and her black hair fell like a curtain to shield her face and again great gulping sobs convulsed her small body.

Josh looked from the sobbing girl to Whitehead. "What'll I do now?"

"She be okay soon. Just pat her some and talk to her, quiet-like. She be okay."

"I've about used all the Mexican I know."

Whitehead smiled. "Don't matter the words. The sound tell her she be safe."

He had sat the girl down facing away from the bodies and as he patted the girl's small arm and murmured soft words, he noticed with a start that they were gone. Dark stains marked the spot, where Slade had gone down and where Buck and Runt's blood had drained away, but the bodies were gone. He whipped around, certain they had only been wounded and Slade now waited, hidden somewhere from sight. He cursed himself for not thinking to check to see if they were breathing, and to pull Buck's gun from its holster. The hair rising on the back of his neck, he shot a swift look at Whitehead.

The old man jerked his head toward a jumble of rocks and Josh glimpsed the heels of a pair of boots. "I done move 'em while you was bringing up the horses," he said. "Figure it be best the young lady don't got to see them debils no more."

Suddenly realizing he knew nothing of how the old man came to be with Slade, Josh, still squatting beside the girl, twisted around to look at Whitehead. "Why were you with Slade?" he asked.

"He pick me up same as the girls. 'ceptin' I be for doing slave work."

"There's only three horses," Josh said. "You don't have a horse?"

"No. I ride behind Runt."

Josh nodded. "You take Buck's horse, then. The girl can ride Runt's."

Whitehead pursed his lips and frowned. "I 'pect the little missy never ride by her ownself before. She feel safer, she be with you."

"All right," Josh said, "But we'll take him along anyway. Maybe, tomorrow, she'll feel like riding alone. We'll turn Slade's horse loose."

They did not look back as they rode away from Slade's camp. Slade's gray horse had disappeared down into an arroyo and several buzzards were already circling high above the bodies of the three men.

Not knowing in which direction lay the closest town and reasoning that the girl had come from one of the border towns, they rode south. On the third day, they came to a well-traveled road and met a wagon coming from the southeast.

"Nearest town is San Felipe del Rio," the driver of the wagon, said. "I just now came from there. You're only six, seven miles out." Josh could see the questions in the raw-boned, middle-aged man's eyes and nearly laughed. They were an odd looking trio all right.

They watered their horses at an oasis of water and grass and trees set in the midst of a dry land of prickly pear and mesquite. They washed their faces and drank deeply of the clear water from the spring. The girl sat down on the bank and put her feet in the water, splashing them up and down, looking for all the world like the child she was. She caught them looking at her and a grin spread across her face.

Josh smiled back at her. He had grown fond of her and in a way, he would miss her. She reminded him of Kit and even of Belle, this little girl whose name he didn't even know.

In town, they rode directly to the sheriff's office and reported the location of the bodies. The sheriff sent someone for a Mexican woman who could speak Anglo to question the girl about her home and her family and to buy her a dress to wear home.

"I'll send someone to take her home," the sheriff said when they discovered she was taken from the streets of a small town, just over the border.

"If it's all the same," Josh said, "we'd like to take her."

The girl, whose name they now knew was Lupé Hernandas, was solemn faced as she sat in a chair in the sheriff's office. No longer in Josh's faded gray shirt, she had bathed and was now dressed in a new bright yellow and red dress, the tangles combed from her black hair. As the Mexican woman translated Josh's words, a smile lit her small face.

The sheriff laughed. "I guess that settles it then," he said.

The girl's family smothered them with words and gestures, joyous over the return of their child and happy to know that the evil Slade no longer lived to plague them.

As they prepared to go, Lupé came shyly forward and extended her small hand. Josh smiled as he closed his over hers, but behind his eyes, tears burned. He knelt down and she came into his arms and hugged him fiercely.

As he and Whitehead rode down the narrow streets of the village, Lupé and her family stood watching. At the end of the street, Josh turned in the saddle and waved at the small figure standing with her parents in the doorway, then he touched Top with his spurs and the horse broke into a canter that took them out to the road leading north across the border.

Although he was extremely conscious of what the black man had said after killing Slade, Josh tried not to let himself think about it until they had left the girl with her family and were riding back toward Texas.

Now, he felt ready to face the fact that Cole Slade had been his father, more than likely by the act of forcing himself on his mother. She had been very young then, like Lupé and all the other girls.

He knew now that his mother had known all along who had fathered him. She had made up the redheaded man to give him a sense of worth and had insisted on him being Anglo, so, if Slade came asking, he might more easily pass as the redheaded man's son.

Angel and Birdy had told Pete his mother's story. At least what she had told them. She had been very young and living with her grandparents when the outlaws came. The men had killed her grandparents, but she had escaped by swimming the Rio Grande. The red-headed man had found her wandering, lost, nearly dead from hunger and exhaustion and he'd brought her to Indianola, to Floss and Angel and Birdy.

Josh knew that if Slade had known about him that night, he would have killed him, too. Slade would not have tolerated a half Mexican son. He was grateful to his mother for making up the redheaded man, instead of telling him who had really fathered him.

Except for Josh's mention of Shadow waiting at the livery stable, Josh and Whitehead did not speak of the future. In fact they spoke very little, even when camped for the night. Josh was still trying to sort though his emotions that ranged from anger to bitterness to sorrow, and he was, he knew, poor company.

When they reached the springs at San Felipe del Rio and stopped to water the horses, he thought of little Lupé sitting on the bank splashing her feet in the water. She had been through hell and she'd sat on that bank, not knowing what would happen next, her hair uncombed, her only clothes, his gray shirt drooping off her small shoulders and falling well below her knees, but the spirit that lived in her had not been crushed. The spirit he imagined to be much like Kit's and Belle's and maybe Mrs.

Rawlins and his mother, too. They all had a natural bent toward happiness that even the toughest times could not destroy.

As they swung back up on their horses and headed north again, he imagined how knowing what he knew now would have affected him. If he had known when he met Belle would he have allowed himself to love her? Would he have taken lessons from Mrs. Rawlins? Would he have thought himself good enough for Belle? Good enough to try and better himself by learning to read and write? Although he had to admit, he'd not thought so much of bettering himself, but as an opportunity to be close to Belle. None of that would have happened, though, if he'd known that Slade was his father, which was another reason to be grateful to his mother for telling him about the redheaded man. Without him to search for, he would not have gone that day to the Lazy R.

They were some miles from the springs when Josh turned in the saddle to look at the old black man riding behind him on Buck's dark bay. "What made you think Slade was my father?" he asked.

Whitehead urged his horse up beside Top and his dark eyes searched Josh's. "I 'spect I shouldn't of said that. If I was to think on it awhile, I don't believe I would. Cain't be no help to a man finding out a low-down snake be his daddy."

"No. It doesn't help me at all and I'd just as soon you hadn't told me, but since you did, tell me what you saw in him and in me that made you know we were father and son."

"Well, you looks a whole lot like him, walk the same way, 'cepting you're darker'n him."

"My mother was a Mexican," Josh said. Even now, with Whitehead, he could not make himself say what she'd been, especially now that he reasoned it had not been her choice, but one of necessity.

"I see," Whitehead said gravely. "My first sight of you I think I see you somewhere before. Then I shave off your beard and I see your chin."

Startled Josh's hand darted to his chin and fingered the deep cleft there.

The old man shook his head. "You don't notice, he got that same chin? A gully near big as a canyon 'tween two mountains and you don't notice?"

Josh frowned. "I guess not. Never gave it a thought, anyway. So we both got chins alike that's no real proof. Could be it's just coincidence."

"No. Cain't say it be certain true. Could be it's what you say. A co…a coinci…"

"Coincidence."

"Yeah. Might be it's that."

They rode the rest of the day with few words between them. At dusk they made camp and after a supper of jerked beef and coffee, shook out their bedrolls and lay down.

Josh lay on his back looking up at the dark sky filled with thousands of stars. So maybe Slade had fathered him. But he'd not been a father like Pete had been, so why should he accept the low down slime as his father? Maybe Slade had had a lot of those shadows Pete talked about that had turned him mean. Maybe so. Maybe not. Maybe he was just naturally mean. There was no way to know now and at this point Josh didn't much care. No one but Whitehead knew Slade was his father so he wasn't going to acknowledge him as such. He'd take Pete, even the non-existent redheaded man, but not Cole Slade.

Pete had said once that a scrub horse will throw a scrub foal, but Mrs. Rawlins' words that people weren't horses was certainly a comfort, now.

He turned his head toward Whitehead lying a few feet away. "Did Slade notice we looked alike? Did he notice we had the same chins?"

"Don't figure he did."

"He asked if I had Mexican blood and I told him it wasn't likely bad as my old man hated Mexicans. Of course I made it all up."

"He'd of killed you, if he'd knowed."

"I figured that."

A silence fell between them and Josh again mulled over the decision he had made lying there in the dark. He knew he needed to say it aloud if he was to shake this ghost of his past. His father had been the lowest scum of a human instead of the honorable one he had imagined.

He turned his head toward Whitehead. "There isn't any way to prove that Cole Slade was my father. Right?"

"Reckon there ain't," Whitehead said.

"Then as far as I'm concerned he's not."

"That sound sensible to me," Whitehead said. "Don't know who my daddy is. Guess a fella gotta make his own way, no matter who done the makin' of him."

"I'd say that's right," Josh said. "So I'm disowning any connection to him. I'm setting myself free of the bastard, and I'm thinking that after I pick up my horse, I'll head up towards Port Lavaca and then on to Victoria. I know some folks near both those places I need to see. If you want to come along, you're sure welcome."

"Ain't got nowhere else to go," Whitehead said. "'Cept if I go with you, could we use my real name?"

"What is it?" Josh asked.

"Isaiah Blue. Slade named me Whitehead, cause of my hair. He give his own names to folks. Don't know Buck and Runt's real names but 'spect they ain't neither one right."

"My name's Joshua Ryder. I had an alias ready, but he never even asked. He just called me Kid."

"He name us, he own us."

"Well he won't ever be owning anyone again."

"No he ain't gonna," Isaiah Blue said, shaking his head.

A welling of excitement began to grow in Josh. Soon he would be riding Shadow and seeing the Pinõs and Mrs. Rawlins, and Lee, and Kit, and all the men he'd come to respect and admire on the drive. First, he wanted to see them. But after that, *Quein sabe*? He grinned to himself. He was definitely going to learn more of his mother's language.

He thought about those cowboys he'd met in the saloon before he'd figured out that if he was to find Slade he'd better frequent the run-down hard luck bars. The one from Vermont had talked of an outfit taking a herd to Montana come spring. It was a long ways, Montana was, but maybe he'd do that, go to Montana.

When sleep at last claimed him, he dreamed he was riding Shadow and eating the dust of a thousand bawling cattle.